W9-CBA-602

CARBS
&
CADAVERS

A Supper Club Mystery

CARBS
&
CADAVERS

J. B. STANLEY

MIDNIGHT INK
WOODBURY, MINNESOTA

FIRST EDITION
Second Printing, 2008

Book design by Donna Burch and Joanna Willis
Cover design by Ellen Dahl
Cover illustration © Linda Holt-Ayriss / Susan & Co.

Midnight Ink, an imprint of Llewellyn Publications

Library of Congress Cataloging-in-Publication Data
Stanley, J. B.
   Carbs & cadavers / J.B. Stanley.—1st ed.
    p. cm.—(A supper club mystery ; #1)
  ISBN-13: 978-0-7387-0913-0
  ISBN-10: 0-7387-0913-1
   1. Overweight men—Fiction. 2. Dieters—Fiction. 3. Clubs—Fiction. I. Title. II. Title:
Carbs and cadavers. III. Series: Stanley, J. B. Supper club mystery ; #1.

  PS3619.T3655C37 2006
  13'.6—dc28
                                               2006044952

Midnight Ink
Llewellyn Publications
2143 Wooddale Drive, Dept. 978-0-7387-0913-0
Woodbury, MN 55125-2989, U.S.A.
www.midnightinkbooks.com

Printed in the United States of America

In gratitude to my friend, Holly Hudson Stauffer,
for sharing books, coffee, and the gift of her time

*If more of us valued food and cheer and song
above hoarded gold, it would be a merrier world.*

—J. R. R. Tolkien, from *The Hobbit*

ONE

CHEESE PUFFS

Nutrition Facts

Serving Size 1 oz. (17 pieces)
Servings Per Container 7

Amount Per Serving
Calories 150 Calories from Fat 70

	% Daily Value*
Total Fat 8g	12%
Saturated Fat 2.5g	13%
Cholesterol 0 mg	0%
Sodium 360 mg	15%
Total Carbohydrate 17g	6%
Dietary Fiber 0g	0%
Sugars 2g	
Protein 2g	
Vitamin A 0% • Vitamin C 0%	
Calcium 2% • Iron 0%	

*Percent Daily Values are based on a 2,000 calorie diet. Your daily values may be higher or lower depending on your calorie needs.

JAMES HENRY WRAPPED A towel around his formidable stomach and stepped onto the bathroom scale. He hesitated before looking down. He hadn't weighed himself in over a year, but his new pants were growing tighter and tighter and several of his belts no longer fit at all. Finally, he steeled himself for the results and peered down, but he couldn't see the numbers as the rotund, protruding flesh of his belly completely blocked them from view. *This is what it must feel like to be eight months pregnant*, James thought glumly.

He leaned forward, trying to read the scale without making the numbers on the dial jump around too much as he shifted his weight. When he was actually able to make out the results, James leapt backward off the scale as if it had suddenly caught fire. He frantically dried the bottoms of his wet feet and the sides of his calves, assuming that an extra thousand ounces of water must have been clinging to his body in order to produce such a number. Exhaling heavily, James stepped back onto the scale and once again examined the truth laid out in bold black-and-white digits: 275 pounds. He was more than fifty pounds overweight.

James sat down on the toilet and put his face in his hands. Over the last few months, he felt like he had been laid out at the bottom of an open grave while shovelfuls of dirt were thrown on top of him. First, his wife filed for divorce after a three-year separation so that she could marry a hotshot lawyer, then James's mother died, forcing him to move back home to care for his sour, reclusive father, and now, on top of everything else, James was fat. The two things he had loved most—his job teaching English literature at the College of William and Mary and his wife, Jane—were both gone. Now he was an overweight, divorced, thirty-five-year-old loser living with his father.

"I've got to *do* something about myself," he moaned aloud. "I've *got* to go on a diet."

After weighing himself, James Henry finally got dressed and trudged wearily downstairs to make breakfast. He cracked three eggs into a bowl and mixed them vigorously with milk. The sound of the liquid slapping about in his mother's tin mixing bowl gave him a small measure of comfort. Next, he poured the pale yellow mixture into a sizzling frying pan and then sprinkled the cooking eggs with parsley and a dash of garlic salt. He popped two bagels in the toaster and poured two glasses of orange juice while keeping an eye on the frying pan. When the surface of the eggs began to look crinkled, like a piece of plastic wrap, James expertly flipped the omelet and then covered its surface with a thick coating of shredded cheddar cheese. The toaster oven beeped. James pulled out the bagels, spread a generous layer of cream cheese over each crisp half, and then slid them neatly onto two chipped plates. He divided the omelet in half with the spatula, pushed a half onto each plate, and then called his father.

"Pop! Breakfast!"

Jackson Henry shuffled into the room wearing his usual attire: a faded plaid bathrobe over a pair of denim overalls. He glowered at the food laid out on the counter and then raised a pair of furry eyebrows as he bent over to examine his bagel more closely, a frown creasing his wrinkled face into deeper furrows.

"What kind are these?" he growled as he carried his plate over to the table.

"Cinnamon raisin," James replied, spearing a forkful of egg. "Why?"

Jackson sat down at the kitchen table and scraped his chair loudly across the linoleum floor as he moved his thin frame closer to his plate. He began to pick raisins out of his bagel like a petulant child.

"I told you, I like sesame seed," he grumbled, tucking a paper napkin into the neck of his shirt.

James sighed. "The store was out of those, Pop. I'll get them next time." He inhaled the pleasant aroma coming from his own bagel as he lifted it to his mouth. He loved the smell of cinnamon.

When James was a boy, his mother would have made homemade cinnamon rolls on a dreary October day like today. They would be waiting, perfectly warm and fresh from the oven, with rivulets of icing cascading down their steep, savory brown sides. When James came home from band practice and Jackson arrived home from a long, satisfying day's work at Henry's Hardware & Supply Company, the scent of cinnamon would fill the entire house.

It was the small things, like the aroma of cinnamon or the gleam on the tin mixing bowls, that made James miss his mother's presence the most. She had died in August, just two short months ago. Physically, Jackson was perfectly healthy, but over the last decade, he had become more and more reclusive. After his hardware store was bought out by one of the big chain stores, something in Jackson seemed to wither up and die. He began to leave all of the errands into town to his wife, tinkering about in the back shed for most of the day. James's mother complained that her husband barely talked anymore. He came inside for meals, which he didn't finish, and to watch TV in the evenings. The only shows he watched were the game shows. He no longer read the paper or seemed to have any hobbies.

James had always assumed his mother would live to a ripe old age. She was vivacious and full of life, constantly working on some charitable venture or volunteering at the local elementary school. She walked three miles every morning and had never smoked a day in her life, so when she had a sudden heart attack in her sleep, James was completely stunned and devastated. He knew her death marked the end of his life as a professor in Williamsburg. He could not leave his father to fend for himself, nor did he feel right putting him in a nursing home. James was their only child and his mother would have wanted him to move back to Quincy's Gap in order to care for his father, so he did.

After painfully handing in his resignation to the English Department chair, James packed his old Bronco full with his belongings—mostly books—and gave the key to his cozy brick townhouse back to the rental agency. He took a final walk through the streets of historic Williamsburg, early in the morning before the crowds arrived, and marveled at how beautiful the trees looked lining the gravel road stretching toward the campus of William and Mary. The morning sun set the autumn leaves ablaze as if bidding James a fiery farewell.

He took the hint, filled up a thermos of Sumatra Blend at the coffee house, and then drove four hours west, to the hometown he only visited during Christmas and summer breaks. Boasting one main street and a population of two thousand Virginians, Quincy's Gap was a picturesque burg nestled in the Shenandoah Valley. Settled beneath the impressive shadow of the Blue Ridge Mountains, it was a pastoral, tranquil place where farms formed an emerald-and-saffron checkerboard when viewed from the air and horses roamed over hilly pastures.

In the middle of these farms, the town arose as a neat square of historic wood and brick buildings. Beyond the town proper were two strip malls. One was comprised of Home Doctor, the mammoth hardware store, and a Dollar General. The second housed the Winn-Dixie, the video rental store, a nail salon, pet groomers, and an Italian restaurant. Other than Dolly's Diner and the drive-in movie theater, which only operated during the spring and summer months, all of the town's shops and eateries were on Main Street. The tiny side streets housed the municipal buildings, lawyers and medical offices, and the three homes listed on the National Register that were open to the public for a small charge.

James Henry had returned to Quincy's Gap just in time to fill the vacancy of head librarian for the county's main library branch. His salary was sharply reduced from what he had earned at William and Mary, but his living expenses were, too. James moved into his old room, lovingly maintained by his late mother as a shrine to her only child. Every toy soldier, comic book, baseball glove, and even the tattered posters of various rock 'n' roll icons were still scotch-taped to the walls as if James were planning to bring a son of his own home to play in his childhood room. But James had no children. What he had instead was a lot of heavy baggage—both emotional and physical.

His life-altering move had taken place almost two months ago, and James had come to believe that returning to Quincy's Gap signaled the end of any chance of happiness. He would grow old in a place where he had spent torturous years as an awkward boy, followed by four more years as a solitary, unpopular teenager, and finally, as an unmemorable college student returning home during semester breaks.

Staring at his half-eaten bagel, James snapped out of his self-pitying reverie and shifted his weight on the uncomfortable metal chair with the cracked seat cushion and tried to read a newly released piece of historical fiction about a boy growing up in Afghanistan. He had a few minutes to spare before heading to work, and he desperately wanted to know if the boy would win the coveted kite contest so exhilaratingly described by the author. As James read, Jackson scraped his chair noisily away from the table and shuffled back to the den, leaving half of his egg uneaten and a completely pulverized bagel on his plate.

It began to rain just as James finished his breakfast, licking globs of cream cheese from his fingers. He peered out at the gray skies, checked his watch, and then fixed himself a tuna sandwich for lunch, wrapping it gingerly in tinfoil along with two dill pickle spears. He grabbed an apple and a snack-sized bag of cheese puffs and packed them all into his leather tote bag. Hesitating, he took a second bag of cheese puffs from the pantry and added those to the tote as well.

James loved cheese puffs. They had been his favorite snack for as long as he could remember. As a boy, he ate them at the movies, in front of the TV, and while doing homework. At the library, he now ate cheese puffs with his right hand so that his left would be clean enough to turn the pages of whatever library book he was reading during his lunch break. Even when he was a professor, he had often gotten the orange dust on his student's papers, for he liked to enjoy a treat while grading essays. James was well aware that he had earned the nickname of Professor Puff, and though he hated the idea that the moniker had a double meaning, the satisfaction he received from the cheesy, crispy crunchiness of cheese puffs far outweighed what his students called him behind his back.

"Pop!" James called over the sounds of contestants screaming on *The Price Is Right.* "There are some cold cuts in the fridge for you to make a sandwich for lunch. And there's some canned beef and barley soup in the pantry."

Jackson didn't reply, but James knew there was nothing wrong with his father's hearing. In fact, he had grown accustomed to his father's silence. Jackson hadn't had much to say since he sold the hardware store, and when he did speak, his words were usually critical or strung together to form a complaint. James preferred it when his father was in one of his quiet moods. He wondered how his mother had put up with such morose company, but then again, she had had a way of bringing out the best in everyone.

Heading out to his Bronco, James ignored his reflection in the glass of the storm door. His handsome face looked swollen and weighed down by a rapidly enlarging double chin. He carried his extra weight well—it was evenly distributed over a big-boned, six-foot frame, but his stomach bulged far out over his waistline and his jowls were becoming a distraction. People no longer noticed his intelligent, golden-brown eyes, sincere smile, aquiline nose, or soft waves of nutmeg-colored hair. They became hypnotized by the shaking flesh on his cheeks, sliding their library books across the desk to be checked out in a bit of a stupor.

"Good Morning, Professor Henry," was the chorused greeting that James received ten minutes later at the library's front door. It was the same one he had heard every day since he had taken the job a month ago. Francis and Scott Fitzgerald, the twins who formed the library's only other staff members, aside from a retired schoolteacher who worked part-time, were always waiting to be let in by the time James arrived at eight forty-five.

The twins were long-limbed, brainy bibliophiles who were given up for adoption at birth and spent most of their lives living in a series of foster homes. Luckily, they had never been separated, and the last of their foster homes, which was the one they lived in throughout high school, was a unique place. Their foster parents, Mr. and Mrs. Sloane, owned a bookstore and were die-hard fans of early American literature. The Sloanes believed that fate had brought them together with the brilliant young men named after one of their favorite writers.

Francis and Scott were encouraged to attend the local community college, and the Sloanes helped them acquire scholarships. The boys were so thorough in applying for grants and scholarships that they were able to graduate without any debt. Immediately after graduation, they searched for a job in libraries across Virginia in which they could both be hired together. Only Quincy's Gap offered them both identical jobs.

Francis raised a lanky arm to hold the door open for James and then for his brother, who issued a forceful head bob in gratitude that shook his wild curls of unkempt hair. The young men had attractive faces well hidden behind thick glasses, and when they were not re-shelving books or helping patrons, both would be peering intently at a computer screen or rifling through the pages of a book. James immediately liked their quirkiness as well as their proficiency and punctuality. So far, things had run smoothly at the King Street Branch.

Perhaps living in Quincy's Gap wouldn't be all that bad, James thought hopefully as he tried to put the morning's negativity behind him. The presence of the tidy stacks of books and the Fitzgerald brothers' quirky optimism always seemed to lend him solace when he was feeling down.

"More cheese puffs, Professor?" Francis asked him as James emptied his lunch from his tote bag in order to store his sandwich in the staff fridge.

James nodded, slightly embarrassed.

"I'm a sour cream and onion chip man, myself."

"Poor choice, F. Salt and vinegar is clearly the superior chip," Scott quipped.

"Oh! Customer!" Francis exclaimed, hurling his lunch onto the rectangular table where the three men took turns eating lunch and reading. He strode out to the circulation desk while Scott carefully arranged everyone's sandwiches in a neat row within the fridge. James could hear Francis whispering to someone even though there were no other patrons in the library. Once the clock struck nine, the twins would whisper until their shift was over at five.

Francis poked his head back in the staff room. "There's a lady out there, Professor. She says she needs to ask you about hanging a notice on the lobby bulletin board."

"Certainly," James said, almost repeating a reminder to the twins that they could call him by his first name, but he had told them several times and they seemed determined to call him "Professor." Truthfully, James liked the title. It made him feel dignified and more significant than a small-town librarian each time one of the brothers uttered the word.

Out at the circulation desk a woman was leafing through the latest edition of *People* magazine. When she saw James, she smiled in a friendly fashion and extended a hand bearing small, delicate fingers. "I'm Rosalind, the art teacher up at Blue Ridge High."

James returned the handshake, staring at the young woman's round face as he introduced himself. In fact, all of her was round. She had saucerlike brown eyes, large breasts, a thick waist, and wide hips that only tapered slightly down to short, plump legs. Her hair was a shiny black that reflected a pleasant sheen from the overhead lights and was constricted into a twist held by two lacquered spikes resembling a pair of chopsticks. Her skin was a very light tan, as if made out of café au lait. James looked back down at her petite hands, one of which held a neon pink flyer.

"I was wondering if I could hang this in the lobby," she said loudly and then covered her mouth with her hand. Whispering, she continued, "The old librarian, Mrs. Kramer, was such a witch. She wouldn't hang anything that wasn't related to 'the literary interests of Quincy's Gap,' which basically meant the personal interests of Mrs. Kramer. She wouldn't even let the Girl Scouts hang up their signs for cookie sales. I'm glad you're here now." Rosalind smiled, revealing a mouthful of perfect teeth. "You already seem nicer than old Mrs. Kramer."

"Thank you," James returned her smile warmly. "Well, let's see what you've got there, Rosalind."

"Rosalind is what my Brazilian mother calls me, but you should call me Lindy. All of my friends do."

At that moment, James would have hung a flyer calling for a book burning. No one had even approached James as a possible friend since he had moved home, and the word itself burned pleasantly through James's memory of once having a social life that included parties, dinners, and conversations mixed with great doses of laughter. He took the pink flyer and immediately tacked it up on the bulletin board, reading it as he pressed pushpins through the soft flesh of cork.

Are You Feeling Out of Shape?
Not So Pleasantly Plump?
Downright Miserably Fat?
Join Our New Supper Club!
We Plan to Get Fit Together!
We Meet Every Sunday Night!
Make Friends!
Lose Weight!
Call Lindy at 555-2846

"What do you think?" Lindy asked.

James creased his brows. "I'm afraid I don't know what a supper club is."

"Oh, it's when a bunch of people get together to cook a meal and talk and form friendships. Some clubs have a theme, like cooking light or cooking different exotic foods. My sister lives in Atlanta and she's in a supper club that focuses on pairing wine and food. I came up with the idea that Quincy's Gap should have one where people can lose some weight. Like a dieter's club but more fun. I know I'll never get into shape on my own." She cast her eyes on the ground and mumbled, "And Lord knows I have to stop making excuses."

"So you're just starting to recruit people?" James asked quickly. He didn't like the way in which Lindy had so suddenly become deflated.

"Oh no!" Lindy perked back up. "We have four members already. Actually, we tried to meet last week to decide what kind of food we were going to eat—you know, like what our theme would be, but two of us wanted to count calories like Weight Watchers and the other two wanted to follow a low-carb diet like Atkins or the South Beach Diet. So, we need a tiebreaker."

"Hmm," James responded, nodding his head sympathetically. He disliked indecisiveness as a rule, but he also didn't relish the thought of being a tiebreaker.

"Wait!" Lindy grabbed onto his arm, her wide eyes gleaming. "Why don't *you* join our club? You're new to town and," she picked up his left hand and pointed at his ring finger, "it looks like you're not married. This would be a great way for you to make some friends!"

Reeling from Lindy's enthusiasm, James hesitated. It would be nice to make a few friends, but he was also a bit offended that Lindy so clearly viewed him as someone who needed to diet. Glancing down at his protruding belly, he knew she was right, but it still made him cross to think about his weight.

Lindy dropped her hand from James's arm and softly said, "I didn't mean to insult you. I just thought you'd like to join us."

Her tone was so gentle that James relented. "I'll give it a try. I've gotten to be a decent cook over the last few years, but I don't know much about diets."

Lindy's face filled with delight. "Don't worry about that! We'll figure something out together. Let's see, today's Friday. It feels weird not to be in school, but we've got parent-teacher conferences and no one ever wants to meet with the *art teacher*." Lindy shook her head as if to shake off her annoyance and returned to the subject at hand. "The supper club is meeting Sunday at my place. We're having a lunch meeting this time since we haven't worked out any of the food details yet. Let me write directions down for you."

"Thanks." James smiled and then wondered aloud, "Who else is in the supper club?"

"There's me, of course, and then Lucy Hanover, who works for the Sheriff's Department, Bennett Marshall—he's a mailman— and Gillian O'Malley. She owns the Yuppie Puppy."

James chewed on the name. "Is she a pet groomer?"

"You got it!" Lindy handed him the sheet of directions. "You must know Lucy. You guys both grew up here. Did you go to Blue Ridge High?"

James squirmed. "I did, but I wasn't much of a socializer. I was pretty quiet back then. I *did* play in the band," he added with a mix of pride and embarrassment. "French horn. I might know her if she had been in the band, too. Otherwise, I pretty much went straight home after school . . ." He trailed off, feeling like an idiot for babbling about his lack of teenage social activities.

Lindy seemed to grow pensive for a moment. "I don't think Lucy was in the band. But that's okay! Even if you didn't know each other in high school, you can get to know each other now. In fact, we'll all be getting to know one another. That's part of the beauty of a supper club."

"Uh, should I bring anything?" he asked, relieved that the subject of his lack of friends from the "good old days" was over.

"No need. We're just going to have sandwiches while we decide what kind of food we'll be cooking for the next meeting. See you Sunday at noon. It was nice to meet you, James Henry."

"Nice to meet you, too, Lindy." James stole another glance at the pink flyer and then returned to his duties at the circulation desk. Without realizing it, he was humming softly under his breath. The Fitzgerald twins looked at each other over a rolling cart filled with books that needed reshelving and smiled. They had never heard their boss hum before. It was a pleasant sound.

It was a crisp, sunny weekend morning and Homecoming Saturday to boot. The counter at Dolly's Diner was empty, but Dolly laid out silverware at every place. James could see that she expected to do a booming business before closing shop early in order to see the Blue Ridge Red-Tailed Hawks "put a whupping to those braggarts from Jefferson High," as Dolly so aptly phrased it during lunchtime a few days ago. According to Dolly, the Jefferson Cougars had pummeled the Hawks last year, and the football fans from Quincy's Gap were looking for a little revenge. Dolly counted herself among the most loyal of all Hawks fans.

After casting her eyes in a satisfactory manner over the counter-top, Dolly put her cloud of white hair into a tight bun on the top of her head and peered into the horizontal mirror behind the gleaming rows of clean glasses. James shared the same belief as most of the townsfolk that Dolly looked like a cross between a sumo wrestler and Mrs. Claus. Nobody cared, though. Dolly was beloved by all. She was the mistress of her own domain and treasured three things most in this world: her business, her husband, and gossip.

James could feel Dolly's eyes boring into his back as she brewed a fresh pot of coffee behind the counter. Dolly had clearly decided it was high time she learned a bit more about the town's newcomer. She questioned him relentlessly whenever he came in for a meal, which was often because the food was delicious, but James Henry had so far skillfully avoided her most personal questions. He was friendly and polite, of course, but close-lipped when it came to answering any queries outside the realm of work or food. Dolly was not so easily put off, however, and James steeled himself for another round of bluster and evade.

Dolly ambled over to the booth where James sat, appearing to be deeply engrossed in a novel. "You want some more coffee, hon?" she asked, holding the steaming pot up in front of her ample bosom.

James looked up, blinking, like someone who has just driven out of a dark tunnel into the bright daylight. "Huh? Oh, yes please. Sorry, Dolly. I was completely absorbed in this book." His act didn't fool the all-seeing eyes of the mistress of the diner for a second.

"So," Dolly began, preparing to squeeze new tidbits out of the librarian before he could escape. "I thought I heard your mama tell me about you getting married a few years back." She waited, withholding the coffee until James responded. "How come your wife isn't here with you?"

"I *was* married," James muttered, absently turning a page of his book. "We just got divorced this summer."

Dolly clucked in sympathy and then filled his cup while giving him the once-over with her eyes. "Well, then, you ought to be socializing with folks, not sitting here reading," she said in a teasing tone, even though she meant every word. "How you ever gonna meet someone with your nose stuck in a book?"

James shrugged, recognizing that Dolly was one of those women who liked to make a project out of matching up all the single people she knew. "It's a good book," he said lamely, wishing she would drop the subject.

Dolly waved off his answer and made a dismissive noise by pushing air out through her closed lips. "Pffah. There are plenty of nice women your age that would love to get to know you better. Why, I know . . ." Dolly trailed off, her attention suddenly caught by some movement out the front window. "Sakes alive! Here comes the parade! They're all gonna want to eat here and I don't have all the pies out yet. Clint!" she bustled off, calling for her husband, who was safely out of range in the kitchen.

"You got lucky that time," laughed the young waitress who came over in Dolly's wake to clear James's empty plates. She was tall and fair with freckled skin and had thick, ash-blonde hair pulled up into a high ponytail.

"That was the best stack of strawberry pancakes I have ever tasted," James exhaled, feeling his belt groaning across his bulging waist. "I'm eating all the junk I can before starting a new diet," he told the girl just to make conversation. He had made a terrific mess with the syrup and felt guilty watching her scrub the sticky droplets from the tabletop while he sat there reading.

"Don't want to get your book stuck," she said kindly. Her name tag read *Whitney* and was pinned on the simple white apron she wore over her jeans.

"Did you go to Blue Ridge High?" James asked.

"Yep. Go Hawks!" she said with false enthusiasm.

James put his crumpled napkins on her tray. "Homecoming parade not your thing?"

"Nah. Plus, I could use the hours. I'm attending James Madison U part-time. I'll need all the cash I can get my hands on just to pay for two classes."

"Good for you," James nodded in admiration. "What's a parade when compared to a college education? Do you know what you're planning to major in?"

"Business." Whitney handed James his bill. "I can't wait to get out of this hick town, and I figure a business degree is my ticket to a better life," she added with a surprising amount of vehemence. "If I can ever afford to *complete* my degree, that is."

"Whitney!" Dolly called. "Can you help Clint slice all the meatloaf? I think we are about to be as packed as feathers on a rooster in a few minutes."

James looked around the diner. Aside from him, there were only two other clients enjoying a late breakfast at Dolly's. The midday sun was making its way into the restaurant, glinting off of some of the exotic souvenirs Dolly and Clint had brought home from their travels around the world. Dolly's husband, Clint, had been in the Coast Guard for almost twenty years. He had been stationed in Guam,

Honolulu, the Philippines, Alaska, and up and down both coasts of the United States. Each time Clint was given personal leave, Dolly got to choose a new country for them to visit. Now the evidence of their global wanderings was forever preserved on the walls and in the rafters of the diner.

From his booth, James could reach out and touch an enormous sequined sombrero, a porcelain Mardi Gras mask, an African walking stick with a carved snake curling up the handle, a rusty tin sign reading *Banheiro* (meaning "bathroom" in Portuguese), a cricket bat, a beautiful black silk kimono spread out in order to show off its embroidered green dragon with the forked tongue, and a corkboard covered with the labels from French wine bottles. James tried to sit in a different booth each time he visited in order to admire a fresh collection of treasures before he began reading.

As he scanned the room, James noticed one of Lindy's neon pink flyers posted on the bulletin board by the front door. A young man in a rather ragged-looking letter jacket was examining it. As James watched, the man yanked the flyer off the board and held it out to Dolly, who was wiping an already gleaming countertop.

"What's this?" he yelled across the quiet diner. "An ad for the Fat Loser Club?"

"You hush up, Brinkley Myers," Dolly scolded without looking up from her scrubbing. "Some folks need a little help gettin' into shape. There's no need for you to be puttin' them down."

"Well, I hope *you* don't join in. We all love you *just* the way you are," the young man named Brinkley oozed with false charm while eyeing Dolly's chest.

Dolly flashed him an amused grin. "Now you hang that back up on the board like a good boy," she gently ordered and then disappeared into the kitchen.

Ignoring her, Brinkley shoved the paper into his jacket pocket and then plunked himself down into a nearby booth. James studied the young man from behind his coffee cup. He was tall and muscular, except for the first hints of a promising beer gut, and looked like he was in his mid-twenties. James was unsure why he was still wearing a high school letter jacket, but assumed that he was a former high school jock who wanted to show his support for the football team. He had a square jaw covered with blonde stubble and a full head of curly, reddish-blonde hair. The unkempt hair combined with deep-set dark eyes gave him a roguish Hollywood look.

Draining his tepid coffee, James wondered if Brinkley had kept the flyer because he was planning to join. He hoped not. The young man seemed to wear a cocksure and slightly malicious aura. Turning away from Brinkley, James took a twenty out of his wallet and laid it on the table. Neither Whitney nor Dolly was anywhere to be seen, so he decided to finish the chapter he was reading while waiting for his change.

Outside, the hum of a large group of people intensified as the front door of the diner burst open and the noise of the crowd erupted into the calm room. Dozens of people came streaming into the restaurant, laughing and cheering. All were wearing red and black hats, scarves, or sweatshirts. James recognized the two shades as the school colors of Blue Ridge High.

A group of boys wearing letter jackets crowded into the booth next to him, elbowing one another and yelling loudly at another group of boys sitting at the largest table across the aisle. They all seemed to pay homage to Brinkley before settling down in their seats. A great deal of backslapping and high-fives were exchanged between the high school boys and the lone adult wearing one of their jackets.

Dolly bustled over to the posse of boys with an enormous smile and proudly eyed the rambunctious group. "Well, gentlemen. I've made a special meatloaf to get y'all good and ready for tonight's game. What's needed today is meat and mashed potatoes and a bit of tail whuppin'. What do ya say to that?"

The boys let out a communal holler and banged their fists on the tabletops.

"Just lemme have your drink orders and then I'll be back with your food. I think y'all should have milk—good for your bones—especially when you've got to stand up to some of those Jefferson linebackers, but I know some of you are addicted to ole Dr. Pepper, so I'll let you decide."

Dolly flipped open her pad and began scribbling down drink orders. James tried to catch her eye but she was fussing over the football players like a mother hen, so he looked around for Whitney instead. However, Whitney clearly had her hands full taking care of the group at the counter, so James grabbed the bill and his money and maneuvered around the posse of excited boys clotting the aisles between the booths.

As he struggled to pass the three booths where the football players milled about, a middle-aged woman with hair bleached beyond blonde into white knocked into him with her elbow.

"Sorry," he said. The woman said nothing, but stepped aside to let him pass. At the counter, Whitney was busy serving drinks.

"I'd better pay up," he said, handing her the money. "I think you're going to need my booth. Looks like you've got some football players here."

"Damn right!" exclaimed a man at the countertop as he butted into the conversation. "Those boys are going to play their hearts out tonight. Yes sir. There's nothing better than a night game in October. Nothing better." He thumped the countertop with his palm in order to emphasize his point. James thought he detected a hint of whiskey in the air.

Other patrons at the counter nodded their agreement and then began discussing which game over the course of the last several years had been the coldest. As Whitney handed James his change, Brinkley Myers suddenly appeared behind his right shoulder.

"Hey, Whit," he casually greeted the pretty waitress as James laid down a five-dollar bill out of his pile of change.

Ignoring the speaker completely, Whitney politely thanked James for her tip and then pointedly turned away from Brinkley. She poured glasses of ice water and served them to two men at the other end of the counter without raising her eyes. Brinkley shrugged his shoulders and turned away.

At that moment, James noticed Whitney throw Brinkley a menacing look as the younger man leaned over to chat with one of the customers at the counter. Her eyes blazed with anger for just a flash before she marched off toward the kitchen, her ponytail whipping back and forth like a rapid pendulum.

"You gonna watch the rookies throw some touchdowns tonight, Brinkley?" one of the men asked the boy. "Think anyone's gonna break your record?"

Brinkley puffed out his chest. "For most touchdown passes thrown? No way. No one's going to do that, but hopefully some Cougar *necks* will get broken!"

The men at the countertop applauded. The one sitting in front of James reached around and enthusiastically clapped him on the back, pinning him in place. James was contentedly stuck in the midst of the townsfolk's camaraderie and anticipation. Normally, he would be uncomfortable being in the middle of the crowd, but everyone seemed to accept his presence as natural. James smiled shyly at the men and women seated around him. Then Whitney returned, bearing plates of meatloaf with sides of mashed potatoes swimming in brown gravy for all. Brinkley once again tried to get her attention, but she continued to ignore him.

"So you think we might win tonight?" a woman asked Brinkley as she waited for her meal to cool.

"Yes ma'am," Brinkley nodded and then smiled and raised his voice, his eyes boring into Whitney's turned back. "I've been looking forward to this game all season. I think we're *due* this game. Sometimes it's just time to pay the piper, know what I mean?"

The woman beamed at him. "So you think our boys are going to get lucky?"

"Sure." Brinkley shrugged. "*I* plan to get lucky pretty soon. Right, Whit?" He laughed.

The sexual implication was lost on the woman, but several of the men at the counter guffawed heartily and exchanged high-fives with one another. The pleasant spell James had been under was instantly broken by the men's coarse response. He felt embarrassed for Whitney and gave Brinkley his most disapproving stare. The young man turned and returned James's look with a flippant grin.

As Brinkley passed James, he leaned over and spoke so that only James could hear. "I bet you've never had a girl like that. Maybe it's because you look like you swallowed a few watermelons." Then he gave James a patronizing pat on the belly and moved back toward the booth where the football players and his meatloaf waited.

Trembling with anger, James watched as the boys held out a playbook for Brinkley to examine. They had obviously asked the former player to join them in order to review their plays for the night, and anyone could see that the boys viewed Brinkley as a living legend.

More and more people crammed themselves into the diner. James had had enough of both the crowd and of the gross display of hero worship for such an obnoxious young man. By the time James could finally squeeze himself out the door, with people pushing past him to get in, every seat had been taken. He suddenly noticed that there were no children present at Dolly's, but once he stepped outside he realized why. All of the children and their parents were continuing to march down Main Street. Curious as to their destination and seeking something to buoy his spirits after Brinkley's disparaging remarks, James followed alongside them.

At the edge of town, one of the side streets had been blocked off and a miniature amusement park had been erected. James spotted a petting zoo, pony rides, popcorn and cotton candy machines, as well as several thrill rides, including a tiny roller coaster and a spinning ride that was guaranteed to make the kids who overindulged on cotton candy good and sick. There was also a row of carnival games where parents could spend inordinate amounts of money in order for their child to win a stuffed animal worth a fraction of the cost of the game.

James watched a little girl run up to a female clown wearing an enormous blue and white polka-dotted bow tie and floppy pink shoes and politely ask for a balloon animal. The clown smiled silently, nodding in agreement, and then made a grand show of blowing up and twisting a yellow balloon into the shape of a poodle. The little girl was thrilled and James watched her run back into her parents' arms with a tinge of envy. He wondered if he would ever have the opportunity to experience fatherhood.

James lingered around the children a bit longer, not wanting to return to the quiet of his house and the grumblings of his father. Finally, he strolled back down Main Street toward the parking lot where he had left his car. The street was littered with a variety of small trash from bubble gum wrappers to cigarette butts, but James knew that the town's maintenance crew would restore cleanliness and order before the day was out. After all, weekends meant the arrival of horse people and tourists, the main economic infusion for Quincy's Gap. The horse people would compete in local shows or purchase animals from one of the Quincy's Gap horse farms while the tourists would visit the Civil War sites, historic homes, and apple orchards, or simply drive through the countryside in order to view the vibrant foliage. With the golden sunlight streaming through the pear trees and the carnival atmosphere pulsing in the air, James was feeling more at peace with his hometown than at any other time since his return.

Back at home, Jackson had locked himself in his shed as usual and had closed all the shades so that James had no idea what he was up to. James didn't even bother telling his father that he was home. He doubted the old man would even notice until dinnertime. He fixed himself some decaf, settled on the davenport to read, and then briefly considered attending the football game. James wasn't very interested in sports, but it might be a topic of conversation at tomorrow night's supper club and James didn't want to appear uninvolved in one of the autumn's biggest events. Then again, he decided that since he was almost done reading his book and that it was sure to be cold at the game, he might as well stay put.

After a peaceful afternoon reading and munching on cheese puffs—he easily polished off a jumbo-sized bag—James decided to cook a hearty pot of stew for dinner. As he was peeling carrots his father shuffled wearily in the back door. Ignoring James, Jackson fixed himself a cup of coffee and headed into the den. The sound of the television filled the silence. After some channel surfing, Jackson found a rerun of *Family Feud*.

James sighed in annoyance. When the stew was ready, he brought a bowl in to his father and placed it on a TV tray. Jackson never turned his face away from the screen. His eyes were red and puffy as if he had not slept well recently.

"What are you doing out there all day, Pop?" James asked in concern.

Instead of answering, Jackson pointed at James's shirt. "You got orange stuff all over you again."

James looked down at the familiar orange dust. "It's from the cheese puffs. It was my last bag. I'm going to start a diet on Sunday."

His father shook his head in disbelief and then focused on the television once more. "Stupid, stupid," he muttered, and James didn't know whether he was referring to the contestants, who couldn't seem to get any of the answers right, or to his son, who couldn't seem to get anything right either.

TWO

COFFEE CAKE

JAMES WENT TO THE early church service. He hadn't been to church in years and he felt like an imposter sitting in the polished pews among the genuinely devout members of the congregation. At least they all appeared to be genuinely devout. None of them seemed to have James's problem of being distracted from the droning words of the sermon by the scenes of the apostles depicted in the glorious stained glass windows or by the coughing of the man in the front pew. It was a wet, racking cough, filled with phlegm, and James was certain that at any moment, the man's entire lung would be deposited in the hand that he was using to cover his mouth while he coughed. The sermon was entitled "How You

Nutrition Facts	
Serving Size 1/12 cake (54g)	
Servings Per Container 12	
Amount Per Serving	
Calories 230 Calories from Fat 110	
	% Daily Value*
Total Fat 12g	19%
Saturated Fat 3g	15%
Cholesterol 15 mg	5%
Sodium 140 mg	6%
Total Carbohydrate 28g	9%
Dietary Fiber 1g	4%
Sugars 15g	
Protein 2g	
Vitamin A 0% • Vitamin C 0%	
Calcium 2% • Iron 4%	
*Percent Daily Values are based on a 2,000 calorie diet. Your daily values may be higher or lower depending on your calorie needs.	

Can Be More Giving," and James thought he really should pay attention, but he had already given up so much in order to care for his father and he felt that the level of gratitude being shown to him by his remaining parent was greatly wanting.

As the sermon wore on, James felt the roof of his mouth grow exceedingly dry. He slid down the pew so that he could reach a hand into his pants pocket without obviously doing so. Deep inside that pocket, nestled in a collection of loose change and keys, was a mint. Just as James began the agonizingly slow unwrapping of the mint, pausing each time his fingers created too much noise in untwisting its crinkly casing, the minister paused for a moment of prayer.

James stopped working at the mint's stubborn wrapper and instantly sat up, afraid that the worshippers seated beside him would realize that he had been caught unawares that the sermon had concluded. As he jerked his body upwards, the loose coins in his pocket spilled out onto the pew and rolled on the floor. James thought that the echoed tinkling of his falling coins could surely be heard in China. Several of the old ladies seated in front of him slowly pivoted around in order to give him reproachful glances.

Stooping to collect his change, not because he wanted the money but because he wanted to hide the red flush of embarrassment that had crept up his neck and covered his fleshy cheeks, James was prevented from seeing that the collection plate had arrived at his pew. Just as he straightened up, his fist closed around the wayward coins, his neighbor held out the large brass plate to him.

Here is my chance to redeem myself, James thought, smiling. He would put a generous contribution into the offering plate and then no one would pay him any more attention. He pulled out his wallet from his back pocket and opened it hastily, aware that his neighbor was still holding out the heavy plate. Her friendly looks soon rearranged themselves into confused ones, and these would soon make way for looks of irritation if James did not produce some money quickly. To his horror, only two singles lay tucked in the folds of his wallet. James had forgotten to go to the bank! And naturally, his checkbook was at home. He only used checks to pay bills, so he never carried it on his person.

Looking around wildly, he finally accepted the plate from his neighbor, who continued to pointedly wait for James to place his money in the plate. In fact, James had taken so long that people all around his pew began looking at him. The hymn, which was usually repeated three times during the collection, had now begun its fourth repetition. Whispering began. In a panic, James pulled out the two singles and folded them into a roll, hoping that his neighbors would be fooled into believing there were bills of a higher notation within the roll. At the last second, he unceremoniously plopped in his loose change as well.

As he handed the plate off, he felt as if the skin on his face had caught fire. The man he handed the plate to shook his head in what James felt was a very un-Christian display of disgust, and the service mercifully continued. James was so flummoxed during the final hymn that he sang louder than he should have and continued to attract odd glances from those seated nearby.

When the service finally ended, James decided to make a hasty break for the door and vowed to wait to until at least Christmas, or possibly not until Easter, before returning to church. Just when James thought he might safely reach the exit doors, Dolly appeared out of the blue and hooked her arm in his.

"Why, Professor Henry!" she exclaimed as if she hadn't seen him in years. "I don't think I saw you at the game last night."

"No, I didn't make it," James stammered.

"Oh! You missed quite a show! Blue Ridge won, don't you know? And guess how close the score was?"

"I can't imagine. One touchdown?" James asked, looking longingly at the front door, which was receding as Dolly tugged him in the opposite direction.

"Not even! There was only one field goal separating us from glory!" Dolly gushed as she cut a swathe through the group of parishioners with her protrusive bosom and maneuvered James toward the refreshment table where several ladies were removing coffee cakes from white bakery boxes and cutting them into neat squares. "Now, Professor, you've just *got* to try Megan's coffee cake. It is *simply* out of this world!" Dolly collected a plate and fork and handed them over to James. "You know, Megan owns the Sweet Tooth, the candy store and bakery. I don't think it was open yet when you were visiting last Christmas. *And*," she lowered her voice to a conspiratorial whisper, "she's single, but she's got a daughter," Dolly plowed on. "Not to worry, the girl's out of high school. Should be living on her own by now but . . . do you like kids?"

James cut off an enormous piece of coffee cake with his plastic fork and hastily shoveled it into his mouth, guaranteeing that he would be unable to reply without illustrating bad manners. However, he was unprepared for the savory sensation of that bite of coffee cake. All at once, he tasted brown sugar, almonds, vanilla, and a powerfully strong jolt of sugary icing. Relishing every chew, he had to close and re-open his eyes for a moment to make sure that he hadn't actually died and been sent straight to coffee cake heaven.

"Good, huh? I told you, honey." Dolly punched James playfully in the arm. "That woman can bake!" She lowered her voice again. "Now I hear she can't actually cook worth a damn—just sweets—but you two could work that out. Lemme introduce you."

James finished his coffee cake in three bites and then made a big show of checking his watch. Thankfully, it was 11:45, time for him to head over to Lindy's.

"I can't right now, Dolly," he pointed at his watch. "I'm actually supposed to meet someone at noon."

Dolly was immediately interested. "Oh ho! And who is this *someone?*" she demanded, refusing to release his arm.

James did not want to offend Dolly, and he could hardly drag himself away while she physically restrained him, so he looked around for a distraction. Not seeing any behavior worthy of repetition at the diner tomorrow, James had to make up something on the spot.

"Is that Clint over there, talking to Luanne Lovett?" he asked slyly.

That did it. Dolly swiveled her head back and forth like an owl. Luanne Lovett was a celebrated flirt. Having just divorced her third husband, she was said to be on the prowl for number four. With a Rubenesque body and a pretense of girlish naivety, which women could instantly see through but men somehow could not, Luanne had become a threat to marriages throughout the county. James hadn't actually seen either Clint or Luanne, but he knew that Dolly would forget about her matchmaking the second she heard the vixen's name. Dolly dashed forward into the mingling crowd and James was free to make his escape.

Driving to Lindy's, he reflected that he was lucky to have eaten that wonderful coffee cake before officially starting his diet. From now on, he would stick to whatever foods his new friends determined they could all eat and still lose weight. At the next red light, James checked his reflection in the rearview mirror. He brushed some coffee cake crumbs from the front of his shirt and chuckled. He would never succeed in losing weight if he were involved with the owner of a bakeshop.

Lindy's house was a small gray bungalow within walking distance of Blue Ridge High. The yard was colorful, with a square of green lawn, neatly trimmed shrubs, a bed bursting with raspberry asters, and a grouping of ochre-colored chrysanthemums set in purple and red ceramic pots astride the front door. Several other cars were parked along the curb in front of Lindy's house, and the sight of a tan Jeep and a mail truck made James nervous for a moment. Lindy seemed nice enough, but what would the other members of the group be like? Would they like him, a divorced librarian?

Suddenly, James felt like retreating. He had never been very good at making new friends. In Williamsburg, he had left his social life in the hands of his capable wife. Most of his friends were just spouses of her friends, but they had all gotten along just fine. Now that he was on his own, he worried that he had little to offer this group of strangers.

Before he could entertain any more second thoughts, a car pulled up behind his truck. The car's front bumper was so close to the back of his Bronco that he was effectively boxed in. There was no turning back now. A woman with what James could only describe as a bird's nest of orange hair stepped out of the compact sedan and waved at him.

"I'm Gillian!" she called, walking up to him with hurried steps. "You must be James Henry."

They shook hands. Gillian ran her fingers through her tangled locks and gestured toward the house. "Shall we?"

James followed behind, noting that Gillian had a barrel-shaped torso carried about by a pair of trim and shapely legs. Her billowy tent shirt and tight purple leggings emphasized the fact that she was as wide in the waist as she was in the hips. On top of the oversized shirt, Gillian had arranged two flimsy shawls in bright purple and blue with strands of sparkling silver threads running through them. These hung far down her expansive back and followed in her wake like two kite tails. Gillian was like a walking rainbow with her orange hair, aquamarine eyes, sapphire shirt, and purple leggings. James had never seen anyone like her before. She reminded him of pictures he had seen of hippies dancing at Woodstock, except that all of those hippies were waif-thin and Gillian, with the exception of her legs, was not.

Gillian rang the doorbell. Inside the house, Lindy called out, "Come on in!" so James and Gillian obeyed. Lindy met them in her tiny front hall carrying a bowl of potato chips. James eyed them hungrily.

"Chips?" Gillian immediately frowned. "I thought we were starting a diet."

"These are baked, not fried. And anyway, we haven't decided which diet we're doing so we're just having sandwiches for lunch." Lindy turned her friendly smile toward James. "Lucy and Bennett are already here. I've just laid out bread and lunch meat on the kitchen counter, so we'll fix ourselves sandwiches and then get down to brass tacks."

As James walked into the kitchen, a short and stocky black man with a toothbrush mustache and close-cropped hair stopped spreading mayo on his bread and held out his hand to James. "Bennett Marshall, U.S. Postal Service carrier. Pleased to meet you."

"You too. James Henry, uh, librarian."

Bennett cocked an eyebrow. "But some of your mail reads 'Professor,' doesn't it?"

"Ah . . . yes it does." James looked over Bennett's shoulder at a pear-shaped woman wearing a plaid flannel shirt over black pants, which were clearly straining against her wide hips and thighs. Her shirt looked oversized, as if she were trying to hide a large chest, but the shape of her ample breasts was as apparent as two loaves of bread extending out of a plastic grocery bag. She was busy folding three slices of turkey on top of a piece of bread and did not notice James studying her. She had shoulder-length hair the color of melted caramel and when she eventually raised her eyes to meet his, James was rather astonished by their unusual shade of blue. They reminded him of bachelor's buttons, his mother's favorite flower. James felt the something stir inside as he gazed at Lucy, but he quickly looked away so that she would not know what he was feeling.

"I *was* a professor," he finally answered Bennett's question, grinning shyly at the woman who he assumed must work for the sheriff.

"James Henry, this is Lucy Hanover." Lindy pointed back and forth at the two of them with a knife covered in mustard. "Behave yourself or she'll have to arrest you."

"Hi," Lucy said, raising her plate in greeting. "Don't listen to Lindy. I'm just an assistant over at the Sheriff's Department. I don't even own a pair of handcuffs," she teased and then grew quickly serious. "I'd sure love to be a real deputy someday, but I've got an uphill road to climb before that can ever happen." She looked at the window as if seeing herself in the sheriff's brown and beige uniform and then turned back to James with a dazzling smile. "We're glad you joined our group, James."

"Thanks." James made himself a ham and cheese sandwich and then sat down next to Bennett at the kitchen table. The space was small, but it gave the group's gathering an immediate feeling of comfort and coziness.

Gillian sat down at the table, picking up one of Lindy's pink flyers, which had been wadded into a tight ball and tossed next to a ceramic napkin dispenser. "What's this?" she asked.

Lindy shrugged. "Oh, someone decided to edit my flyer. Probably one of my students. I'm sure they thought it was funny, but *I* don't."

Gillian straightened out the crumpled sheet and read the revised version.

> *Are You Feeling Like a Total Lard?*
> *Do You Look Like a Bowling Ball?*
> *How about a Beached Whale?*
> *Join Our New Loser's Club!*
> *We Meet in the Grocery Store!*
> *Make Friends with Other Losers!*
> *Lose with Losers!*
> *Call Lardy Lindy at 1-800-EAT-MORE*

"Very original," Gillian nonchalantly tossed the flyer into the garbage. "Whoever wrote that is a regular Shakespeare."

"I saw that kid, Brinkley Myers, mowing the lawn across the street," Bennett said, chewing on his sandwich. "I bet it was him. He always looks like he's up to no good—just got one of those faces."

"It wouldn't surprise me," Lindy agreed. "He was one of my worst students. He thought he was so great at football that he didn't have to apply himself to any of his academic subjects. I was stuck being his academic advisor. What a nightmare! He barely graduated and now he's mowing lawns. Guess he might be a little bitter," she sniggered. "He still wears that letter jacket all over town. And *we're* the losers? Ha! Pass me the chips please, Bennett."

"That might be the last sandwich with three slices of American cheese and regular mayo you have for a while," Bennett taunted Lindy. "That is, if we go on your Weight Watchers plan."

"Gillian wants to do that plan, too," Lindy said defensively.

"Well, I just *cannot* eat all of the meat they have on those low-carb plans. Gross!" Gillian shivered dramatically, her hair floating in front of her eyes.

"Are you a vegetarian?" James inquired.

"I eat some chicken and fish, but I'd *really* like to be. I can almost *sense* the pain of those animals . . ." Gillian paused and then continued. "The problem I have is if I don't eat any meat, I end up eating too many heavy starches like bread and potatoes. It all sticks right on me. I don't even have a *dent* to indicate a waist anymore. I'm like a walking marshmallow."

The rest of the group nodded empathetically. "I used to be a lean, mean, wrestling machine," Bennett said, wiping the potato chip grease shining on his fingers onto his paper napkin. "All that muscle has turned to flab. Know why? 'Cause I eat during my deliveries. Lots of snacks from the 7-Eleven."

"What do you eat that's so bad?" Lucy asked.

"Donut holes mostly," Bennett answered. "You know, the little ones that come in a box. I just pop 'em right in. I eat a whole box every day, and I am not a tall man." He turned to James. "You can carry some extra weight pretty well. Me, I can't."

Lindy piped right up at that comment. "I'm short, too! My deal is that I can't stop eating candy. I keep bite-sized pieces in my drawer at school as a reward for kids who help me with something, like unloading the pottery kiln. Problem is, I keep eating it." Lindy patted her stomach. "I've eaten myself out of all the clothes in my closet. I have *got* to do something. You see, I'd love to catch the eye of our new principal. He's Latino and *so* handsome . . . but he looks right through me whenever we meet in the hall. I want to make him look twice!"

"Here, here!" Gillian raised her cup of water in salute to Lindy's romantic dream.

Feeling safe enough to contribute, James decided to volunteer his own problem with food addiction. "I'm a cheese puff man. Once a bag is open, I just can't stop eating them. I guess . . . well, the real trouble is that they actually . . ." he paused, "make me feel good."

Everyone was quiet for a moment and James wondered if he had confessed too much with that last statement. Lucy looked at him kindly with those lovely blue eyes and nodded in understanding. He felt his heart pounding beneath his ribs.

"I know exactly what you mean," she said. "For me, it's frosting. You know, like birthday cake or cupcake frosting. When I've had a really bad day, I'll actually eat it right out of the can. It's gross, I know, but that sweet taste just makes me forget about whatever is going wrong. Until later. Then I feel really terrible for eating it. I keep saying that I want to become a deputy and I know I have the brains for it, but until I can control myself, I'll *never* have the body for it. And every time I even think about passing any kind of physical, I feel so lousy that I might actually go back and eat *more* frosting." She sighed. "It's a pretty vicious cycle."

Everyone bobbed his or her head in agreement. They all knew the feelings of pleasure followed by guilt that Lucy described.

"I have an *issue* with peanut butter cups," Gillian whispered. "I sit there, trying to meditate . . ." She turned to James to explain. "I do a lot of yoga. Anyway, I'm trying to get to my state of Zen but instead of visualizing emptiness, I'm picturing peanut butter cups! I'll never achieve enlightenment at this rate." Gillian was being serious, but the other four people around the table chuckled and then tried to hide their amused grins.

"So we have two items to cover today," Lindy redirected the conversation to more proactive territory. "We must choose a diet plan and then decide where to meet for our first *official* supper club. Gillian and I want Weight Watchers. Bennett and Lucy want to try a low-carb diet. I'm afraid it's up to you to choose for us, James."

James shifted in his chair. He had been feeling entirely comfortable a moment ago but now he had suddenly been put on the spot. He really didn't have a preference as to which diet, he just wanted to be involved with a group that he felt he had something in common with. James looked at each expectant face. When he gazed at Lucy across the table, he noticed that she had a faint peppering of freckles across the bridge of her nose. She gave him a shy smile as he looked at her and then turned away to take a few more potato chips out of the bag.

James decided to pick the low-carb diet, as he didn't think he had the discipline to count points or calories. He assumed from listening to commercials that he would need to keep track of his food on a Weight Watchers type of diet. Plus, he had an inexplicable desire to please his new friend Lucy, and if choosing the diet would make him look good in her eyes, then that was reason enough for him.

"I think I vote for low carb," he said hesitantly.

Lucy and Bennett happily exchanged high-fives and then Bennett clamped James on the shoulder. "You're *all right*, my friend."

"Since I'm thrilled with this choice, we can meet at my place for the first supper next week," Lucy offered.

"Just as long as you put those dogs of yours *outside*," Bennett grumbled and both Lindy and Gillian laughed.

"I can't even get near her mailbox," Bennett explained to James wryly. "She's got three of the most terrifying German shepherds known to humankind, and I am *not* afraid of dogs."

"This is so exciting!" Lindy exclaimed. "We are going to have so much fun helping one another lose weight!"

"But how do we know what to eat?" Gillian complained.

No one said anything for a moment and then James spoke up, feeling more confident now that his decision had been given and accepted. "We've got several diet books at the library. And I'm sure I could look some menus up on the Internet, so I volunteer to figure out what meal we should eat on Sunday. I'll give everyone an idea for an item to bring."

Lindy got up and retrieved a pad of paper and a pen from one of her kitchen drawers. "Why don't we exchange e-mails and phone numbers, and then James can tell us what to bring? Is that okay with everyone?" They all agreed and thanked James for his initiative. "And I think that whoever offers their house shouldn't have to cook," Lindy continued. "It's enough to have to clean up before and after."

"Oh!" Gillian exclaimed dramatically. "I truly hope we can lose some weight together, but it won't be easy. Do you think we need a slogan or a name or something to psych us up?"

Everyone grew silent as they tried to conjure up a witty moniker for their supper club group.

"There are five of us. How about the Fab Five?" Lindy offered.

Lucy shook her head. "That's taken. Besides," she spread her arms out to encompass everyone at the table. "We're not exactly fabulous . . . yet."

"Yeah, more like flabulous," Bennett cackled.

"So instead of the Fab Five, we're the Flab Five," James mumbled, grinning to himself. Everyone turned to stare at him and then four round faces lit up with laughter.

"That's it!" Lindy shrieked. "That's what we are! And when we've knocked off the flab, we'll change our name. We need to *earn* that name change though. I mean, really earn it. Together." Lindy put her hand in the middle of the table. "Put your hand on mine if you are willing to be a member of the Flab Five and pursue a low-carb diet until your personal weight loss goals have been met."

Everyone put a hand on top of hers. James was last and as his hand covered Lucy's, he felt the warmth of the room and the people seated at the table beside him fill up an empty space within him. It had been so long since he had shared any feelings of true companionship that he believed he might actually start to cry. Quickly withdrawing his hand, he covered up the emotions welling up inside his throat by saying, "I'll prepare a food list of what we're allowed to eat during my lunch break tomorrow. You can all stop by the library at the end of the day and pick one up. This way, we'll all be eating low-carb foods during the week. Maybe we can share how much we've lost when we meet again next Sunday."

"*If* we've lost anything," Gillian said glumly.

Just as all of them were pondering the enormity of their individual tasks, a siren screamed outside the window and a parade of three brown cars with lights blazing zipped past.

"That's the sheriff! And Keith and Luke and—" Lucy exclaimed, jumping up. "I'm going to call over to the station and see what's going on! Can I use your phone, Lindy?"

"Sure," Lindy gestured toward the wall phone in the kitchen. As the sirens moved off in the distance, she mused out loud. "You know, while we're all here we should talk about some ideas for exercise."

Bennett groaned. "Seriously," continued Lindy as Lucy listened to a loud voice coming over the phone line. "Maybe we could meet at the high school track and walk or something."

"I don't know," Gillian replied, tossing the end of one of her scarves over her shoulder. "We all have such different schedules. And I am *not* a morning person like you folks are."

"What about you, James?" Lindy peered at him hopefully.

James didn't answer. He was too distracted by Lucy's puzzled facial expression. She looked completely bewildered.

"Anything the matter?" James inquired softly, afraid of being too nosy.

"I'm just talking about a little cardiac activity, people," Lindy plowed on defensively, believing that James had been speaking to her. "It's not like I'm trying to . . ." She paused as she read the curiosity depicted on the others' faces. Everyone was watching Lucy. Swiveling in her chair, Lindy joked, "What's going on Ms. Sheriff?"

"No one is answering at the station," Lucy replied, shrugging her shoulders. "It's just unusual. They've got the machine on." Lucy silently put on her jacket, her eyes showing both concern and a twinkle of exhilaration. "Maybe they need some help. I'd better get down there. This might be my big chance to prove myself indispensable. I'll call you guys and let you know what's going on." Lucy hurried out to her car.

The remaining foursome exchanged perplexed looks but said nothing.

"You don't think . . ." Lindy began and then trailed off. After a moment she spoke again. "Why would every deputy be at one call? Something *big* must have happened!"

"What are you suggesting?" Gillian asked, eyes wide.

"You know," Lindy whispered. "Something *bad*. Maybe even a *murder*. I wonder if our local boys could handle that. Maybe they'd have to get help from some cute forensic guys from Harrisonburg or Charlottesville. Maybe *Unsolved Mysteries* or *CSI* would want to do a story based on our little town . . ." She trailed off, absorbed in her own fantasy.

"That's ridiculous. We don't have that kind of violence in Quincy's Gap, Lindy. It's simply impossible." Gillian tried to sound doubtful, but her voice caught a little on the word "impossible." She pulled out a crystal pendant from the depths of her shirt and began to rub it fiercely.

Bennett calmly folded his napkin into a tiny square. "Well, homicide rates in the South have increased more than in any other part of the United States, especially when guns have been involved. We may be a small town, but we're a small Southern town. Statistically, I guess we're due." He turned to James. "Statistics are my hobby."

"You might be useful to a TV producer, Bennett," Lindy said, fixated with her idea. "I think you'd be a great character for a detective show."

"You really think so?" Bennett asked, his dark eyes glowing.

James noticed that the group's initial concern had gradually turned to excitement as the speculations grew. He was ashamed to think that he was feeling a kind of thrill over the mystery, but he had to admit to himself that he was extremely interested in what Lucy might discover down at the station.

"I wonder where those patrol cars were headed," he mused aloud.

"I can answer that." Bennett pointed toward the mail truck parked outside. "I've got a police scanner in there. If anything's going on, we'll hear it."

The foursome practically ran to the mail truck. Though it was only parked at the end of Lindy's front walkway, they were all short of breath after hustling their normally sedentary bodies at such speed out to the street.

Bennett hopped into the driver's seat and began to turn dials on the scanner. There seemed to be a lot of static and the voices were not coming through clearly. Eventually, the garbling ceased long enough for them to understand the words "Sweet Tooth" and "901H."

"A 901H," Bennett muttered morosely.

"What the devil is that?" Gillian demanded.

"It's a code. Most law enforcement agencies share a common set of codes which—"

"But what does it mean?" Gillian shook her fists with agitation. "Is it . . . what does it stand for?"

"It's a call for an ambulance," Bennett replied, glancing nervously at Gillian's fists, "to pick up a dead body." He sighed lugubriously. "Looks like the sheriff and his crew are too late to help anyone."

"A body in the bakery? I hope it's not Megan Flowers or her daughter." Gillian grabbed Bennett by the sleeve. "Let's go find out what's happened!"

Bennett's eyes lit up. He had never actually witnessed any of the codes he could so skillfully translate on his police scanner. "Hop in, folks. It's against regulations to have you in here, but . . ."

As they sped off downtown, Gillian frowned and said, "I hope Lucy stayed at the station. It's obvious that she's dying to wear a uniform, but the Sweet Tooth wouldn't be the best setting to start offering her investigative services."

Bennett seemed lost in his own thoughts. "Who knows what kind of situation the sheriff is dealing with right now? All we know is there is a body involved."

"It's not *what* he's investigating that Gillian's worried about, Bennett, it's *where* he's investigating. I hope Lucy is staying put at the station, too, answering phones or whatever it is she usually does," Lindy added as they raced well over the speed limit toward Main Street.

"What would be the problem with her meeting us at the bakery?" James asked in Lucy's defense. "She must be as curious as the rest of us. You could see she was hoping to be able to offer some kind of assistance."

Lindy looked at him as if he were a mental patient. "James, we just started a diet. We've got to keep Lucy away from the Sweet Tooth. The place is *filled* with frosting!"

THREE

CHOCOLATE CHIP COOKIE

Nutrition Facts	
Serving Size 1 cookie (71g)	
Amount Per Serving	
Calories 350 Calories from Fat 160	
	% Daily Value*
Total Fat 18g	28%
Saturated Fat 7g	35%
Cholesterol 20 mg	7%
Sodium 330 mg	14%
Total Carbohydrate 46g	15%
Dietary Fiber 1g	4%
Sugars 27g	
Protein 3g	
Vitamin A 2% • Vitamin C 0%	
Calcium 0% • Iron 10%	
*Percent Daily Values are based on a 2,000 calorie diet. Your daily values may be higher or lower depending on your calorie needs.	

BENNETT WAS ACCUSTOMED TO driving a mail truck bearing the weight of thousands of letters, hundreds of magazines, and dozens of packages, but the painful squealing of tires as his official vehicle of the United States Postal Service turned the corner of Elm and Main streets made him cringe. Apparently, four overweight human bodies shifting around the interior were harder on the truck's axles than all the mail delivered during the Christmas season.

"Hurry!" Lindy yelled excitedly. Her long hair whipped about her face like a licorice-colored tornado and her round cheeks were tinged pink with expectation. Bennett had his window cranked down in order to escape the overpowering scent of Gillian's patchouli perfume, but Gillian constantly leaned over his headrest in order to convey a list of impatient questions about the conversations taking place on the police scanner.

"They're saying that there are two women inside the Sweet Tooth," Bennett shouted over the wind. "Megan and Amelia Flowers. The police are going to question them."

"Good, that means that they're alive, but who's the victim?" Gillian demanded.

James couldn't make out a word coming from the scanner. All of its garbled noises sounded like voices shouting underwater. He looked out his window at the quiet town. Church services had ended and most folks ate a large midday meal at home and then piddled around their houses crossing jobs off of their honey-do lists, tending to the fall gardens, or taking leisurely strolls. Very few businesses were open on Sunday, but James knew that some people would wander into town for an afternoon treat from the bakery or to pick up fresh bread for supper sandwiches. Whatever happened at the Sweet Tooth would soon be discovered. Perhaps that was why he and his new friends hoped to get there first. It would give each of them something exciting to talk about at work Monday morning.

Barreling down Main Street, the mail truck made record time before it finally slowed to a crawl before the bakery. Three sheriff's cars with blue lights flashing had parked helter-skelter along the curb, indicating how quickly they had arrived at the scene.

"Nice work, Bennett. We made it in three minutes. It looks like we even beat the ambulance here." Lindy clapped Bennett on the back. "We'd better park next door, in that back lot behind the stationary store."

"Good idea," Bennett agreed, maneuvering the truck into the gravel lot. "Look! There's Lucy's Jeep!"

The mail truck groaned to a halt and its four passengers clambered out. Sticking as close as possible to the cement wall on the alley side of the bakery, they crept as stealthily as they could in the direction of the back door. Lindy, who was leading the inquisitive foursome, turned the corner into the bakery's parking lot and then leapt backward right onto Bennett's big toe.

"Ow!" he yowled. Lindy clamped a hand hastily across his mouth.

"Sorry," she whispered, making frantic hand gestures commanding everyone to retreat. "Lucy is standing right outside. She's talking to one of the deputies. Listen."

Sure enough, voices floated to their corner of the building. The town's Sunday afternoon tranquility, defined by a noticeable lack of traffic noise, allowed their eager ears to clearly hear the strained conversation taking place just outside of the bakery's back door.

"Look, Keith," Lucy was saying in a pleading tone. "I just want to observe, see if I can learn something. I've mentioned that I want to take the deputy's exam in the future and I—"

"I thought you were *joking*!" the man laughed maliciously. "Come on, Lucy. You'd never pass the physical. Besides, being a deputy is a *man's* job."

"I don't think so," Lucy replied timidly. "There are plenty of women in law enforcement and even in the Armed Forces. If they—"

Keith interrupted her once again, "I'd *love* to get into a philosophical debate with you, Lucy, but right now I've got a dead body to examine and some witnesses to interview." He paused. "You ever seen a corpse, Lucy?"

"No."

"What makes you think you can handle seeing one? I mean, most dead bodies are not pretty things. There's blood and nasty smells and all *kinds* of bodily fluids involved, if you get my drift. It takes a tough person to look at one. You think you're tough enough?"

Listening to the deputy's patronizing tone, James suppressed an urge to come to Lucy's defense. Why didn't the jackass just give Lucy a chance? But instead of running to her side, James bit his lip and took a quick peek around the corner of the building in order to get a look at Lucy's crass coworker.

Keith stood with his hands on his hips and his legs drawn apart in a cowboy-like stance. His red hair glinted in the October sunlight, and even from a distance, James could see that his face was covered so completely with freckles that it was difficult to see the pallid skin underneath. Keith wore mirrored sunglasses that reminded James of the cool cop shows on TV during the 70s, but seemed startlingly out of place in a small Virginia town in the twenty-first century.

"Let me see if I *can* handle seeing a dead body, Keith. If it upsets me, then I won't bother thinking about taking the exam." Lucy's pleading was pathetic. Her new friends looked at one another, their eyes replete with sympathy.

"Donovan!" another male voice called out from within the building. "Get your tail in here!"

James saw Keith do a little jump and then hustle inside, leaving the door ajar. Lucy hesitated for a fraction of a second, and then pulled a small notebook from her purse, turned to a fresh sheet of paper, and resolutely followed in her redheaded tormentor's wake.

"Come on!" Lindy moved forward, tiptoeing up to the back door.

The heavy metal door had been propped open and the sounds of a woman's hysterical voice could be heard from within. Aside from the view of cooking equipment and the tantalizing smell of freshly baked cookies that curled around the foursome like an alluring, invisible boa, there was nothing to be seen through the back door.

"They must be up front," Gillian suggested. "We can't go in, so let's sneak around to the street side and see if we can peak in the front windows."

At that moment, the honk of a nearby horn sliced through the stillness.

"Hurry! That could be the paramedics!" cried Bennett as he led the group around the building. "It is! Look!"

The yellow van from Quincy's Gap Fire & Rescue moved quietly but briskly past them into the bakery's small parking lot. The driver honked again, but the breathless group was too far away to see why he was making such unnecessary noise.

The first window they reached took up most of the storefront. Megan Flowers always displayed examples of her decorous wedding cakes in that window, along with a sampling of items she would bake during the week. Today, her display shelves had been covered with black and orange crepe paper. Plastic pumpkins were brimming over with miniature banana nut and pumpkin spice muffins. A black plastic cat with glowing purple eyes drew attention to a platter of donuts dripping with white icing and showered with orange sprinkles. Beneath the shadow of a friendly scarecrow, another platter featured Megan's latest creation: a variety of cookies in the shapes of various monsters. Each cookie looked like it had been slathered with an inch of homemade buttercream. James's eye was particularly drawn to the Dracula cookies. Each pale-faced vampire had two rivulets of bright ruby icing dripping down from fangs fashioned out of white sprinkles.

"I've never seen such a good-looking mummy," Gillian said, pointing at a cookie.

"Forget him," Lindy drooled. "I'd take that Frankenstein's monster cookie any day. Look at all the black sprinkles making up his hair."

Bennett tried to see beyond the display. Standing on his tiptoes, his view was blocked by a shelf crammed with miniature éclairs swollen with custard.

"James," Bennett croaked, his mouth dry with longing. "You're the tallest. See anything?"

James finally drew his focus beyond the display of delicious goodies. Unfortunately, he could only make out the backs of three people as they stood looking down at something. There were two women and one man. From this angle, he couldn't tell what their eyes were riveted on. He *could* see Lucy, however, standing off to the side, and it was clear that she was fighting to control her emotions. Her lovely face had turned rather gray and the hand that gripped her notebook was shaking. Someone must have addressed her, for she wordlessly nodded and began writing notes with a tremulous hand.

"I can't see what they're looking at. We're going to have to move to the other window," James informed the others. "That will mean going right past the front door. It will seem kind of odd if all four of us slink past the door and then stop to stare in the window."

"Well, the sign still says 'Open,' so it won't be so strange that we're walking past the bakery," argued Gillian. "And from the looks of Lucy's face, there is *definitely* something worth seeing in there!"

Crouching as low as they could, the foursome shuffled past the entrance and to the smaller storefront window. The display in this section was mostly an array of breads. Beyond the plump mounds of rye, pumpernickel, egg, and raisin breads, along with baskets brimming over with dill and rosemary rolls, James was able to get a clear view of the three people whose backs he had gazed upon a few seconds ago.

The first was a burly, middle-aged man with an enormous mustache. He appeared to be asking questions of a tall woman wearing a red-and-white striped apron with the words *The Sweet Tooth* written across it. Her slender arms were folded across her chest in a pose of self-preservation and her eyes were filled with a combination of fear and confusion. Standing next to her, close enough to touch, was a younger, more curvaceous version of the woman wearing the apron. The younger woman had dull blonde hair that fell forward into her eyes as she stared fixedly at the floor. She held a rolled-up magazine in her right hand, tightly enough to cause her knuckles to turn white.

"That's Sheriff Huckabee talking to Megan Flowers and her daughter, Amelia," Lindy whispered before James had a chance to ask who he was looking at.

Though he didn't know Megan or Amelia, James remembered Huckabee. He had been a deputy when James was in high school and had often been visible at athletic events at the school. Sometimes the crowds could get a little rowdy at football games and the presence of a few deputies helped keep things in order. James remembered

Huckabee because of the unique name and also due to the fact that the man closely resembled a walrus.

Finally, James leaned forward until his nose was a millimeter from pressing against the window glass and looked down toward the floor. A paramedic, wearing a yellow jumpsuit, turned his body in order to retrieve an instrument from his case. In the moments that it took for him to search his bag, James had an unobstructed glimpse of the vision that had caused Lucy's hands to tremble. It took his mind several long seconds to register what he saw.

It was the body of a man, one that James had just seen two days ago at Dolly's. He recognized the worn letter jacket immediately, as well as the unkempt hair and the wide, muscular shoulders. Brinkley Myers had collapsed onto his stomach with his head turned toward the window. His open eyes were glazed over and his nose and mouth were covered with fresh, bright blood. Tiny droplets still leaked from his left nostril, slowly, like a dripping tap. All around his face and head an unbelievable pool of crimson had formed, widening into an ellipse that markedly contrasted with the black-and-white-checkered linoleum.

"I couldn't stop the bleeding!" Megan shouted, loud enough for them all to hear. She held up a collection of blood-soaked dishtowels. "I tried! I tried!"

Beside her, Amelia's face crumpled and she began to cry.

James could see little else on the floor except for the inordinate amount of blood, and then he spied what looked like a shattered cell phone near Amelia's foot.

"That's Brinkley Myers," Lindy whispered, peering between loaves of pumpernickel and marble rye. "And he's definitely dead."

"But from what?" asked Gillian after exhaling loudly. "I've never seen so much blood."

"Looks like it all came from somewhere on his head. There's no blood near his chest or legs." Bennett clucked his tongue in sympathy. "Point of fact, it sure seems like he had a nosebleed that just wouldn't quit."

The others remained silent as they confirmed Bennett's theory by casting their eyes once more on Brinkley's inert form.

"What's that in his right hand?" James asked, unable to get an unhindered view over the shoulders of the paramedic.

"Dunno," answered Bennett. "Can you see, Lindy? Hurry, they're going to move him."

Lindy let out a deep sigh. "I see it! Of course I know what that is. It's one of Megan's famous cookies; a 'chocolate chipped and dipped.' Those cookies are so—" The rest of her statement was cut short by the sudden appearance of Sheriff Huckabee's face in the window. He did not look at all pleased to see four faces pressed up against the window glass. Waving them off with a brusque flick of his hand, Huckabee drew the green shades over the bakery windows and then turned the store sign to "Closed."

James stepped back and gazed at his open-mouthed companions. "Guess the show's over," he said, unable to think of anything else to say. "I don't know about the rest of you, but *I've* just seen my first dead body and I feel kind of weird."

"Yeah, me too," Bennett muttered quietly. They all stood on the sidewalk in motionless silence.

"Let's go back to my place and have some coffee," Lindy offered. "I feel kind of strange, too. It would be nice to have some company right about now."

Everyone nodded in agreement and walked back to the mail truck like a row of automatons. James's mind was buzzing with all that it had just absorbed.

"Fine time for us to start a diet," Gillian laughed awkwardly as Bennett started the engine. "In a few days we're *all* going to wish we had one of those cookies."

Lindy cast an uneasy glance at Gillian. "That's the stress . . . making you talk like that." Lindy held onto Gillian's arm and released a sigh. "You know, I never liked that Brinkley Myers," she stated glumly, "but at least *his* last meal was a good one."

FOUR

DRY-ROASTED PEANUTS

Nutrition Facts	
Serving Size 1 oz. (about 39 pieces)	
Amount Per Serving	
Calories 170 Calories from Fat 130	
	% Daily Value*
Total Fat 14g	21%
Saturated Fat 2g	10%
Cholesterol 0 mg	0%
Sodium 190 mg	8%
Total Carbohydrate 5g	2%
Dietary Fiber 2g	10%
Sugars 2g	
Protein 8g	
Vitamin A 0% • Vitamin C 0%	
Calcium 0% • Iron 2%	
Percent Daily Values are based on a 2,000 calorie diet. Your daily values may be higher or lower depending on your calorie needs.	

COFFEE AT LINDY'S HAD not lasted long. All four of the supper club members found that they needed some time alone to digest the fact that a young man had suddenly died. True, he was a distasteful young man, but one belonging to the Quincy's Gap community nonetheless.

Monday at work, James busied himself researching acceptable foods for a low-carb diet plan. He grew quickly confused between the definition of low carbs, good carbs, useless carbs, and the overall abundance of nutritional phrases even mentioning the term "carbohydrates." James decided to pursue the good carbs, good fats approach as at least the adjectives put a more positive spin on the mountain of depravity he and his new friends were about to climb.

After skimming through several books, James realized that he had already exceeded his daily allowance of carbohydrates by having a bagel for breakfast. True, he had skipped his regular layer of cream cheese and had used a generous measure of strawberry jam instead, but he had innocently added on even more bad carbs cleverly disguised as sugar.

"How can they expect anyone to lose weight with all of these conflicting menus? This book says no fruit, this book says only berries, and this one says eat all fruit!" James snapped a weight loss book shut and stared at the cover. A shirtless man with washboard abs and a pair of biceps that looked like they were actually concealed cannonballs had a veined forearm around the trim waist of a busty and toothy blonde who gazed up at her bronzed diet-mate with a look of rapture.

In order to keep his fingers occupied during his lunch break (so that they would not be tempted to buy a package of cheese puffs from the lobby snack machine), James surfed the Internet. He was able to achieve a tenuous idea of the types of foods the supper club should be eating. Energized, he was busily typing up a shopping list and a list of acceptable snacks when Lucy arrived.

Francis and Scott had already left for the day. James seemed so preoccupied with his typing on the computer that the twins simply disappeared after softly calling, "Until tomorrow, Professor!"

James should have realized that his workday had officially come to an end, but he only grunted in reply as he consulted yet another website created for hopeful dieters. Even when Mrs. Waxman, the part-time librarian in charge of the evening shift, arrived and began to assist a group of boisterous high school students at the reference desk, James remained absorbed with his task.

"Hello, Lucy," Mrs. Waxman whispered. "Haven't seen you in here for a few weeks. What true crime books are you reading these days?"

Mrs. Waxman had taught eighth grade English at the Thomas Jefferson Middle School for so many years now that no one could remember who had occupied the position before she moved to town. She had taught both Lucy and James and remembered the names of every one of her students as well as the reading habits of each library patron within a three-county radius.

"Hi, Mrs. Waxman," Lucy smiled. "I'm still working on that Ann Rule paperback."

"I bet you finished those M. C. Beaton novels, though," Mrs. Waxman chuckled. "I think you have a thing for that fictional detective."

"Hamish Macbeth?" Lucy shrugged. "He *is* a dog lover, but he's too tall and skinny for me. Plus, I'm not really attracted to redheads."

"My . . . aren't *we* fussy?" Mrs. Waxman clicked her tongue in disapproval. "How old are you now, Lucy?" she asked wickedly.

Lucy flushed. She knew where this conversation was headed and she did not want to admit that she was thirty-five and had never even come close to walking down the aisle. Not even as a bridesmaid. "Actually, I'm not here for books, Mrs. Waxman. I'm here to see . . . ah . . . Professor Henry."

"*James* is in his office." Mrs. Waxman called everyone by his or her first name, regardless of title or occupation. Dr. Morris, the town vet, was still Emily, and Reverend Beasley of the First Baptist

Church was and always would be Mike Jr. "He's doing something on the computer. Go on back."

Lucy tapped lightly on the door separating James's tiny office from the shelving area behind the circulation desk. James jumped up in surprise and put his hand over his racing heart. "You startled me."

"Sorry." Lucy offered a shy grin, pointing at the wad of papers James clutched in his hand. "Is the diet starting to make you a little tense?" she teased.

James looked down at his hand and then put the pile of papers onto his desk. Smoothing the wrinkled edges with his fingers he said, "Actually, I was so busy this afternoon I kind of forgot to be hungry. Of course, I've had about five diet sodas and none of them were decaffeinated, so I'm a little jittery."

Lucy sat in one of the office's uncomfortable wooden chairs. "This chair reminds me of school," she said, thinking glumly of Mrs. Waxman. "How did the research go? Are we going to survive this, or will we be eating carrot sticks and Swiss cheese for the rest of our lives?"

"Actually, it's not that bland. There are a lot of foods on our list that are pretty good. Of course, it helps if you like any vegetable known to man, which I don't."

Lucy shrugged. "I like potatoes."

"Yeah, who doesn't? Fried; scalloped; baked with cheese, chili, and sour cream; hash browns with ketchup; tater tots—"

"Stop! You're killing me!" Lucy begged. "All I had for lunch was a Caesar salad with grilled chicken and I'm starving!"

"I know. Right now, I could eat a miniature pony. I had tuna salad without the bread. Man, I already miss not crunching on something."

James consulted his food sheet and smiled widely. "Hey! At least what you had for lunch was good!" He paused. "Did you eat the croutons?"

"Yes," Lucy admitted sheepishly. "I wasn't supposed to though, was I?"

"No, but you didn't know that." He handed her a stapled packet of menu ideas. She flipped through some of the meals and groaned. "There are so many fish dishes on here. I'm not a big seafood fan."

"That's okay," James said, coming to sit down next to her. "You can make the same recipes using chicken."

"You did all this today? That is wonderful, James. Thank you." Lucy looked into his eyes and he held her look for a long moment. Feeling that something intimate had suddenly passed between them, they both dropped their embarrassed gazes to their liberal laps and tried to think of something else to talk about.

They were saved from any further awkwardness by the appearance of Lindy and Bennett. As they came into the office, chattering away about the coolness in the air and what they had eaten for lunch, James pulled two of the plastic chairs from the kitchen area into his office. When Gillian arrived a few minutes later, James gallantly offered his own chair. Everyone seemed genuinely impressed with his work.

"Why, James!" Lindy gushed. "You've made this so organized. We won't have any excuses now, except that we all have to start cooking."

"Great," Gillian sighed dramatically, curling a strand of orange hair around her finger. "That's going to take up a lot of my reflection time. Still," she brightened, "I'm really getting a strong *feeling* like there's a good change ahead for all of us."

Bennett cleared his throat. "I see some menus here, but what do we eat for a snack? A diet including five smaller meals is more successful than three large ones."

James was so busy basking in the joy of having four friends gathered around his little desk that he almost didn't hear Bennett. When the words finally sank in he leapt up and grabbed a sheaf of paper from his printer tray. "I almost forgot. Here's a list of acceptable snacks."

The Flab Five's "Good" Carb Snack List

Celery sticks with Swiss cheese
½ cup low-fat cottage cheese
(add chopped tomatoes or cucumbers if you want)
Cucumber slices with feta cheese or sugar-free ranch dressing
4 ounces nonfat yogurt
Hard-boiled egg
Beef jerky
Hummus (no pita! Use a vegetable to dip instead)
Low-fat ham or turkey slice wrapped up with mozzarella
Mozzarella string cheese (2)
Two pieces Canadian bacon
Granny Smith apple wedges with 1 Tbsp natural or light peanut butter
Dry-roasted peanuts (about 25)
Almonds (¼ cup)
Pistachios (about 30)
Fat-free, sugar-free pudding
Sugar-free Jell-O (1 cup)
Sugar-free popsicles
Sugar-free gum
Sugar-free hard candy
Diet soda
Coffee with fat-free half and half
Artificial sweeteners

"What about all those low-carb bars I've seen at the grocery store?" Lindy asked. "They look just like candy bars."

"You'd have to check the calories," James replied. "Any bar with more than 150 calories isn't going to help us. Plus, they're pretty expensive."

"Where, in Buddha's name, is all the fruit?" Gillian demanded, shaking her list.

"I think we're supposed to go light on fruit until we lose some weight. This is kind of our put-it-in-high-gear snack list. We can add more foods once we've lost some weight."

"I don't think sugar-free gum is going to get me through an afternoon of art class with twenty-five hormonally imbalanced seniors," Lindy moaned.

"And not too many of these are good for eating in my truck." Bennett frowned. "Did you know that there are thirty-two thousand motor vehicle accidents a year caused by drivers distracted by either talking on their cell phones, reading, putting on makeup, eating, or drinking? That's why I need something that goes in nice and easy." Bennett opened his mouth in a wide "O."

"Look, everyone." Lucy stood and put her hands on her formidable hips. "No one said this was going to be easy."

James reddened, feeling that Lucy was defending him and not just their diet plan.

"You're right," Lindy agreed. "And I *do* appreciate your work, James. After yesterday, I've just felt so distracted. It's been hard to concentrate on a diet." She turned her round face to Lucy. "Is there any word on what happened to Brinkley?"

Lucy relaxed and sat back down in her chair. "We had to wait for the medical examiner to come over from Rockingham County.

61

Sheriff Huckabee went on home and left Keith, that's Deputy Donovan, and Deputy Truett to stay with the body and wait. They interviewed Megan and Amelia, too. I was there for everything." Lucy sounded proud. "I know I was only taking notes, but they've never let me go to a scene like that before."

Gillian shuddered dramatically. "The poor Flowers women! I should bring them some homemade chamomile tea. It's very soothing, you know. How are they holding up?"

"Fine, I guess." Lucy hesitated. "Though there's this one thing about Amelia that I keep turning over in my head. Something that just doesn't sit right."

"Like what?" Lindy asked, leaning forward in her chair.

"When Keith was questioning Megan, I saw Amelia sneak back to the front to look at Brinkley's cell phone. Doesn't that seem odd?"

"Where was the other deputy? Wasn't he supposed to be guarding the body?" Gillian seemed shocked. "How could a person lose focus at such a *significant* time?"

"Um, I think he couldn't resist the temptation of one of those mummy cookies Megan makes. I saw him squirrel a broken one out of the showcase. Guess he went outside to eat it." Lucy smirked. "Not that I could blame him. I could eat a few dozen of those right now."

The others murmured in agreement, fantasizing about the monster cookies.

"Where were you all this time?" James asked quickly, fearing that he might start drooling. "Did you see . . . uh . . . us?"

"Just your backsides as you hustled off to the parking lot," Lucy giggled. "Don't worry, I'm not mad. I tore down there faster than a speeding bullet so I can hardly blame anyone else for being curious." She resumed her narrative. "Anyway, I was taking notes while

Keith interviewed Megan. Both of them were really upset and Amelia clung to Megan like a baby chimpanzee, but after a few minutes, she excused herself to use the restroom. Now, we were interviewing Megan in back, near the ovens. There are a few stools there and it was toasty and comfortable back there. Amelia *did* head for the bathroom, but then she snuck up front."

"How could you see that if you were in the back?" Gillian asked dubiously. "Do you have the gift of *second sight*?" She grew excited, tugging on her violet overshirt. "I've read about people who can *see* things happening in another room, they—"

"Sorry to let you down, Gillian, but I could see her reflection in the oven doors. Once I noticed her heading to the front, I kind of sashayed sideways until I could see what she was up to out of the corner of my eye. I saw her pick up the cell phone, but then she turned her back to me and I couldn't see anything else. Keith was being his usual charming self with Megan, so she was too distraught to notice anything and it all happened in under a minute."

Bennett's eyes shone with interest. "How did Amelia seem when she came back?"

Lucy grew thoughtful. "She was only gone for a few seconds, but when she turned to face me again, I could tell a weight had dropped off her shoulders. Kind of like when a huge pile of snow goes sliding off a rooftop. 'Course she was still upset when she looked down at that pool of blood again, but who wouldn't be? Lord knows *I've* never seen anything like that before."

"The human body holds about five liters," Bennett casually informed them. He pointed at a plastic liter bottle of Diet Coke sitting on the break room's countertop. "That's five of those, folks."

"*That's* exactly what was bothering the ME," Lucy also gestured toward the bottle. "For the life of him, he couldn't figure out what had caused so much bleeding."

"So, I take it neither Megan nor Amelia bludgeoned him to death with a rolling pin," Lindy stated, sounding disappointed. The others regarded her curiously. "Well, let's face it, the guy was a total jerk."

"Certainly to women," James added, and all eyes turned toward him. He filled them in on the belittling remarks Brinkley had made in reference to Whitney, the sweet waitress at Dolly's Diner.

"She's such a good girl, too!" Lindy exclaimed. "A wonderful art student and a hard worker. Her daddy had to quit his job last year 'cause of health issues and so Whitney stopped going to college full time. She started taking shifts at Dolly's in order to help out with household expenses. I always chat with her when I'm there. How many kids these days would be so selfless?"

"None that *I've* seen," Gillian harrumphed. "That's why I work with animals. They're as loving and as spiritual and as selfless as you can get."

"I don't know if you could call Lucy's three hounds of terror loving *or* spiritual," Bennett mumbled, and then his stomach grumbled so loudly that everyone turned to look at him. "No donut holes today," Bennett said, looking embarrassed. "See? My gizzard is staging a revolt."

Everyone laughed in sympathy. Their own stomachs were complaining about not receiving their daily doses of fatty carbohydrates or tasty sugars as well.

"So there's no indication of what caused Brinkley's death?" James asked Lucy once the room had grown quiet again. She shook her head with an air of regret. "Besides one powerful nosebleed, it's a mystery. The ME did send a blood sample away to the lab in Charlottesville, but it could take a week or even longer for them to respond. They have to go with their priority cases first and I doubt Brinkley Myers will qualify as a priority."

"What does qualify?" Lindy asked. "This case seems pretty unusual to me."

Lucy shrugged. "I guess a suspicious death or the death of someone famous. We've never had something like this happen since I've been working at the Sheriff's Department so I'm not so sure. Who knows? Maybe the lab won't be busy and we'll know before I see y'all at my house on Sunday."

Lindy turned to James and raised her brows playfully. "Okay, Mr. Drill Sergeant Henry, what are we having for dinner on Sunday?"

Lucy looked at him expectantly. Her gaze made his heart beat faster as he shuffled through the menu packet he had created. The light from the fluorescents stained her blue eyes a deep indigo. "Ah, let's see . . . page 6. It's all there, including what every person needs to bring. I wasn't trying to be bossy, I was just trying to make things easier on everyone." His shoulders slumped. "We can divvy out all of the menu items out on Sunday for our next meeting. I had found this website on running a supper club so . . ." He trailed off.

"Oh, James," Lindy was instantly apologetic. "I was just teasing you! You have done a terrific job and, speaking for all of us, I'm glad we were able to recruit you. We'd still be trying to decide on a diet plan if it weren't for you. Now, since I don't have a single one of those snack items at home, I'm off to the grocery store."

"Man cannot live on celery . . . at all," Bennett stated seriously. "I'm going to pick up some cheese and a whole mess of peanuts."

"Me too," echoed the others as they shuffled out of the office, wishing James a good night and warmly thanking him again for the menu packets.

James was so unused to praise that he just stood behind his desk, soaking up the moment. The library was quiet, as most of the high school students had retrieved the information they needed to complete their projects and had gone home. Mrs. Waxman was busy flipping through the pages of *Time* magazine as James walked past her with a cheerful wave.

"Have a good night, James," she whispered and waved in return.

Outside, darkness had fallen among the pine trees, dragging with it a multitude of glittering stars. "I believe I *will* have a good night," James answered. As he headed to his car, he walked a little taller, like a man with a purpose.

FIVE

SIRLOIN STEAK

Nutrition Facts

Serving Size 10 oz.

Amount Per Serving	
Calories 644 Calories from Fat 414	
	% Daily Value*
Total Fat 46g	71%
Saturated Fat 2g	10%
Cholesterol 190 mg	63%
Sodium 150 mg	6%
Total Carbohydrate 0g	0%
Dietary Fiber 0g	0%
Sugars 0g	
Protein 54g	
Vitamin A 0% • Vitamin C 0%	
Calcium 0% • Iron 48%	
*Percent Daily Values are based on a 2,000 calorie diet. Your daily values may be higher or lower depending on your calorie needs.	

JAMES WAS REPAIRING A loose page from a hardback copy of *The Old Man and the Sea*. He lovingly applied a thin line of glue along the inside gutter and then carefully replaced the page. Closing the book, he wrapped it with a rubber band and then set a brick covered in muslin on top so that the weight could help set the glued page. Scott had given him several lessons in book repair and now sat beside him using fine-grade sandpaper to rub away ground dirt smudges from the page corners of a copy of *Tender is the Night*.

"There you are, Mr. Hemingway," James handed Scott a newly covered copy of *The Sun Also Rises* to be placed on the reshelving cart.

"Think you could ever run with the bulls, Professor Henry?" Scott asked, pushing his heavy glasses farther up on his nose.

"Not unless they counted me as one of the bulls," James replied grumpily. It was only Thursday and he felt as though he couldn't survive another second without having a bag of cheese puffs or a slice of pepperoni pizza. He was irritable and hungry and felt completely devoid of energy.

"The F. Scott Fitzgerald books must be in the best shape out of our entire collection," James said, meaning to be critical, but Scott beamed as if he had just received a compliment.

"We try," he answered modestly, glancing across the room at his twin brother as he sat at the reference desk. "They see so much wear because they're on the reading list at Blue Ridge High. Imagine, a Fitzgerald classic every year! What a great school that must be."

James ignored him, wishing a patron would arrive with a challenging question so that he might be distracted from his powerful cravings. By eleven thirty, the stillness of the library began grating on him. He strolled restlessly to the lobby, telling himself that the books for sale needed to be straightened. Of course it just so happened that he had a perfectly unwrinkled dollar bill inside his wallet that would slide effortlessly into the snack machine's slot in exchange for some crunchy, orange heaven. Checking over his shoulder to make sure that the twins were occupied, James fed the money into the machine and desperately punched the E6 buttons until the splendid thumping sound announced the arrival of a precious parcel of cheese puffs.

"It's just a snack-size bag," James muttered aloud defensively to the vacant lobby. Slipping outside, he sat down on the front steps and, heedless of the cold, devoured the bag in under a minute. He felt an incredible sense of elation from having granted himself his favorite treat. He crunched blissfully, examining the blazing colors on the maple and oak trees dotting the library parking lot. The contents of the bag disappeared all too soon. James stared longingly at the bottom of the bag and then wadded up the evidence, stuffed it in the lobby trash can, and was just about to suck the orange dust from his fingertips when Francis came outside.

Without thinking, James frantically wiped his hands on the back of his pants as Francis leaned on the stair railing and blinked in the face of daylight like a bat.

"Nice day, huh?" Francis asked, his breath hanging in the air like wet lace.

James agreed, rubbing off more orange dust stuck between his thumb and index fingers.

"Do you remember the Halloween Carnival from when you lived here?" Francis asked nervously.

"Sure," James replied. "All the local businesses can enter a float for a chance to win a cash prize."

Francis shuffled his feet. "Mrs. Kramer never let us build one. She said we didn't have funds for it in the budget, even though Scott and I came up with a design that would only cost three hundred dollars to build."

James smiled. "So you two want to enter a float in this year's parade?"

"Yes, Professor, we sure do."

"Let me review the budget for this month, but I'm sure we can come up with a few hundred dollars. I think it would be great to have the library represented."

"We have a drawing." Francis held out a rolled piece of paper.

James examined the drawing with a smile. "This is great. Are you certain that you two can build this on your own?"

Francis looked sheepish. "We started it last year, hoping we could change Mrs. Kramer's mind. We just need to add on some final touches, like special effects. Thanks, Professor! I can't wait to tell Scott!" Francis bounded up the steps and went inside. A few seconds later, James followed.

At lunch, he stared at his chef's salad, suddenly feeling guilty about cheating.

"You're really sticking to it, Professor," Francis said as he came into the kitchen. He folded his long, lanky form into the chair across from James and began to eat one of his three peanut butter and banana sandwiches while reading the latest paperback release by Piers Anthony. James was still unenthusiastically picking at his salad when Scott arrived and switched places with Francis, who had consumed his entire meal within five or six minutes. Scott ate two salami and cheese sandwiches, a bag of pretzel twists, and a jelly donut while speed-reading the October issue of *Popular Mechanics*.

Midway through his donut, Scott wiped his sugar-speckled lips with a napkin and then exclaimed. "Sorry, Professor Henry! I didn't mean to eat this kind of stuff in front of you."

"Don't worry, Scott." James sighed. "Just be glad you have the metabolism of a goat."

Scott guffawed. "'Cause their stomachs have four chambers. Good one!" He cocked his head to the side and then said, "But hummingbirds have the fastest metabolism of all animals. I wouldn't want that, though, as you'd have no time for anything except for eating." The phone in James's office began to ring.

"Sounds good to me," James murmured crossly and got up to answer the phone. It was Lucy.

"James? Do you have a second?" she asked hopefully.

The black cloud that had been orbiting James's head disappeared with a poof. "Of course," he answered brightly. "What can I do for you?"

"The lab results came back," Lucy paused and took a deep breath. "I kind of eavesdropped on Sheriff Huckabee as he talked to the ME in Rockingham. All I heard was the sheriff repeat the word . . . um . . ." James heard the rustle of paper. "Sorry. Here it is. *Coumadin*. Do you know what that is?"

"No idea."

"Well, I can't look it up from work or they'll wonder what I'm doing. Plus, I have to type up the incident report and all of the interviews, even though Keith is supposed to do his own." James could almost feel Lucy shrug at the other end of the line. "Guess it's better this way, 'cause I get to stay in the loop. Do you have time? I don't want to keep you from—"

"No problem. We're really dead today," James assured her. "I'm not positive, but Coumadin sounds like the name of a drug. Give me a sec and I'll grab a *PDR*."

"A what?"

"It's a hundred-pound book called the *Physicians' Desk Reference*. Hold on a sec." James placed the receiver on the desk as gently as if he were placing a bird's egg back in its nest. He grabbed the blue tome from the reference section and returned to his desk, his lethargy completely dissipated. Glancing through the index, he spotted Coumadin under the heading "Blood Modifiers." He picked up the phone again. "Lucy? Looks like it's a kind of blood thinner." He scanned the microscopic font describing Coumadin's uses. "Comes in tablet form or can be injected. Let's see here—if I'm translating this medical-speak correctly, it looks like people are mostly given Coumadin after they've had heart valve replacement or after having a heart attack, if that's what *myocardial infarction* means."

Lucy digested the information. "Weird," she said after a pause. "I doubt Brinkley has had heart problems. I mean, he was a football star in high school and then he mowed lawns all day long. What would Coumadin have to do with his sudden death?"

"I dunno. It doesn't make much sense to me either."

Lucy was quiet for a moment "I'll have to just wait and see, I guess. Sit here answering phone calls about lost pets until one of the *real* deputies gives me a report to type or something," she added bitterly, her voice trembling a little, as if she might begin to cry. When James failed to respond, she said, "See you Sunday," and quickly hung up.

James held the receiver aloft until the grating noise blaring out of the earpiece signaled the conclusion of his call. Returning it to its cradle, he thought back to the many times when his wife had been upset about something and he had felt incapable of finding a way to comfort her. It's not that he didn't want to, but something in him seemed to shut down and go numb in the face of a woman's tears. He didn't know whether Lucy had been on the verge of crying, but that same reaction of idiotic silence had taken a hold of him during the last few seconds of their conversation. He was going to have to be especially attentive and charming on Sunday to make it up to her—two character traits he had never been known for.

As he was about to return to his work at the circulation desk, Scott tapped him on the shoulder.

"You've got somethin' on your pants, Professor."

James looked down at his clean khakis and saw nothing amiss.

"On the back," Scott pointed at his own non-existent derriere.

James craned his neck over his shoulder and still saw nothing. Excusing himself, he went into the men's room and turned his back to the mirror. There, on his wide bottom, were two perfect handprints made of orange dust. James sighed and dampened a paper towel with water. Rubbing at his pants while watching himself in the mirror, he noted that tiny dots of white paper towel were now sticking to his pants along with the orange dust. He moved closer and closer to the mirror above the sink, so that his rear end was practically hanging in the bowl. He was so focused on his reflection that he didn't hear the door open.

An older man entered the restroom and gasped in shock at the sight of the head librarian thrusting his full buttocks toward the mirror. He pivoted immediately and exited with a huff. James groaned. He would never be able to look at that man in the face again. This is what he got for cheating.

Sunday evening finally rolled around, signaling the end of a gray and rainy week that seemed to have dampened the spirits of everyone in Quincy's Gap. James stopped by Dolly's to pick up one of her famous "After Church Pot Roast" specials for his father's dinner. The diner buzzed with a pleasant air of vivacity. Silverware clinked, people chatted between booths, and Dolly bustled about, laughing heartily as her mighty bosom shook beneath her "Kiss My Okra" apron.

At home, Jackson eyed the take-out container with a frown. "What's this?" he demanded, sniffing the lid as if the Styrofoam package was filled with fresh manure.

"Pot roast." James opened the fridge. "There's a bowl of Caesar salad in there for you, too. I'll be back around ten-ish."

"You got some kind of hot date tonight?" Jackson cackled gleefully. "Maybe she could come over and fix our leaky roof instead of you wastin' yer money throwin' food down her neck."

"I told you, Pop. I'm in a supper club," James said as he glanced at the two plastic buckets sitting on the counter. He had used them to catch the water seeping in through the ceiling of the upstairs bathroom and hallway. James knew that the entire roof needed to be replaced, but he didn't have that kind of money saved up. As it was, he was completely supporting himself and his father on his librarian's salary. Jackson never offered his son any money and didn't even glance at the bills in the mail pile, most of which were in his name. James didn't know if his father even owned a credit card any longer.

"There are five of us altogether. There will be *three* women at the meeting tonight," James added proudly.

Jackson's caterpillar-like eyebrows crawled higher on his forehead in a mocking expression. "Oh yeah, the *Fat* Club."

"Not for long." James jerked on his windbreaker. It was an old jacket, left in his closet during a visit home years ago. James now found that he couldn't zip it closed. Jackson smirked and suddenly anger whirled up from deep inside James like a scorching tornado. "At least I'm getting out of the house!" he yelled. "Do you think Ma would have wanted you to sit inside that shed doing God knows what or waste the rest of your life watching game shows? *You're* more of a ghost than she is, and *she's* the one who died!"

Both men were stunned into silence by the fury in James's voice. He had never spoken to his father in such a tone. Jackson's eyes flashed with a mixture of ire and pain. Before his father could deliver one of his scathing responses, James fled.

———————

James was the last one to arrive at Lucy's house. Bickering with his father had caused him to run late. His mouth had gone dry just thinking about how he had screamed at his remaining parent—he felt both ashamed and liberated at the same time. His father was obviously having trouble dealing with his wife's death and James should be more sympathetic. On the other hand, he had spent a lifetime accepting his father's criticism and dour moods and he was simply growing tired of being treated like an uninvited houseguest.

Lucy lived about five miles out of town in a clapboard farm-house. It was painted a cheerful, butter yellow and it had teal-green shutters. Two large planters filled with sedum and marigolds flanked the green door and an ancient maple tree dropped fiery leaves all over the front steps leading up to the small porch, where Lucy had installed a porch swing and two white wicker rockers. Three lop-sided pumpkins squatted on the porch swing, covering up several large rust-colored stains. Everything looked like it could use a fresh coat of paint.

Mail was stuffed in the black metal mailbox and dead leaves blew across a ratty doormat. The word "Welcome" was so faded that only the "l" and the "o" were discernible. The lawn had an air of neglect and Lucy's dormant azalea bushes were in dire need of pruning.

As James approached the house up an uneven brick walkway, a ferocious chorus of barking erupted from behind a green chainlink fence. This barricade surrounded a seemingly endless backyard, where dense woods suddenly swallowed the dandelion- and thistle-pocked lawn. Lucy materialized at the front door and held the screen door open for the final supper club member.

"Come on in." She smiled thinly. James noticed that the skin beneath her eyes looked swollen, as if she had been crying or had had too little sleep. He wondered if the diet was taking a big toll on her.

"I like your house," James said brightly, trying to boost her spirits.

"Thanks. It was my grandparents' place. Built in 1939." She beckoned him into the eat-in kitchen. "They raised four kids in a two-bedroom house. I've managed to fill it up all by myself, though. I'm kind of a pack rat."

"Don't forget your roommates, the Hounds of Hell," said Bennett, coming forward to greet James. "What are their names again?"

"Benatar, Bono, and Bon Jovi, after the three greatest band leaders of the 80s." Lucy's eyes twinkled for a fraction of a second. "The best decade of music ever."

James wasn't so sure of that, but he wisely decided to keep quiet. Lucy's kitchen was decorated in blues and creams. She collected blue pottery roosters and had an array of ivory-colored cow creamers displayed on a baker's rack. There were a number of dirty dishes in the sink, and a pile of *Cosmopolitan* magazines looked like they had been hastily dumped on top of the refrigerator.

Gillian was preparing their side dish—fake mashed potatoes. Every few seconds she stopped stirring in order to yank the bottom of her mango-colored turtleneck over her love handles. Yet no matter how much she tugged, the shirt was too short to completely cover her lowest roll of fat. It snapped upward after each tug like a roller shade. Whenever she lifted her arm toward the stovetop, a pale fold of skin poked out above the waistline of her pants. Finally, Gillian gave up and let her flesh hang out, exposed.

"I *am* among friends," she said, mostly to herself.

"What's actually in there, Gillian?" Lindy asked as she gazed into the steaming pot, unconsciously pulling her own shirt down over her round, wide bottom. "It smells really good."

"It's in this menu packet James made for us. Here it is." Gillian pointed to the recipe.

The Flab Five's Phony Mashed Potatoes

Ingredients

1 head of fresh cauliflower
1½ teaspoons of minced garlic
1 teaspoon rosemary
1 tablespoon of whipped cream cheese
¼ cup grated Parmesan cheese
A generous sprinkle of salt and pepper
1/8 of a teaspoon of chicken bouillon powder
1 tablespoon of butter substitute such as Smart Beat or Smart Balance

Boil cauliflower for five to six minutes until soft. Drain water. Using a potato masher or large spoon, mash the cauliflower, adding in the rest of the ingredients. Don't use an electric mixer or food processor—it won't taste as good. Plus, mashing by hand burns calories! Makes 4 servings.

Gillian paused in her mixing. "I was only supposed to use one tablespoon of butter substitute but I used two. I *really* like the flavor of butter."

Bennett placed two bottles of diet soda on the counter. "You look like you could make this in your sleep."

Gillian beamed. "I actually did a trial run for myself as I was feeling a little pressured about cooking for others." She cast a sideways glance at the packages of meat sitting in the sink. "I actually doubled this recipe as I will not be partaking in . . . in the *tragic* consumption of animal meat this evening," she added theatrically.

"Great. James and I will split the extra one." Bennett nudged James in the arm. "Right?"

Lindy scowled at Bennett for being insensitive and patted Gillian's shoulder. "Looks like you did a great job. Bennett and I shared the cost of the meat, but I was in charge of prepping the steaks. I just covered them with some Southwestern meat rub and they're all ready for the grill. I picked the ones with the least amount of fat. Bennett, did you bring the herb butter?"

Bennett bowed with a toothy grin. "Surely did, ma'am. Half cup butter substitute, one teaspoon rosemary, one teaspoon parsley, and a sprinkle of garlic salt. I then rolled them into balls with a spoon. They'll melt nice and fast on those hot steaks. That is, if the dogs don't attack me on the way to the grill." Bennett eyed Lucy.

"I'll protect you. Come on, I'm starving." Lucy led him to the deck where her grill was fired up and ready to cook their sirloin strips.

A few minutes later the supper club toasted their first meal with glasses of diet soda. They agreed to put off the discussion of their weight loss progress (or lack thereof) until after the meal. As they ate Caesar salad, cauliflower potatoes, and steak with herb butter, the conversation naturally drifted toward the most interesting event of everyone's week—Brinkley's death.

"So what's new with the Case of the Has-Been Football Star, Ms. Sheriff?" Lindy teased Lucy.

Lucy's lip quivered. Wordlessly, she hid her face in her hands as a pregnant silence descended on the table.

Lindy leaned over to clasp Lucy's arm. "Lucy, honey. What is it?" she asked with concern.

Lucy wiped a tear track from her cheek and tucked a strand of lustrous hair behind her ear. Sniffing, she said, "I'm sorry, everyone. I've been trying to act normal all night but . . . oh, I might as well tell you. The sheriff is going to arrest Whitney Livingstone tomorrow on suspicion of murder."

"What?" Gillian squeaked, dropping her fork onto her empty plate with a clatter.

"The only reason she's not in jail now is that the sheriff is hosting a family reunion tonight. First thing tomorrow, though, he's gonna pick her up."

"That's absurd!" Lindy banged her fists on the table. "That girl wouldn't hurt a soul! Are you saying that she *supposedly* killed Brinkley Myers?"

"That's ridiculous," Gillian harrumphed.

James looked at Lucy. "Does this have something to do with Coumadin?"

"Isn't that a drug?" Bennett asked questioningly. "What do *you* know about all this, James?"

James hastily explained Lucy's telephone call on Thursday and gave a brief definition of Coumadin and its uses.

Lucy issued a heavy sigh. "The problem is, Whitney's daddy is the only person in Quincy's Gap taking Coumadin. He had that massive heart attack earlier this year and had to have emergency surgery. I remember Mrs. Livingstone telling me that he needed a heart valve replacement. According to Donovan's interview with the pharmacist, Mr. Livingstone was prescribed Coumadin right after that surgery. Seems he needed a blood thinner to prevent clots from forming on the new valve. Donovan believes Whitney gave Brinkley the entire contents of her daddy's bottle."

James frowned. "So Whitney's father used the drug. Whitney wasn't fond of Brinkley. Those are pretty flimsy pieces of evidence. There were no eyewitnesses, right?" Lucy shook her head. "How can an arrest be made on such insubstantial facts?"

"There's more," Lucy began.

"Let me hazard a guess," Bennett interrupted. "It was what she said yesterday at Dolly's that did her in, wasn't it?"

Lucy looked at him in surprise. "How did you know?"

"I was there." Bennett explained. Looking at the perplexed faces of his tablemates, Bennett went on. "I only work until noon on Saturdays, so I always go to Dolly's for lunch after my shift. I had a package to deliver to Clint so I went in through the back. Whitney was working behind the counter. I could see three customers sitting there. Two of them were football players, catching some lunch before tonight's game, and the third was Lucy's favorite person since Milli Vanilli, Deputy Keith Donovan."

"Who, in this overly polluted world, is Milli Vanilli?" asked Gillian, momentarily distracted from the main narrative.

"Pseudo-rock stars from the 1980s with cool hair," Lindy replied. "Go on, Bennett."

Bennett took a swallow of Diet Dr. Pepper and continued. "As Whitney was handing a check to the football players, one of them asked her if she missed Brinkley. She looked as though she could fire missiles out of her eyeballs when he asked her that, but she just said 'No, why should I?' Apparently, the boys thought Whitney was one of Brinkley's girlfriends."

"Ha! She's *way* too good for pond scum like that!" Lindy asserted.

"That's about what *she* said, except not in such nice terms," Bennett smiled. "But the boys wouldn't let up. They taunted her, saying, 'Brinkley said he would meet you behind the movie theater so you could give him what he had comin.'" Bennett tugged on his toothbrush mustache and then laughed nervously. "My mama would have put all those boys over her knee if she had heard the rest of what they hinted at."

"And Deputy Donovan just let this go on?" James asked, shocked. It was a man's duty to intervene when a young lady's reputation was being insulted. Then he remembered how he had done nothing to stop Brinkley's insinuating remarks to Whitney on Homecoming Day.

Lucy jumped in. "That man is a walking toad. He was probably enjoying every minute of it. He loves to see any woman kept down."

"If we could all just learn to *love* one another!" Gillian wailed.

Bennett ignored her and turned to Lucy. "He *did* seem to be wearing a sheep-eatin' grin, Lucy, I won't lie to you."

"So that was it?" James wondered.

"No. Whitney leaned over the counter and grabbed one of the boy's shirts. She practically pulled him out of his chair she was so spittin' mad. 'I'm glad that son of a bitch is dead!' she yelled. 'I hope it was slow and painful and bloody as hell!'"

There was a long stretch of silence.

"Right in front of Donovan." Lucy looked at her friends mournfully. "He hears her say that and then finds out about her daddy's Coumadin and . . ."

"So she hated Brinkley for how he treated her." Lindy threw her hands in the air. "Who wouldn't? Doesn't mean she killed that boy."

"I've got to find a way to help her." Lucy gave an appealing look around the table. "Any ideas?"

"Can you get in the . . . ah . . . prison cell to talk to her privately?" James asked.

"I think so. Why?"

"The more we all know about Whitney and her relationship to Brinkley, whatever it was, the more info we'll have on what both of them are like as people. It could only help."

"That's true," Bennett agreed. "But aside from trying to clear this little lady, we need to put our sights on who could have given him the Coumadin instead of Whitney."

"Exactly!" Lindy joined in. "Do you know when he was supposedly given the drug, Lucy?"

"Yes, sometime during his meal Saturday at Dolly's. It was in the ME's report. I found it on Donovan's desk while he was out for one of his two-hour lunch breaks." Lucy smirked. "Of course, *he* never gains a pound."

"I'll ask Dolly if she noticed anyone near Brinkley's food after Clint dished it out. You never know." Bennett volunteered.

"And I'll discreetly ask some of my current students if they know of any enemies Brinkley had," Lindy said.

"*Or* who he hung out with," Gillian added. "Ten to one I see some of their mamas in my shop, and my place is a hotbed for gossip."

James searched for something to say that would show his willingness to assist Lucy. "Do you want me to come with you to see Whitney? I could bring her some books and magazines to read." He cleared his throat nervously. "And give you moral support."

"And I'll send you some prayer beads and a healing crystal. That girl's going to need all the help she can get." Gillian pronounced.

Lucy smiled. "Thanks, guys. I feel so lucky to have y'all here tonight. I may have only lost two pounds this week, but look what I've gained. Four friends."

"I lost four pounds!" Lindy declared triumphantly.

"Three for me," Gillian added.

"Me too," said James. "Bennett?"

Bennett's dark eyes twinkled. "Five big ones!"

"Good for you, Bennett. Though, truth be told, I guess I was expecting more," Lindy said. "But I have to admit, I did some cheating this week. Being on a diet was harder than I thought."

James listened as all four of his friends confessed that they had cheated several times by eating their favorite treats.

"What about you, James? Any cheese puffs?"

"Four snack bags," he groaned. "I just felt hungry in the afternoon sometimes and didn't want celery or an egg or whatever I was supposed to have. I wanted . . . well, a treat that actually tasted like one."

"Amen to that! Speaking of cravings, what's for dessert, James?" Lindy asked hopefully.

"Sugar-free chocolate pudding."

Everyone sighed collectively.

"We should be proud about losing what we did," Gillian said enthusiastically as they were eating the pudding. "But I think we could do even better."

"I told you we need to be exercising," Lindy muttered.

"I've been reading this book," Gillian went on, "called *Filling Your Life With Light*. The author suggests that when you make any kind of life-altering goal, you should use something physical to keep you on track. *Most* people need visual reminders of what they're reaching for. Now *I*—"

"What kind of reminder would we use?" Lindy quickly asked before Gillian could get too much wind in her sails.

Gillian clasped her hands together as if in prayer. "We could all bring a piece of clothing to our next dinner. Something that we can't wear now, but hope to fit in within, say, two months."

"What would yours be, Gillian?"

"Oh, I have this *psychedelic* tank top that I got on a trip to San Francisco. The thing is, it's got horizontal stripes." She placed her hands around her torso. "Right now, I am a human barrel supported by a decent pair of legs. I want smaller arms and a waist that is smaller that my hips, not the other way around. When I've got one, I will wear that top."

"Okay." Lindy smiled. "I've got something I'd like to wear one day as well. This is a great idea, Gillian. I like the idea of fitting into clothes as our goal instead of seeking certain numbers on the scale."

"Whose house shall we go to next week?" James inquired, anxiously. Eventually, he would have to have them all over. That would mean introducing the Flab Five to his father and he was not looking forward to that event.

"We can use mine," Bennett volunteered. "It's small, but there's room enough."

Lindy put one of her delicate-looking hands on top of Lucy's larger one. "Please e-mail us after you talk to Whitney. I'm sure we'll all want to see if there's anything we can do to help her. We may need to get together before next Sunday."

"After James and I visit her tomorrow, I'm hoping we'll have something new to tell Sheriff Huckabee. Something that will prove her innocence."

"*If* she's innocent," James almost whispered. Four pairs of eyes let him know that for the second time in one evening, he had said exactly the wrong thing.

SIX

STRING CHEESE

QUINCY'S GAP HAD ONLY one jail. It had been in place in the basement of the old brick courthouse since the early 1800s. James had dawdled at the library, undecided as to which books or magazines to bring to an incarcerated young woman. Finally, he had appealed to the twins for help and now he bore a paper grocery bag filled with beauty and celebrity magazines as well as Mitch Albom's *The Five People You Meet in Heaven.*

Nutrition Facts	
Serving Size 1 oz.	
Amount Per Serving	
Calories 70 Calories from Fat 35	
	% Daily Value*
Total Fat 4g	6%
Saturated Fat 3g	14%
Cholesterol 10 mg	3%
Sodium 180 mg	7%
Total Carbohydrate 1g	0%
Dietary Fiber 0g	0%
Sugars 0g	
Protein 2g	
Vitamin A 4% • Vitamin C 0%	
Calcium 25% • Iron 0%	
*Percent Daily Values are based on a 2,000 calorie diet. Your daily values may be higher or lower depending on your calorie needs.	

"That's to give her hope," Francis had said, handing James the book.

"Good luck, Professor Henry." Scott shook his hand gravely, as if he were headed out to war. "We've known Whitney for years." He wiggled the arms of his glasses back and forth in a fidgety manner. "Not well, you know. But she likes fantasy books and science fiction. We talk about that kind of stuff with her."

"She has always been nice to us," Francis added, implying that not all of the women their age had been as kind.

At twelve thirty, Lucy appeared at the top of the white slate steps leading up to the courthouse. She wanted a few minutes alone with Whitney before Keith Donovan returned from lunch. Keith was treating himself to a meal at the Italian restaurant, Il Pomodoro, in celebration of his excellent police work. If Keith returned and noticed that Lucy was not at her desk, ready to answer the phone or Donovan's smallest whim, then he might discover that she was visiting Whitney. For now, Lucy wanted to keep her investigation separate and hidden from Keith.

"This is one benefit over my old job," James remarked as he and Lucy stepped into the courthouse lobby. "I can take an extra long lunch break if I need to without checking with a superior. I mean, I had a schedule at William and Mary, but sometimes my office hours or the endless department meetings made me feel so trapped. Here, I can take off knowing that the library is in good hands with the Fitzgerald twins."

"I wish I had some of that freedom," Lucy replied wistfully. "But let's worry about getting Whitney hers first."

James followed Lucy down a dimly lit stairwell leading to the basement. Here, there were storerooms, filing areas, and holding cells. A sleepy deputy sat at a wooden desk guarding the entrance to the cells.

"Mornin' Glenn," Lucy offered a dazzling smile. "Brought you some Krispy Kremes from the Winn-Dixie. You been here all night?"

"Yep." The young deputy sat up straighter as he examined the box of donuts. "Chocolate frosted. Thank you kindly."

"Professor Henry, this is Deputy Glenn Truett. Glenn, Professor Henry has brought Whitney some library books. We'd like to take them to her and see how she is. That okay?"

Glenn was already happily occupied with his breakfast. Wiping his hands on a paper napkin, he did his duty by taking a quick glance through the bag of books and magazines. He paused for a long moment to admire a photo of Angelina Jolie in a low-cut dress, and then brought Lucy and James back to Whitney's cell. She was in the third cell in a row of six. The other cells were empty except for one. The last cell of the row contained a middle-aged man who was snoring like a locomotive as he lay splayed out on his narrow cot.

"Old Wilbur's sleepin' off another one?" Lucy asked conspiratorially.

"Yep. Gotta keep him away from his old lady when he gets like this. How's ten minutes, Lucy? It's not officially visitin' hours yet." Glenn unlocked Whitney's cell. The young woman had her face buried in her hands and did not even look up as the barred door was slid open with a squeak.

"Just fine," Lucy replied gratefully.

"I'll give a holler when it's time." Glenn called over his shoulder, hustling back to his box of donuts.

"That's some willpower, Lucy," James said with admiration as they waited for the deputy to return to his desk. "Having Krispy Kremes that close to you."

"Believe me, I was tempted." Lucy answered under her breath as they went into the cell. Lucy leaned over the cot so that she could whisper to Whitney.

"Whitney. Look at me, honey. We don't have much time."

The young woman met Lucy's eyes reluctantly. "I already told the sheriff that I didn't do it." Whitney turned a blotchy face toward Lucy. "And I don't know who did, but it wasn't me."

"We don't think you did it either. I'm not a deputy. I'm here just as a friend. You've met Professor Henry, right?"

Whitney sat up a tad straighter and managed a small smile for James. "I'm glad you've come, but . . ." She gave a helpless shrug.

"You're wondering what we can do?" Lucy finished for her as James sat down on a stool in the corner of the cell. "We don't know either, and we can't promise to get you out of here, but we'd like to help. Okay?"

James was impressed by Lucy's gentle, forward manner. He watched Whitney's shoulders relax and her creased forehead slacken as she placed her trust in them.

"Now, the whole town knows that Brinkley Myers was a horse's ass, pardon my language," Lucy began. "And that afternoon at Dolly's, before the football game, he was harassing you, right?"

Whitney nodded.

"Did he do stuff like that all the time?"

"Only when he had an audience," Whitney replied, grimacing. "He didn't have much to say to me if no one else was around. He was a show-off, ya know?"

"Sure as the crow flies. Now, I'm sorry, but I have to ask. Were you two ever an item?"

"God, no!" Whitney was clearly appalled. "I may not be in school full-time now, but I'm going to finish college and get a good job. I'm only going to date men who have the same ambitions as me. That boy wanted to do as little work as possible and still act like the town's greatest gift." She clenched her fists. "Trust me, the only feeling I have ever felt toward Brinkley Myers was that he grossed me out."

Lucy put up her hands in a placating gesture. "Just checking. I didn't really think you were ever together. Not for a second. Back to Saturday, did you serve Brinkley his meal?"

"No, Dolly did. I was busy behind the counter for most of the shift. The professor was pretty much my last table on the floor."

"And do you know what Brinkley ordered?"

"Everyone got the same thing. Meatloaf, mashed potatoes with gravy, and collard greens. That's what Dolly always serves for Homecoming. No one gets to order off the menu. She's superstitious about that meal. Says that we always win if the whole town eats her meatloaf." Whitney smiled fondly.

"That's true." Lucy laughed. "I had forgotten about the Victory Loaf." She was lost in thought for a moment. "And neither Clint nor Dolly bore any grudge against Brinkley?"

Whitney waved the suggestion off. "No. You know them, they love everybody."

"Isn't that the truth? How about other girls your age? Was he ever obnoxious to any of them that you know of?"

Whitney looked down at her hands. "I'd imagine so, but I don't know which ones."

"Hmm." Lucy gazed around the cell, unseeing. "Guess it still keeps coming back to your daddy's pills. You never touched them?"

"Never. Daddy keeps them in his bathroom and I don't go through his things, let alone steal them to kill somebody with," she added with a trace of sarcasm.

Lucy allowed silence to fill the cell. Finally, she turned to James. "Professor?" Her blue eyes bored into him. "Can you think of anything?"

James shook his head, feeling immensely useless. He handed Whitney the bag of books and magazines as Lucy stood to leave.

"Hang in there," he offered foolishly, but Whitney clamped an anxious hand on his arm and squeezed, as if trying to communicate her appreciation more forcefully. "Thanks so much for coming. It's nice to have people who believe that I didn't . . . that I would never . . ." Her eyes welled up with tears.

"Time's up!" Glenn barked down the short hall.

"I'll be back, Whitney. You won't be here long." Lucy gave the younger woman a hug and thanked Glenn as he walked down the corridor, jingling his key ring.

Glenn had consumed three donuts and, hunger satisfied, his interest in Lucy's actions was suddenly aroused. "Whatchya talkin' about to our prisoner?" he asked in a proprietary tone, picking his teeth with a decrepit toothpick.

"Just books," James blurted quickly, smiling. The spark of curiosity in Glenn's eyes died immediately.

"Good thinking," Lucy said in approval as they walked back upstairs. On the landing, they both found themselves short of breath from having climbed the steep flight of stairs. "I've got to go back to work, but would you be willing to meet me afterwards to pay a visit to Whitney's parents?" Lucy fanned herself, her face pink with exertion.

"Think they might know something?" James wondered, trying to contain the pleasure he felt in having been asked to accompany her again.

"Doesn't hurt to talk to them. We've got to find out every detail," she added with a serious expression. "That's how all of the world's great detectives work."

———————

Lucy offered to pick James up at the library after her shift was over. He waited in the lobby, hungry, excited, and doing his best to ignore the celestial glow of the snack machine. He had completely forgotten to pack the green apple and Tupperware of peanut butter meant for his afternoon snack. He could just visualize taking a dollar bill from his wallet and inserting it into the snack machine. Only the possibility of Lucy's imminent arrival prevented him from indulging in another cheat. For the third time, he peeked out the front door for any sign of Lucy's brown Jeep. Finally, running fifteen minutes late, she pulled erratically into the parking lot and honked the horn.

Slightly irritated, James opened the door to what appeared to be Lucy's garbage can on wheels. Empty paper cups sprang from the doorjamb to the ground and a pile of papers, fast food bags, and receipts prevented him from even seeing the surface of the passenger seat.

"Sorry," Lucy said, hastily scooping up the debris on the seat and hurling it into the back seat.

James climbed in reluctantly. He was a man who cherished neatness and order. He cast a sideways glance at Lucy. Her caramel hair was pulled back into an untidy ponytail and her turquoise blouse, which was so tight that James could see glimpses of skin in between the straining buttons, had several stains along the neckline. While her hands were neatly manicured with shapely, rounded nails, the polish was a garish red and was chipped around the ends. James began to wonder if he was really compatible with someone as sloppy as Lucy.

They pulled up in front of the Livingstones' brick house a few minutes later. Lucy had thoughtfully brought some pumpkin muffin tops from the Sweet Tooth as a gift for Whitney's troubled parents.

"They're open again?" James pointed at the bakery box.

"The next business day. Megan's a single mom, so she can't afford to stay closed. They just mopped the floor Sunday night and opened up again first thing Tuesday morning."

"And . . . the sheriff," James was going to say Keith but thought better of it, "allowed that?"

Lucy shrugged, ringing the doorbell. "Guess he felt there was no more evidence there once they had removed the body."

James was about to ask what had happened to Brinkley's cell phone when a woman in her late forties with Whitney's ash blonde hair and heart-shaped face opened the front door. Wringing her hands together anxiously, she took a step back. "Come on in. We sure appreciate you visitin' our gal this mornin', Miss Hanover."

"Please, call me Lucy. And this is James Henry, our new librarian." She handed Mrs. Livingstone the box of muffin tops.

"How nice. Thank you, kindly. I'm Caroline. Sorry not to have met you yet, Mr. Henry. I'm not much of a reader," she added apologetically and led them to a living room in which all of the furniture looked like it had come from an earlier decade. The floral fabric on the sofa, curtains, and rug was worn, but the room held a comfortable, lived-in air instead of one of neglect.

"This is my husband, Beau." A middle-aged man with receding hair and a beer belly stood up from a faded leather recliner and switched off the TV. He gave James a powerfully firm handshake and thanked Lucy profusely for the muffins.

"We told the deputy everything we know, which is basically not a thing." Caroline smiled wanly. "But ask us anything you want. If we had the bail money to get Whitney out of there . . ." she trailed off, embarrassed. "We're trying to borrow from my sister, but she's got her own troubles."

Beau cleared his throat. "We just don't have a nest egg anymore after all of the medical bills."

Lucy bobbed her head in sympathy. "This might seem like going back a ways, but could you tell us about your surgery. I want to understand anything I can about this Coumadin stuff."

Beau nodded. "It's easier to talk to y'all, anyway. That Keith Donovan comes in here like he owns the place, struttin' about and tryin' to scare us. Why, I remember when that boy . . ." He checked himself. "That doesn't help right now though, does it? Well, as you probably know, I was a roofer. Ran my own business," he added proudly. "Things were goin' along just swell. We had enough to send Whitney to James Madison and were putting more away for my retirement. I wanted to quit early enough to take Caroline to some real nice places."

James could see Caroline smiling at her husband with a mixture of pride and sadness.

"One day last spring, I had just come down off the ladder, thank the Lord, when this pain shot up my left arm like an electric shock. Don't remember a thing until I woke up in the hospital the next day and the doctor told me I had had a heart attack. He said he had to give me a new heart valve, the mechanical kind, and that he had some more bad news." Beau paused, no doubt recalling the exact conversation. His eyes went to his lap and James could feel the painful memory coursing through the older man. His heart went out to him, but once again, he had no idea what to say or how to gently coax the difficult narrative along.

"It's alright, Beau." His wife put her hand on top of his. "The doc told us that Beau had a stroke during the surgery. His heart was gonna be fine, but his balance was never going to be the same again. They said he could never go up on another roof. They don't even want him to drive. So he sold his business to George Dundy, his right-hand man, and now Beau's workin' real hard doin' other kinds of jobs."

James filled the silence following Caroline's explanation with his first question. "And you've been taking the Coumadin since the spring?"

"Five milligrams a day," Beau answered.

Lucy asked, "That's a bottle per month?" When Beau nodded, she frowned. "Is there any possibility that you lost one or got an extra bottle once?"

Caroline laughed at that. "Mr. Goodbee would have your head if he heard you talk like that down at the drug store."

"I know it," Lucy grinned. "Still, you never lost one?"

"No." Beau sighed morosely. "It's the thing I keep comin' back to in my head. But you know, my memory just isn't what it was before that stroke. I didn't tell that deputy this, 'cause he'd just use it against my little girl, but that's the truth."

Caroline patted her husband's hand again. "Sweetheart, you can't blame yourself for what happened."

"Who else should I blame then?" Beau roared, causing everyone to jump. His anger subsided as quickly as it had flared and he rubbed his face with calloused hands. "I'm sorry. I know you folks just wanna help."

Lucy sat thoughtfully gazing out the window.

"Would anyone like some coffee?" Caroline offered. "One of my friends brought me back this terrific blend from her trip to New Orleans."

Suddenly, Lucy's eyes sparkled. "Wait a minute, Mrs. Livingstone, ah, Caroline, did y'all go anywhere after Beau got home from the hospital? Any trips out of town?"

Caroline screwed up her lip as she thought. "I don't think . . . Yes! We did! My sister's anniversary party. We went to Baltimore for the weekend, 'member, Beau?"

Beau shot out of his chair like a rocket. "Sweet Jesus, Caroline! I forgot my pills that weekend! I forgot to pack them!" he yelled excitedly. "Do you remember? *I* do!" He grabbed James enthusiastically by the shoulder, his hand squeezing like a vise.

"Oh my stars, that's right! We had to go to one of those twenty-four-hour pharmacies to get you a refill."

James could feel the energy flowing through the room. It was as if tiny streaks of lighting were filling every person with the radiance of hope.

"Was Whitney home alone?" Lucy asked breathlessly.

"Yes. It was Labor Day weekend, just over a month ago. Whitney had to work most of the weekend, poor darlin', but she didn't want to go to that old-folks party anyway." Caroline returned to her chair, the coffee forgotten.

James hadn't forgotten dinner, however. In fact, he was downright starving. As glad as he was that they were making progress, he couldn't think of anything but the demands of his empty stomach at the moment.

"I didn't want to go to that party either," Beau added sulkily.

"Do you know if Whitney had anyone over?" James wondered, trying to keep his mind from thoughts of crunchy, savory cheese puffs.

"Never thought to ask." Caroline shrugged. "She's such a responsible girl. If she wanted to have one of her girlfriends over, she could have, without checking with us first. We ask so much from her as it is." Caroline's eyes filled. "Do you think this could help?"

"I'll talk to Whitney first thing tomorrow morning, find out if she had anyone over. At least this takes some of the heat off her." Lucy assured the Livingstones. "Someone *else* could have taken that bottle of pills from your house."

"If someone was here and also at the diner before the Homecoming game . . ." James mused aloud.

"Then we might just have ourselves a *genuine* suspect," Lucy said, almost in a whisper.

Beau and Caroline thanked them both for coming, their faces uplifted with the knowledge that their daughter might be released from jail. The couple decided that they would pay a visit to Sheriff Huckabee in the morning, explaining that their house could have been entered by anyone the weekend they had gone to Baltimore.

"We never lock the house. It's one of the reasons we live in a town like this. They can't hold Whitney after we talk to the sheriff." Caroline insisted and Lucy and James hoped she was right.

On the way back to the library, Lucy handed James two sticks of mozzarella string cheese.

"Thought you might like a snack."

"Would I? I'm dying!" James gulped one down immediately. Lucy did the same. "You know, you're really good at talking to people," James said as they pulled next to James's old Bronco. "Really. You've got a gift."

Lucy's face glowed with pleasure. She flashed him one of her beautiful smiles and for the moment, he forgot all about the slovenly condition of her car.

"We make a good team," she said. "I talk, you listen. You have a gift, too, James. It's . . . your presence. You don't even need to say anything. It's like, your humbleness or something."

James was completely tongue-tied. After all, his wife had always told him that he was a dull conversationalist and that he needed to pipe up more at social events. James had always preferred listening, but Jane claimed that he was too much of a wallflower and that no one even noticed when he had gone home.

Now, Lucy was complimenting him for being himself. He was so stunned with the wonder of it that if he had been standing in front of Lucy at that moment, he might have taken her boldly in his arms and kissed her. But she was in her car and night had fallen around them as he stood there, the passenger door ajar, trying to figure out how to react to all he was feeling. And just like that, he felt the moment passing him by.

"Let me know what Whitney says," he murmured hurriedly, before closing the door. "Just give me a call at work."

Lucy nodded, her expression of happiness evaporating in the face of his indifferent manner. With a brief wave, she pulled away without looking back.

SEVEN

CANDY CORN

Nutrition Facts

Serving Size 26 pieces

Amount Per Serving	
Calories 140 Calories from Fat 0	
	% Daily Value*
Total Fat 0g	0%
Saturated Fat 0g	0%
Cholesterol 10 mg	3%
Sodium 115 mg	5%
Total Carbohydrate 35g	12%
Dietary Fiber 0g	0%
Sugars 28g	
Protein 0g	
Vitamin A 0% • Vitamin C 0%	
Calcium 0% • Iron 0%	
*Percent Daily Values are based on a 2,000 calorie diet. Your daily values may be higher or lower depending on your calorie needs.	

THERE HADN'T BEEN A murder in Quincy's Gap since 1913. A few days before Christmas, Barnaby Forrester stole the mayor's horse after losing his entire fortune in a high-stakes poker game. Everyone told Barnaby not to play Robbie MacDougal in poker as MacDougal was the best player in the Shenandoah Valley.

Barnaby Forrester entered the town's only tavern, asking for a shot of whiskey and a card game. After losing all of his cash and jewelry, Forrester also signed over the deed to his family's horse farm sometime after midnight, and everyone thought he was defeated at last. But Forrester insisted on playing one more hand, for the very mare on which he had ridden into town.

Most of the witnesses present for this notorious last hand were several jars into their moonshine, but all would have sworn that MacDougal tried to bow out gracefully. Forrester insisted, however, and had even called MacDougal "yellow." Just after the stroke of midnight, the final hand was dealt. Forrester thought he had it in the bag as he held two pairs of kings in his smooth, citified hands. MacDougal, a man who labored as a farmhand most of his days, held a full house in his rough and work-worn fingers. When the bets were called, Forrester saw his opponent's cards, shot up as if struck by a whip, and bolted outside.

Most of the men who chased Forrester outside assumed he was only trying to mount his horse and make a getaway, but Forrester didn't grab the bridle of his own horse. He mounted the mayor's horse—a fine bay gelding newly purchased for a dear price from one of the nearby farms. Acting on a command from the incensed mayor, MacDougal raised the tavern keeper's shotgun and hit Forrester square in the chest as the thief attempted to ride him down.

There had been no trial. The mayor put a word in the judge's ear and several witnesses came forward to attest the necessity of the shooting. Horses were (and are still) a treasure greater than gold in the Shenandoah Valley and MacDougal was never brought up on any charges. *The Shenandoah Star Ledger* printed the story of Forrester's final gamble on its front page for a week straight. It had taken ninety-three years for another murder to occur to occupy that prominent position in the county's only daily paper.

Murphy Alistair, reporter and managing editor, had entitled her front-page piece FORMER FOOTBALL STAR SLAIN! She splashed photos of Brinkley over the next three pages, including interior and exterior shots of the Sweet Tooth, and a file photo of Megan on the bakery's opening day. Every day since whispers of Whitney's arrest had crossed her desk, Murphy had been zealously writing about the untimely death of Brinkley Myers.

Whitney was released early Tuesday morning. As she and her parents exited through the courthouse doors, Murphy leapt toward them, snapping photos with her digital camera as she shouted questions at them. Beau tucked his daughter behind him and faced Murphy with an expression that could have stopped a charging bull in its tracks. He raised his hand in front of the camera lens and moved so close to the exuberant reporter that he could smell oranges on her breath.

"Ms. Alistair, my girl has had a hard couple of days and we'd like to get her on home." He gently pushed the camera downwards. "This is not the time for your questions."

"*The Star*'s readers have a right to know what's happening in their county, Mr. Livingstone. And your daughter has been falsely accused." Her eyes widened in feigned shock. "Don't you want to set the record straight on her account?"

Caroline shoved past her husband. "Look here, missy. This was just all a misunderstandin'. Anyone with a lick of sense knows that Whitney wouldn't do something like this."

"Of course not!" Murphy exclaimed, switching tactics. "Whitney, it must have been horrible to have spent the night in jail. Poor, innocent lamb. Would you like to comment on the treatment you received while you were incarcerated?"

The Livingstones walked briskly past the reporter.

"I'll call you at home. Just to get a few quotes!" Murphy called after them. Scurrying inside, she hoped to corner the sheriff or one of the deputies to ask about the lack of developments in their case.

Nothing stirred up her readers like the belief that their tax dollars were going to waste.

―――――――

As the work week marched on, another of Murphy Alistair's headlines stared at James as he organized the newspaper rack. From WAITRESS FALSELY ACCUSED! on Tuesday to WILL MURDERER STRIKE AGAIN? on Wednesday, the headlines had everyone in the town talking.

E-mails among the Flab Five flew back and forth like witches on brooms. The first was from Lucy, describing her quick visit to Whitney's cell prior to her release.

Dear Fellow Flabs,

I saw Whitney this morning and was able to ask her if she was alone at home during the weekend her parents were away. She said she worked most of the time, which is what her parents said, too. Still, I asked her again if she had any friends over. She denied it, but there was something in the way she said "no" that makes me think she's hiding something. I don't know why she would, but my gut (and it's big enough to know!) feels that something's not right about all this. Lindy, do you remember who Whitney was friendly with in school? It's only been two years since she graduated, so maybe she still hangs out with the same crowd.

Hope to see you all at the Halloween Parade Saturday night. Should we meet somewhere and watch it together?

☺ Lucy

Lucy's reference to the Halloween parade reminded James that the twins were planning to enter a float in the upcoming parade contest. He tracked Scott down dusting shelves in the audio/video section.

"We've got to update some of these audio books, Professor." Scott pointed at the scant number of plastic book boxes with his duster. "We haven't added a new release in this section since 1998. Mrs. Kramer didn't believe in patrons listening to books instead of reading them. We only have these because people donated them."

James agreed. "I know that many elderly members of our clientele prefer to listen. Especially if their vision isn't that great."

"Mothers, too," Scott added, nudging at his glasses. "They're so busy that they can play a book while they're getting stuff done at home, like folding laundry or cooking dinner."

"You have amazing insight about the habits of our patrons." James gave Scott a fatherly pat on his scrawny back. Scott beamed with pride. "How's the float coming along?" James asked.

"Pretty well. We've been working on it 'til late at night."

James noticed telltale shadows beneath Scott's Coke-bottle glasses. "Listen, you and Francis should work half-days for the rest of the week. I think the float is great publicity for the library and you two shouldn't have to spend all of your free time building it."

Scott blinked in surprise. "Really? But . . . how would that affect our . . ." He looked down at his boatlike feet, clearly trying to phrase his question delicately.

"Your paychecks will be the same. I can handle the afternoons alone for a few days. Tell Francis that you can both take off after lunch." James lowered his voice even more than his usual library murmur. "It'll be our secret."

"Yes, sir!" Scott saluted, his face aglow with happiness. As he dusted the top shelf on his tiptoes, Scott whispered to the empty space surrounding the audio books, "We're going to win that money. Then we'll get more audio books, more videos, and maybe, just maybe, a decent computer in this place!"

By the time James returned to his desk, thinking of how fortunate he was to work with the industrious and big-hearted Fitzgerald twins, a new e-mail was awaiting him.

Dear Dietmates,

If we can help Lucy find out what Whitney may be covering for (or who!), those good old boys down at the sheriff's office might just treat her with new respect. I don't know who Whitney might have had over that weekend, but I do know that Whitney and Allison Shilling, of Shilling's Stables (you know, the richest family in Quincy's Gap!) were best friends when they were Seniors here at Blue Ridge High.

Speaking of friends, it seems like Brinkley had a lot of girlfriends but really only hung out with one guy. This boy was on the football team with Brinkley. His name is Darryl Jeffries. He works at the gas station over by the highway entrance.

That's all the news I have. Did you all see the headlines in *The Star* this week? That woman has gone completely nutso!

Let's meet outside of Dolly's Diner to watch the parade. I will bring us some snacks so we won't be tempted by all the candy thrown out off of the floats.

'Til then,
Lindy

By the time Saturday arrived, James was worn out. Taking over for the twins had been harder than he expected. For the first time, he had had to conduct the children's story times. On Wednesday, reading *The Square Pumpkin* to a group of a dozen children under five had been easy. Helping them create and decorate their own square pumpkin trick-or-treat bags had been almost impossible. Cutting and gluing seemed to be gargantuan tasks for his pint-sized audience and James had never imagined the amazing mess of having glitter cover every surface area of the trick-or-treat bags, the table, and half of the children's clothing.

When one of the children said, "You look like a nice, fat pumpkin, Mr. Henry. I'll just draw *you*," James thought he was going to give up on the whole project. Luckily, the mothers had all pitched in and helped him hand out Dixie cups of orange Kool-Aid and square pumpkin cookies (graham crackers covered with orange frosting with a smiling mouth and eyes made out of candy corn).

Francis had made the treats during his lunch break the day before, carefully wrapping them with cellophane and hiding them in the fridge inside a brown grocery bag so as not to tempt James. James was not to escape temptation so easily, however. When a 5-year-old girl dressed as Raggedy Ann removed all of the candy corns from her cookie and placed them delicately in James's hand, he stared at them as if they were gold nuggets.

"I don't like those," the little girl said in a soft, sweet voice. "Mommy says not to waste food 'cause there are hungry children in . . . in . . . somewhere. Will you eat them so I don't waste them? Pretty, pretty please?" She gazed up at him with imploring eyes, the circular spots of makeup on her cheeks glowing apple-red.

"Of course I will," James smiled, popping the candy into his mouth.

Relieved, the girl bit into her treat, spraying graham cracker crumbs all over the carpet. "Fank oo," she mumbled through a mouthful of cookie. Her mother looked on, beaming at James as if he had suddenly sprouted a halo.

James conducted two children's story hours on Thursday, followed by an adult book discussion on Alice Hoffman's *The Ice Queen* on Friday. During the book club, two of the older women got into a heated argument over who wrote the fairy tale about the Snow Queen, Andersen or the Brothers Grimm. After calmly playing referee to the squabbling women, James was ready to call it a week. He had done the work of three people and he sincerely hoped that the Fitzgerald brothers were creating a float that would make it all worthwhile. Being so busy had kept him from the snack machine, however, so while he had eaten a couple of candy corns, he had stayed away from his beloved cheese puffs for a record-setting five days.

The scale reflected his good behavior on Saturday morning, depicting the loss of an additional three pounds. That made a total of six in two weeks. James had expected more, but he also knew that he hadn't been 100% true to the food requirements—more like 70%—and he was still not exercising.

Downstairs, Jackson waited at the kitchen table for his breakfast. As James reached up to the pot rack for a frying pan, his father held up a gaunt arm and hollered, "Goddamn it all! You're *not* makin' me more eggs! Are you tryin' to kill me? 'Cause if you are, I'd just as soon you used my Colt to do it."

James doubted his father's ancient revolver still worked, but he decided against starting an argument over an old gun. "What would you prefer?" he asked his father as pleasantly as possible.

Jackson's furry eyebrows creased in thought. A malicious twinkle sparkled in his narrow eyes as he said, "Blueberry pancakes."

An inaudible moan escaped through James's lips. He loved blueberry pancakes and his father knew it. "You're deliberately trying to sabotage me, Pop, but it's not going to work. I'm going to cook a scrambled egg with mozzarella and salsa and then I will make you pancakes. By then, I won't even be hungry so I won't want to eat them."

"Suit yourself," Jackson shrugged. He shuffled into the den and turned on the Game Show Network. "Call me when they're done!" he ordered.

Muttering to himself, James savagely broke one egg after another into the mixing bowl until he had half a dozen eggs ready to be scrambled. Looking at the partially empty egg carton and back to the bowl overflowing with eggs, James cursed.

———————

Driving into town that afternoon, James felt a sense of excitement that he hadn't experienced since he was a young boy preparing for a night of blissful and greedy candy gathering. James's mother allowed him to stay out until ten o'clock on Halloween night, or nine if it fell on a school night. She loved Halloween. Every year, she lined the dirt driveway with a dozen jack-o'-lanterns, carved with an array of different expressions ranging from silly to downright fearsome. Jackson always helped with this time-consuming project and although he grumbled about cleaning out the pumpkins, he loved to stand with his wife and son at the end of their road and gaze down at the diverse row of glowing faces.

The jack-o'-lanterns made the Henry house a favorite stop for trick-or-treaters, and once a year, the kids at school found something to praise James for.

"Sweet pumpkins," they would say, and for a moment, James would feel accepted by the in-crowd. Even in November, the pumpkins continued to draw attention from passersby. The day after Halloween, James and his mother would turn the faces on the pumpkins around and decorate the uncut orange skins with feathers. For the whole month, a line of colorful turkeys flanked the sides of the driveway. By Christmas, the pumpkins were gone and so was James's popularity with the cool kids. Like Cinderella at midnight, he returned to being the shy bookworm he was for the rest of the year.

Of course, there would be no line of carved faces this year. James hadn't even bought a pumpkin and didn't want to pick up any Halloween candy until the very last second, knowing he would be unable to resist eating some. As he got closer to town, he slowed down in order to admire the decorations adorning the houses bordering Main Street. He saw skeletons swinging from low tree branches, cardboard tombstones with glow-in-the-dark epitaphs, figures of witches on broomsticks flattened against tree trunks as if the two had collided, electric eyes peering out of bushes, hairy black spiders creeping along picket fences, and strings of purple lights shaped like bats spiraling up lampposts.

Every storefront in town was decorated for Halloween. Paper ghosts announced special sales in the window of the stationary store, while a line of motorized vampires asked for blood donations as they popped out of their coffins in the bay window of Goodbee's Drug Store. James slowed down to about 10 miles per hour as he pulled up next to the Sweet Tooth so he could get a good look at the delectable things he wouldn't be eating this holiday. Fortunately for him, traffic was practically at a standstill as people searched for places to park before the parade got underway.

Megan Flowers had always done a great job preparing her window for each and every holiday. In honor of Halloween, she had draped boxes with orange crepe paper so that a variety of bugs made out of chocolate cakes with licorice stick legs could crawl into the line of sight of even the smallest child. Black widow spider cakes were granted their famous red markings by use of red hots, while a millipede had gumdrops to lend it some colorful stripes. James almost crashed into the car in front of him as he noticed the line of chocolate ant cakes covered with chocolate sprinkles carrying away one of Megan's famous meringue bones to a hive made of mounded brown sugar. Every Halloween, Megan made trays of "skeleton bones" out of meringue and much to the children's delight, spattered them with "dirt" (which was really only cocoa powder). It wasn't truly the Halloween season until the bones went on display inside Megan's giant plastic cauldron.

James met Lindy and Bennett at their designated spot in front of Dolly's Diner. Everyone got settled into folding chairs as Lindy showed off Murphy Alistair's latest headline: IS THE HALLOWEEN PARADE SAFE THIS YEAR?

"Gillian would say that this woman is putting a lot of negative karma out there with this kind of writing." Lindy slapped at the paper.

"And she's having the time of her life doin' it." Bennett laughed. "That reporter hasn't had an event this excitin' since Trent Riggsby's sow bit the judge's finger off at the State Fair a few years back."

"I remember that!" Lindy squealed like the pig in question. "Oh, here comes Lucy. Scoot over a bit, will you," she asked James, indicating the tiny space between their chairs. "Lucy hasn't lost *that* much weight yet."

"Hey!" Lucy greeted everyone and placed her chair in the spot created by Lindy and James.

"Where's Gillian?" James asked.

"She's sharing a float with the ladies from Shear Elegance, the hair salon next door to the Yuppie Puppy," Lucy replied.

James tried to search Lucy's face for any trace of what she might be feeling after their awkward goodbye the other evening, but she seemed to be exhibiting her customary sunny disposition. At the far end of Main Street the band from Blue Ridge High began playing "The Monster Mash." The Halloween Carnival had begun.

"Look! Here comes the first float!" Lindy shouted happily.

Dolly's Diner led the parade of floats. The entire float was shaped like a giant pumpkin pie. Dolly was dressed up as an oversized dollop of whipped cream while Clint, dressed as a giant fork, tossed out coupons wrapped in rubber bands for $1 off any entrée at Dolly's. As the float went by, everyone clapped and cheered, trying to get Clint to toss them a coupon. Bennett caught one and so did James.

"I feel like I'm ten years old!" Bennett yelled, zealously unwrapping his prize.

"Free stuff brings out the kid in everyone," Lucy said, pointing at the next float. "Here comes Gillian!"

Like most of the floats, the one Gillian shared was a decorated flatbed trailer drawn by either a car or tractor. Her float, which bore a sign reading "Beauty Queens on Halloween" in glittering purple, included a coven of witches and their dogs. Steaming cauldrons, birdbaths filled with neon potions, and dogs with green-, purple-, and orange-tinted fur sat at the feet of women with hooked noses and waist-long locks of black hair. Each witch had lime-green talons with which she threw out pieces of Mary Janes to the noisy crowd.

"Why Mary Janes?" James asked Lucy, watching the yellow and red candy wrappers zipping through the crisp air.

"Mary Jane Pulasky is the name of the woman who owns Shear Elegance." Lucy picked one off of the street in front of her feet. "I'm kind of glad I don't like these."

"I do!" Lindy held out her hand. "I may as well tell you, I'm going to eat some candy today. It's a celebration, after all."

"Me too." James agreed heartily.

The next float was sponsored by Blount Realty. It featured a two-story, miniature Victorian with patches of gray paint and purple trim. The house, which had a faded "For Sale" sign posted near the cracked front steps, was clearly haunted. Bare trees with spiky branches led up to a crooked door and cracked glass windows. Ghosts flitted back and forth around the graveyard in back of the house and spooky noises such as high-pierced screams and boards creaking emanated from within. A woman dressed up as a dead Victorian bride tossed marshmallow and peanut butter ghosts out to the throng.

Troy Motors followed the haunted house. Instead of a float, their entry was an antique black car, just like the bizarre vehicle used in the TV show *The Munsters*. The car was complete with a curtained "coach" section where Lily and Marilyn Munster sat waving as their show's theme song played from speakers hidden inside. The car even had the red leather jump seat in the back, in which Eddie and Grandpa Munster sat, hurling chocolate vampires to the back rows of bystanders. Herman Munster (also known as Bradford Troy of

Troy Motors) drove the hodgepodge on wheels, blasting a comical horn and pretending to drive off of the road as he turned around to blow kisses to his Munster wife.

Right behind the Munsters was the float designed by Megan and Amelia Flowers for the Sweet Tooth. Gasps and exclamations of delight from the children preceded the float well before it clearly came into view. The entire float was a mammoth trick-or-treat bag, which was being dumped out so that its contents spilled everywhere. However, the scale of the treats was giant-sized. Candy bars the size of ladders hung suspended in mid-fall, sticks of gum as large as mailboxes littered the floor of the float, and candy corns the size of beach balls dangled in space, with the help of invisible wires, as they waited for time to begin moving forward again. On one side of the float, Megan Flowers, dressed as an angel, threw out toothbrushes and dental floss to a chorus of boos. Amelia, dressed as a sexy devil in a skin-tight Lycra suit, tossed out fireballs and swung her tail in a flirtatious circle. Every motion she made charged the air with sexual electricity. She coyly posed with her pitchfork and blew playful kisses to the handsome young men watching her with slack-jawed expressions.

"Get a load of Amelia!" Lindy exclaimed. "She always turned the boys' heads in school. You can see why."

James and Lucy both stared at Amelia's long and shapely legs, tiny waist, and high, firm breasts. Her red cat suit had a plunging cleavage and showed the perfect roundness of her buttocks as she reached into a papier mâché fire pit in order to grab another handful of fireballs.

"And she works in a bakery, too. It's just not fair," Lucy muttered under her breath.

Several other floats passed them by. Goodbee's Drug Store featured a mad scientist float with bubbling potions and a group of children modeling the Halloween costumes for sale at the store. Home Doctor, the town's home superstore, the very one that put Henry's Hardware out of business, featured a pumpkin field with enormous glowing jack-o'-lanterns bobbing up and down in time to "Bad Moon Rising" by Credence Clearwater Revival. Above the pumpkins, a scarecrow waved a pair of mechanical arms and laughed maniacally.

At long last, the library float came into view and when James saw it, his eyes widened with wonder. Pulled along by an old pickup truck, the Shenandoah County Library float was entitled "The Magic of Words." The Fitzgerald Brothers had created several books the size of small cars. Standing on top of one of the open books was the Headless Horseman from *Rip Van Winkle*. The fearsome rider, astride a real black horse, held a menacing jack-o'-lantern in the crook of his arm as he pointed an accusing finger at the townsfolk. On top of another book was the monster from *Frankenstein*. James certainly hoped that the misshaped and stitched figure was a dummy as bolts of electricity seemed to be jolting the figure right off of its metal lab table. The last book was what excited the crowd the most. Standing upward, so that people behind the float could read the title on the spine as well as on the front cover, the text was the much beloved *Harry Potter*. On top of the pages, Francis had dressed himself as Harry and sat astride a broomstick. Waving to the cheering masses, he flew in an arc around the book, dispensing Tootsie Pops as he pretended to chase the Golden Snitch.

Bennett caught one of the candies in mid-air and it was then that James noticed tiny pieces of paper wound around the lollipop sticks. Apparently, each lollipop came with a recommended read for those who "dared to be scared," as the slips' text challenged.

"What book did you get?" Lucy asked, holding out an orange Tootsie Pop.

"*Faust*," Bennett replied. "Never heard of it."

"Mine's *Picture of Dorian Gray*." Lucy frowned. "I never heard of that one either, but I'm curious about it now. I think I'll check it out."

"Me too," Bennett agreed.

James didn't think he could contain the pride swelling within his heart. The library float was fantastic and the reading suggestions distributed by way of lollipop were nothing short of magical. All of the spectators were pointing at their slips and discussing the book titles written there. The twins had managed to excite literary curiosity in addition to being delightfully entertaining. He applauded as loudly as he could and caught Francis's eye. In Harry Potter's round glasses, Francis looked like a young boy, himself. He winked at James as fog from beneath the Headless Horseman's horse began to roll off the float and into the first rows of spectators.

The final float held the Carnival Queen. Typically a high school senior, the Carnival Queen was elected by her peers and wore a shimmering black velvet robe and a glittering tiara made of amber-colored rhinestones. Two members of her royal court, the Halloween princesses, flanked her golden throne, decorated with wheat stalks and bejeweled masks. The front of the float bore the members of the Sheriff's Department, symbolically guarding the Queen of Quincy's Gap.

Sheriff Huckabee and Keith Donovan took the honors of riding the float for the fourth year in a row.

"Someday *I'm* gonna be up there!" Lucy announced bitterly. "It's always been two *men*."

"Of course you will," Lindy replied soothingly and then squawked, "Who is that on the throne? That's not Heather Gilchrist. Why, that's Allison Shilling! That girl graduated two years ago! What—"

"Looks like the float's been sponsored by Shilling's Stables, too," Bennett interrupted, pointing at the logo covering the entire side of the float. "Guess Allison's daddy bought her a crown."

"But she's not even in high school!" Lindy panted.

A woman standing behind their row leaned in and shouted. "Heather and her two attendants all had such bad food poisoning today that they couldn't even stand up. Poor things. Biggest day of their young lives and they're all home, puking their guts out."

"So who are the Queen's attendants?" Lindy asked the woman.

She shrugged. "Trainers from the stables, I s'pose."

As the float passed by, the entire town followed, preparing to surround the podium where the float prizes were to be awarded.

The mayor, a portly woman with a booming voice, took the microphone. She thanked Blue Ridge Savings & Loan for donating the prize money as well as the table of judges who had cast their votes for the winning float.

The runner-up prize, a check for $1,000, went to the Sweet Tooth. Megan came forward in her angel costume and thanked the mayor as well as the people of Quincy's Gap.

"I don't give a hoot what anyone says," she said, staring directly at Murphy Alistair as she snapped Megan's picture. "This is the most wonderful town in the whole world and I can't think of a better, *safer* place to spend *my* Halloween! Come see us at the Sweet Tooth tomorrow. I'll have a whole new batch of bones for y'all."

After the applause died away, the mayor stepped forward again, holding up an oversized cardboard check in the amount of $3,000.

"And this year's winner, by unanimous vote, is our very own Shenandoah County Library float!"

James hollered out a joyful "Hurrah!" as Lucy and Lindy hugged him in celebration. Scott, disrobed just enough to allow his own head to appear above the Headless Horseman's garb, bounded up the podium's makeshift stairs to accept the check. He took the microphone from the mayor's outstretched hand and announced, "We, the library staff, are going to use this money to give this town the best library ever! Come by next month and see all of the new things we're going to have for you folks to do and don't forget to investigate your lollipops for some *real* magic. And thanks to Professor Henry for letting us build this float!" Scott held the check into the air and waved to James.

"That's a lot of money," Lucy yelled over the cheers of the throng. "You must be so proud."

James popped a chocolate vampire in his mouth. "You know, I don't think I've ever been happier," he said, chewing, the liquid sweetness spreading over his tongue like ambrosia. "And that's not just the chocolate talking."

EIGHT

HERB-ROASTED CHICKEN BREASTS

Nutrition Facts

Serving Size 1 piece (5 oz.)

Amount Per Serving	
Calories 254 Calories from Fat 63	
	% Daily Value*
Total Fat 7g	11%
Saturated Fat 2g	10%
Cholesterol 200 mg	67%
Sodium 930 mg	39%
Total Carbohydrate 2g	1%
Dietary Fiber 2g	1%
Sugars 0g	
Protein 43g	

*Percent Daily Values are based on a 2,000 calorie diet. Your daily values may be higher or lower depending on your calorie needs.

"I THINK WHITNEY MADE a bargain with the devil," Gillian announced with her usual dramatic flair over dinner Sunday night.

In honor of Halloween, Bennett had draped his glass dining table with a black vinyl cloth and had laid out five orange place mats and paper napkins covered with flying ghosts. He had also lit two human-sized skull candles to add to the spooky-but-festive ambiance. The candlewicks were located deep behind the eye sockets of the skulls, and their flickering light created the appearance of life within the waxen orbs.

After dining on lettuce wedges covered by blue cheese crumbles, bacon bits, fresh ground pepper, and blue cheese dressing, the supper club had moved on to their main course. Lucy had volunteered to cook the chicken—boneless breasts seasoned with garlic cloves, olive oil, rosemary, parsley, salt, pepper, and lemon juice—and James was pleasantly surprised by how flavorful and tender the entrée turned out to be.

"I thought this would be like eating a dry rubber band," Lindy confessed, "but this is delicious! Any secrets from the chef on how to cook this on our own?"

Lucy dabbed at her lips with a napkin and said, "Honestly, I called my mom for a bit of advice. She told me to use fresh herbs instead of the stuff in the jars. Guess she was right, as usual."

Lindy laughed a trifle bitterly. "I've got one of those mamas, too."

"Wait a minute. Gillian was talking about devils, not angels like our mamas," Bennett said. "What did you mean about Whitney?"

Gillian stared at her forkful of chicken and then, looking as though she were about to swallow a cyanide capsule, replaced her fork on her plate. "No offense, Lucy. It *is* really good. I'm just apologizing to the spirit of the chicken for eating its flesh."

"I told you, I bought the Amish chicken," Lucy huffed. "They're fed an all-organic diet and are completely free range. Shoot, they're probably treated better than my dogs!"

"And they probably *deserve* to be better treated," Bennett sniggered under his breath. "At least those chickens never tried to attack innocent civil servants."

"Back to Whitney . . ." James prompted, taking a long gulp of orange Diet Rite.

"Yes, let's not lose focus." Gillian inhaled and exhaled deeply. "After we all got off our floats to hear the mayor talk, I realized I had forgotten my evil eye protector. It's a key chain that I bought a few years ago in Greece and is basically a blue bead painted to look like an eye. Every driver has these beads hanging from their rearview mirrors to prevent accidents. I had tucked it under one of our big potion bottles to ensure that there would be no driving mishaps during the parade. And see!" Her face gleamed. "Not a scratch! I bring it every year to protect the parade."

"We're all mighty grateful for the power of your evil eye protector," Lindy teased, but Gillian took her seriously.

"Thank you." She bowed her chin as a cascade of marmalade curls fell over her eyes. "So I *had* to return to the float for my luck charm. I always keep it in my car and I'd be *terrified* to drive without it. It was then that I saw Whitney, talking to someone dressed up as a devil."

"What were they talking about?" Lucy asked excitedly.

"I couldn't hear the exact words, but both of them were upset. Whitney looked like she was pleading with the devil while the devil was waving her hands around like she was really *disturbed* about something Whitney said. Of course, I have no idea who the devil was, as she had a mask on."

"How do you know it was a 'she'?" Bennett asked.

"She had the body of a *Sports Illustrated* swimsuit model, for starters. She wore a Lycra cat suit like it was her second skin. Not an ounce of flab on that woman!" Gillian snapped. "And like I said, I couldn't hear what they said, but I could tell the voices belonged to two women."

James sprinkled salt over the remainder of his chicken and told Gillian, "The devil was Amelia Flowers."

"Yes sir. Hard to forget *that* outfit." Bennett cackled. "Man, she can take me to the fiery pits of hell *anytime!*"

The women glared at Bennett.

"So Amelia and Whitney may be friends," James quickly suggested before Bennett's flesh was burned to a pile of ash from the heated stares given by their female dinner companions.

"They *are* the same age." Lindy rubbed her round chin pensively. "I don't remember them hanging out in high school, but maybe Amelia was the one at Whitney's house Labor Day weekend."

James stood up with his plate, heading toward Bennett's sink. Some connection between Amelia and Brinkley was tickling at his mind, but he couldn't think what it was. Clearing his head with a small shake, he said, "We'll need to find out if Amelia was at Dolly's on Homecoming Saturday."

"But what would *her* motive be?" Gillian asked, exasperated. "Why can't some crazy person, a stranger, have gotten into the Livingstones' house and stolen the drugs?"

"That's not very likely." Lucy sighed. "I wish it were, but according to my law enforcement textbook, most small town homicides are committed by people who know the victim and have a motive."

"Still, out of all the nation's homicides, only 10 percent are committed by women," Bennett added argumentatively.

Lucy looked over at him wearing a scowl of irritation. "How do you know this stuff, Bennett?"

Bennett examined his palms and shrugged. "I like statistics. I read books of facts in my spare time. One day, I'd really like to be a contestant on *Jeopardy!* I think I could give those lawyers and stockbrokers a run for their money." He patted the bulge of his belly and laughed. "One goal at a time though, right?"

"Right," James answered with an empathetic nod.

"Listen, I'll go to the bakery this week and find a way to ask Amelia," Lindy offered. "It would seem a natural thing for me to do, since I used to teach her. I chatted with her all the time when I *used* to go in there. These days, I've been trying to stay as far away from that place as possible." She gestured toward the bowl of candy they had been using for trick-or-treaters. "It's bad enough to have to be in the same room with that bowl of candy—my biggest weakness!"

"Never fear!" Gillian rose, her lemon-colored shirt floating behind her as she marched into the kitchen. "I've made us a special holiday dessert. And don't worry, it's still on our diet."

"Wow!" James exclaimed as he looked at the contents of Gillian's tray. "What exactly is that?"

"Dessert pizza," Gillian replied proudly. "Halloween style. I used low-carb bake mix, cinnamon, and artificial sweetener to make the crust and sugar-free vanilla pudding with sugar-free candies to make the tombstones."

James could feel his mouth watering as he examined his tombstone. The letters R.I.P. had been formed using chocolate chips and his name was spelled out with red shoestring licorice. Tiny gumdrops formed a floral design on the top of the vanilla grave marker. Without waiting for anyone else, James took an enormous bite of his pizza. As he chewed, his tongue was immediately accosted by the strange flavor of the crust. In his mind, he had prepared for the taste of a sugary dough like that of a donut or at the very least, the satisfying richness of French toast. This dough was dry, crumbly, and carried a strange and unidentifiable tang to his dejected taste buds.

"Too many chemicals." Gillian grimaced as she bit into her own dessert. "That's why real sugar tastes so much better. It's a *real* plant.

A *real* part of nature. I think we're supposed to eat things grown from our Mother Earth." Her shoulders slumped. "I can't even pronounce half the ingredients in that bake mix. No wonder it tastes awful."

"You did a great job with these, Gillian." Lindy pointed at her own tombstone. "You've saved us from eating a bunch of empty calories and you displayed creative artistry in decorating these."

"You must be a fabulous teacher," Gillian replied, a slow smile igniting her freckled cheeks. "You're one hell of a good cheerleader when any one of us is feeling down."

"Well, speaking of feeling down," Lindy smacked her dainty hands together. "I brought my item of 'goal clothing.' I'm going to assume the rest of you didn't chicken out on me."

"I hope that means you're going first, then," James answered gloomily.

"I don't care. You two men will probably be more embarrassed by what I brought than I will."

"Bring it on, sister," Bennett declared, having finished clearing off the table.

Before Lindy could speak, the doorbell rang.

"Your turn, James!" Lucy sang out, thrusting the candy bowl into his hands. James opened the door to a pair of teenage boys, about five years too old to be out asking for candy.

"Give us a shitload of candy or we'll egg your mailbox," the one vaguely dressed as a punk rocker threatened.

"And I'll toilet paper your trees." The second boy bared a pair of plastic fangs. It was the only attempt the boy had made at pretending to wear a costume.

James looked out at Bennett's lawn. Even in the dark, he could see from the light shed by Bennett's lamppost that the only trees in the yard were mammoth pines. They would be very difficult to paper.

"Be my guest," James shrugged, withdrawing the candy bowl from the boys' reach. "The man who lives in this house works for the United States Post Office. If you tamper with his mailbox, which is a federal crime, you're going to get a hefty fine and I'm going to stand right here and serve as his witness."

"Yeah right," the rocker scoffed. "You're just a fat lard ass *and* you're totally full of crap."

Lucy appeared from nowhere and grabbed the rocker by the oversized shoulder pad of his leather jacket. "Jason Stein, you get off of this doorstep by the time I finish this sentence or I will call your father *at work* and let him know you are threatenin' folks to give you candy! You too, Bobby Wilcox!"

The boys hesitated for less than a second, torn between indignation and genuine fear. When Lucy yelled "Git!" they jumped up in their shoes and scrambled across the lawn. James watched them as they ran down the street and were swallowed up by the shadows beneath the hillside.

"I was handling them and didn't need any help," James growled at Lucy. "I'm a grown man, after all," he added huffily.

"Sorry," Lucy countered defensively. "I just thought we could get rid of them faster so we could get back to business."

"Fine, let's go then." James sulked his way back to the table.

"Before I show you my clothing item," Lindy said as James and Lucy took their places around the table, "I have to show you a photograph first." Lindy slid a glossy 8 x 10 toward the middle of the table. It was a picture of a young woman in a one-piece bathing suit, leaning backward into a narrow waterfall. The woman's body was long and lean. She had waist-length ebony hair and an hourglass figure that Marilyn Monroe would have been envious of. She also had the same light coffee-colored skin as Lindy.

"That's my mother. She was a famous teen model in Brazil. I'm half Brazilian, but all I seemed to have inherited from my mother physically was her skin tone. My father is a short, round southerner from a podunk town outside of Birmingham. My parents met in an art history class at Washington & Lee and fell in love. Everyone was shocked when they got married, but I think they were even more shocked when I was born. Right away, people could tell I was never going to be any model. In fact, I looked nothing like my mother. At three years old I was already overweight and my father said that I was the spitting image of his own mother. Trust me, being compared to Grandma Bertha wasn't exactly a compliment. I've seen smaller rumps on a water buffalo."

"Where are your parents now?" Gillian asked as she examined the photograph.

"They live in D.C. My mother manages an art gallery and my father does restoration work for the Smithsonian." Lindy took the picture and returned it to her purse. "My mother was always putting me on diets and trying to get me to exercise. It drove a wedge between us. My father loved me no matter what I looked like. I tried to teach in D.C., but the schools there are too crazy and I wanted to escape all of the comparisons to my mother. Here, no one knows me. This is *my* town, a place where I can be myself."

"You *did* get her huge eyes and that killer smile, Lindy," Lucy said soothingly. "And there are a lot of kids who are lucky you came out to Quincy's Gap."

"Thanks." Lindy rummaged around in her duffle bag-sized purse. "But if you thought I was opening up before, then look out." She pulled a black satin bra out of her bag and tossed it on the table.

"Good morning!" Bennett leapt back as if the bra were a coiled rattlesnake.

"I wore this in high school." Lindy held out the slinky-looking bra. "Nice size, dainty shape, alluring demi-cups—to me, it was the kind of thing a movie star or one of the prom queens from school might wear. Right?"

The ladies nodded in agreement. James and Bennett looked at one another in helpless embarrassment.

"Now this," Lindy began, yanking a flesh-colored object out of her purse, "is what I wear now. This is a full-cupped, reinforced underwire bra, size 44 EE." She tossed it on the table next to the black one.

James couldn't help but notice that each cup of Lindy's current bra looked like it could successfully hold an entire cantaloupe.

"Watch this. This is the scary part." She held up the enormous biscuit-colored bra and then placed the black bra inside of it. "At one time, my bra size was a 38 D. My, how I have grown." She sat back, hands folded across the round shelf that formed her chest, and frowned at the amazing difference between the two bras.

Lindy's current bra could hold five cups the black bra's size. It was like comparing small, sweet oranges to massively overripe and distended honeydew melons. She picked up the high school bra and held the delicate piece of lingerie over her chest. James could clearly see that only a portion of each breast would be able to fit into the old bra.

"I could never fasten this around my back, either. I'm just too wide now." Lindy dropped the bra back into her purse. "It would take an entire box of rubber bands to close the space between each set of hooks. So that's my goal, my friends. I want to slim down enough all over, but I especially want to get back into that bra. After all, can you imagine me out on a date with Principal Chavez, things getting kind of hot and heavy, and . . . Bam! He sees my fat lady underwear and drops me off at the curb."

Lindy's audience of four remained silently stunned. Luckily, the doorbell rang and the supper club members could hear a group of children giggling outside, along with the sudden patter of raindrops hitting the metal roof of Bennett's carport.

"I'll get it!" the men shouted simultaneously and dove for the candy bowl.

"That was very brave of you," Gillian said, gently covering Lindy's hand with her own. "You've given us all the inspiration to bare our souls to one another."

James returned from answering the door to a pack of hobbits hiding under umbrellas. He held out an old belt. "Wow, the rain is really coming down out there. Um, I don't have anything quite so interesting as Lindy, but this is a belt I could wear about five years ago. I *might* be able to use the last hole these days."

"I want to fit into these," Lucy said, holding up a folded pair of pants. "If I can get myself into these, then I might be inspired to keep losing weight and get in good enough shape to pass the physical I need to enroll in the deputy training program." She looked down at the faded denim on the table. "Fitting into these would be a big step toward a whole new me."

Bennett coughed. "Mine's a little embarrassing, too. It's a wrestling outfit. Lemme give ya some background on this thing. See, I didn't go to college like you folks. I had to work two jobs out of high school to help raise my brothers and sisters. There were eight of us and I was the oldest."

"So you felt responsible?" Gillian asked.

"I didn't *feel* anything." Bennett pulled roughly on his mustache, a flash of annoyance sparking in his dark eyes. "My folks said 'you've got to help,' and that was that. We lived in an even smaller town than this outside of Lynchburg. My folks scratched out a living working on other people's farms. White people's, mostly. Now I'm forty, a bit older than the rest of you, and back then, the black families all still lived in one part of town. Our neighborhood was growin' poorer and poorer and way too rough around the edges. My folks wanted to move to a better place but there just wasn't enough money. So I started commuting to Lynchburg College to work as an assistant wrestling coach. I was an all-American wrestler at my high school and I had a whole bag of tricks to pass on to those college boys. The only other job I could work while coaching was a part-time postal route. That's how my family got to Quincy's Gap and also how I became a mailman."

Lindy pointed at Bennett's uniform. "What happened to your wrestling gig?"

Bennett frowned. "Budget cuts. Not in the football program, of course, but wrestling was cancelled altogether. The sport just wasn't popular enough with the alumni, I guess. Anyway, this is a suit I wore a couple of times to demonstrate moves with my players. I'd look like a pound of soft butter sitting in a hammock if I wore it now. I'd sure like to leave this spare tire on a car somewhere and build up some of that muscle I used to have."

James smiled as Bennett held up the wrestling uniform, gazing at it nostalgically. It looked a bit like a mustard-colored slingshot.

"I ordered a set of weights a few weeks ago," Bennett continued, lowering his voice to a self-conscious whisper. "They were so heavy they had to be delivered by *the men in brown*. I ripped open this giant box with an *Iron Bodies* label, bent down, and pulled out two thirty-pound dumbbell weights. Meanwhile, a whole pile of those packing noodles flew all over the carport." Bennett scowled. "Took me half an hour to clean those damned things up. Anyway, I started lifting the weights by curling them inward toward my chest. Shoot, there was a time when I would stand in front of the TV, doing repetition after repetition while watching SportsCenter on ESPN. Man, my arms were once like pythons of muscle and my legs were thick as logs. Not anymore."

"But you started working out right away. That's great!" Lindy congratulated him.

"Hold the phone, Lindy. Those dumbbells were too damned heavy. After just a few reps, I had to drop them on the grass. Here I thought that loading and unloading that mail truck would have kept me in decent shape. Ha! I also got an exercise video to go with my weights. It's called *Thirty Days 'Til Iron*. I haven't watched it once and that's the truth."

"I didn't go to college either, Bennett," Gillian said. "But at thirty-seven, I'm smart enough to know that the human mind can accomplish wonders. And if you want to be an ironman, then you will be. Me, I just want to look like a *woman*. Right now, I am wearing a girdle under this top." She pulled at her loose shirt and then let go. The sound of elastic snapping back into place caused everyone to blink in surprise. "On top of the girdle, I'm wearing another flesh-restraining shirt. They're like control top pantyhose for your torso. It's awful. I can barely breathe in all of these shirts and they make me all sweaty. I have marks all over my skin every night when I finally take them off, and I *still* look like Spongebob Squarepants." She held out a tank top with horizontal rainbow stripes and a plunging neckline. "I'd like to wear this and look good in it. I have meditated on acquiring the strength to lose weight for months, but it wasn't until I joined this supper club that I felt the *power* to reach this goal." Her eyes glistened with tears. "I am deeply grateful to have all of your support."

The Flab Five planned their next dinner for the following Sunday at James's house. Gillian would have offered her house but said she was having some remodeling done in her kitchen and asked for a week's reprieve. James swallowed nervously as he realized that his private life was soon to be revealed to his friends. The leaky roof, torn kitchen chairs, and the knowledge that he had no idea how his father would react, had James sweating like a bridegroom. James decided to tell Jackson ahead of time so that he could determine what his father's behavior would be before next Sunday rolled around. Maybe Jackson would stay out in the shed all night.

"Don't forget to send e-mails after you've talked to Amelia," Lucy reminded Lindy. "You might discover a clue. So far, Donovan is stumped and that means we've got as good a shot as he does in solving this mystery."

James bid his friends goodnight and quickly shuffled out to his truck, getting unpleasantly wet beneath a curtain of chilly raindrops, which showed no sign of slackening. Bennett's brick ranch was on the opposite end of town from the Henry house, and no one followed James as he headed directly west. The trick-or-treaters had long since gone home and there were no other cars on the road as James crossed over the Stony Creek Bridge.

Suddenly, a deer leapt out of the cover of trees at the far end of the bridge and James instinctively slammed on his brakes. The deer locked eyes with his car headlights, unblinkingly frozen in terror as James struggled to control his Bronco on the slick bridge. His tires could not seem to find purchase and the truck skidded sideways dangerously close to the rusted guardrail lining the low bridge. James jerked on the wheel and pumped the brakes desperately as the Bronco careened wildly across the bridge. Passing by the immobile deer, his truck came to an abrupt stop on the side of the road, its headlights facing downwards, illuminating the shallow gulley below.

Breathing heavily, James laid his forehead against the steering wheel and whispered a brief prayer of thanks. When he looked over his shoulder through the driver's side window, the deer was gone. He sat still for a moment, calming himself and trying to cease the trembling of his limbs. Finally, he was composed enough to get out of his truck and survey his situation.

Dark black skid marks made an erratic track like that of a roller coaster across half of the bridge. The tires of his truck had bit deep into the muddy embankment, but James felt confident that once he put the Bronco in four-wheel drive he could easily back out of the mud using low gear. He couldn't help gazing down into the gulley, which was destined to fill with water if the rain continued at its current pace.

James turned his face into the rain, welcoming the sharp points of moisture on his skin. As he did so, a glint of metal was caught in the glare of his headlights. He peered into the darkness of the sloping hill, trying to make out what object was shining in the copse of trees. Torn between fear and curiosity, James took a step down into the long, soggy grass, and then another. As his eyes registered that the wink of metal came from the twisted spike of an umbrella, his mind tried to comprehend that an outstretched hand lay just a few feet away from the broken apparatus.

"Hold on! I'm coming!" James called, a sense of desperation flooding through him as he moved forward. The hand lay immobile as James raced down the hill, tripping and absurdly repeating his cry, "Hold on! I'm coming!" His fright completely forgotten, James reached the inert form and paused over the mat of dark tangled hair. He reached for a hand. The thin fingers were cold and unresponsive. James gently pushed back a mass of wet hair from the face, noting that it was clotted not only with mud, but also with a thicker, stickier substance that could only be blood.

As the visage became visible, James gasped in horror. "NO!" he cried, looking down at the smooth skin and the lovely and youthful features belonging to someone he knew. It was the face of Whitney Livingstone.

NINE

HAZELNUT COFFEE

JAMES DROVE HIS BRONCO as fast as he could down the dark, slick roads of Quincy's Gap, heading for the Shenandoah Valley Memorial Hospital. Back on the rainy slopes, he had hesitated to move Whitney, but after listening to what sounded like awfully shallow breaths, James checked her neck for any obvious breaks or injuries and loaded her into the Bronco. He could reach the hospital in the same amount of time it would take the paramedics to arrive at the scene.

Nutrition Facts		
Serving Size 6 fl. oz.		
Servings Per Container 1		
Amount Per Serving		
Calories 2 Calories from Fat 0		
		% Daily Value*
Total Fat 0g		0%
Saturated Fat 0g		0%
Cholesterol 0 mg		0%
Sodium 4 mg		0%
Total Carbohydrate 0g		0%
Dietary Fiber 0g		0%
Sugars 0g		
Protein 0g		
Vitamin A 0% • Vitamin C 0%		
Calcium 0% • Iron 0%		
*Percent Daily Values are based on a 2,000 calorie diet. Your daily values may be higher or lower depending on your calorie needs.		

At the moment, James was questioning the wisdom of his actions. He knew nothing about medicine and was filled with fear that he had caused Whitney more harm than good. After wrapping her in a woolen blanket and laying her as gently as a wounded bird in the back seat, her shallow breathing developed a liquid sound that bothered James immensely. His focus was torn between the road and the nearly inaudible sounds of life coming from the seat behind him.

Once the Bronco reached the highway, James was able to pick up speed. A luminescent moon broke through a collection of spidery clouds and momentarily illuminated the shadowed horizon. James used the eerie moonlight to dial 9-1-1 on his cell phone. He alerted the dispatcher that he would be arriving at Shenandoah Memorial with a seriously injured woman within ten minutes.

"Can you identify the extent of her injuries, sir?" the dispatcher asked calmly.

"No, but her breathing is funny—it sounds wet—and her color isn't good. She's way too pale."

"Does she respond when you speak to her?"

James shook his head and then remembered that he was on the phone. "No," he spoke so low that it was almost a whisper. "She can't hear me."

He was greatly relieved to see a team standing by as he pulled up to a screeching halt in front of the red Emergency doors. Two male nurses whisked Whitney onto a gurney and rolled her into the recesses of the hospital before James could even close the Bronco's back door.

"I'll just park!" he feebly called after one of the nurses and drove into the parking garage. As he pulled into a space in the nearly empty facility, his hands began to shake. Staring at them as if they were foreign objects, he noticed traces of wet dirt mixed with dried blood on his fingers. It was apparent that the shock of finding Whitney had finally set in. Without thinking about what time it was, James pulled out his cell phone again and dialed the only number his distressed brain could concentrate on.

"Hello?" a voice croaked.

"Lucy? It's James. I'm sorry to call so late. I . . . I just . . ."

James could hear Lucy sit up in bed. Next, he heard the switch of a lamp being turned on. "James? What is it?" Lucy's voice seeped into James's ear like a balm and he immediately felt himself clinging to her like a lifeline.

"Something awful has happened." He paused, letting his emotions take charge of his words. "Could you come be with me? I need a . . ." James broke off and told her briefly what had happened.

"I'll be right there. Just sit tight," Lucy assured him as soon as he was finished.

Feeling much stronger knowing that Lucy was on the way, James headed into the hospital and told his story again to the triage nurse.

"We'll inform her parents immediately." The nurse quickly located the Livingstones in the white pages, picked up a phone, and began dialing. James could feel the fist in his stomach tighten into a hard knot. What if the Livingstones were told that James had harmed their daughter by moving her? Assailed by doubt and anxiety, he paced the hall like a caged tiger until he saw the pear-shaped and comfortingly maternal figure of Lucy Hanover hurrying down the hall toward him.

Wordlessly, she enfolded him in a hug. James was engulfed by feelings of warmth and safety. "Thank you," he whispered into her hair. "Thank you for coming."

When she pulled away, her eyes were glistening. "Anytime, James. I'm right here."

At that moment, the nurse arrived to tell James that Whitney's parents were on their way. James sighed heavily and expressed his concerns to Lucy.

"You did the right thing, James. She was freezing cold and, from what it sounds like, in grave shape. If you had left her out there another moment, who knows what would have happened?" She tugged on his damp sleeve. "Look! You're soaked to the bone yourself. I'm going to get us some coffee and dig up a blanket for you." And before James could protest that he didn't need a blanket, she was gone.

Minutes later she returned, wrapped a blue blanket around his shoulders, and handed him a steaming Styrofoam cup of coffee with the most delicious aroma.

"It's hazelnut." Lucy took a tentative sip of the scalding coffee. "My favorite. I just added a drop of half-and-half for you. I don't know if you take cream. And I've got some rat killer here for you, too."

James looked at the pink, blue, and yellow packets of artificial sweeteners displayed on her palm. "Rat killer," he smiled for what felt like the first time in ages. "I like that."

They sat and sipped their coffee in comfortable silence. James thought a better cup of coffee didn't exist anywhere.

"Here comes Beau and Caroline." Lucy pointed and then put her cup down. "I'll tell them what happened, James. It'll be easier for you that way."

James watched helplessly as the panicked couple entered the waiting area. Lucy met them and gestured toward the cluster of seats where she and James were sitting and began to explain how James had found Whitney in the gulley. Caroline burst into tears at the image of her daughter, lying helpless and hurt in the rain. Beau gathered his wife in his arms as Lucy finished relaying the kind of story every parent dreads to hear.

"We haven't had word from the doctors yet." Lucy got the couple seated in the waiting room's uncomfortable plastic chairs and handed Caroline a tissue from one of the boxes on a nearby table.

James leaned forward and said, "I am deeply sorry that this has happened. I hope that I did the right thing in moving her. I'd never forgive myself if I made things worse."

Beau reached across the empty space between the seats and clasped James's hand. "My friend, my little girl would still be lyin' there if it weren't for you. No matter what happens, we sure are grateful that you got spooked by that deer." For a moment, Beau's deep voice got stuck in his throat. "We're just thanking the good Lord that you were out when you were." He turned to Lucy. "And thanks to you, for being here for all of us."

Caroline nodded her head in tearful agreement. Lucy rose and went to get two more coffees. While she was gone, James asked Whitney's parents what she had been doing out on a rainy night.

"She worked the dinner shift tonight," Caroline answered eagerly. Talking made the waiting easier. "She usually rides her bike home afterwards. It's only a ten-minute ride and she's ridden into town since she was seven. If it's raining real hard, I go get her or she gets a ride home from Dolly or Clint. I guess the rain just caught her by surprise tonight."

James frowned. "I didn't see a bike."

The Livingstones exchanged looks. "That's funny." Beau was perplexed. "I saw her ride off on it. I can't imagine what happened to it."

136

"But does that mean"—Caroline's face filled with horror—"someone ran her off the road while she was walking home? How else would she end up in a . . . ditch!" She cupped her hands together and held them over her mouth, as if to contain the anguish that continued to rise like a tide inside of her.

"Now, honey. We don't know nothin' yet. That nice nurse said the doc would be out soon. He'll tell us everything is gonna be just fine. I know it."

Caroline gazed at her husband with renewed hope. Even James was comforted by the strength and determination of Beau's pronouncement. The minutes dragged by. James and Lucy absently flipped through the pile of random magazines spread around the waiting room. Beau sketched something on the back of a piece of paperwork given to him by the triage nurse. As James walked over to Beau's chair, hoping to find a magazine that wasn't about investing or fly-fishing, he noticed that the older man had drawn blueprints and the exterior of what looked like a Tudor-style doghouse.

"That's some house," James said with admiration. "Good enough for the president's dog."

Beau looked pleased. "Think so? I call them 'Pet Palaces.' I've been building a few cat and dog houses to sell at the big Veteran's Day parade in Harrisonburg next month. I started with birdhouses." Lucy put down her magazine and came over to look as Beau continued. "I began selling those out of my truck. Caroline drives me to a busy shopping area and drops me off for a few hours with just a table and a chair. I set up my stuff and sit and wait. We've hit most of the towns in the county, so I decided to try to expand my product line a bit."

"He's done very well," Caroline added proudly. "Sold every single birdhouse he's built."

"Were the birdhouses in different architectural styles, like this Tudor doghouse?" James asked, pointing at Beau's sketch.

"Yep. Mostly red and white Amish barns or real colorful Victorians. Those sold the best." Beau gave them an ironic grin. "Figures. All those tiny pieces of gingerbread take me forever to make."

"I'd like a Pet Palace for *my* dogs!" Lucy exclaimed. "You know what? Our friend Gillian owns the Yuppie Puppy, the grooming place in town. I bet *she* would love to see your products. Maybe you two could go into business together or something."

A spark lit in Beau's eye. "That would sure be great. I don't even want to think about the cost of . . ." He trailed off, embarrassed about bringing up the expense of medical care while his daughter's condition remained unknown. Lucy quickly distracted him by asking for the sketch he had made to show Gillian. Once again, James was amazed by Lucy's ability to say the perfect thing during a difficult moment.

Finally, close to two in the morning, a doctor wearing royal-blue scrubs came out of the operating room area and approached Whitney's parents.

"How is she? How is my baby?" Caroline jumped up, clinging to the doctor's scrubs.

The doctor gently removed her hand and held it with his own. His bright blue eyes were filled with intelligence and compassion. He eased Caroline back into her chair and sat down beside her. "I'm Doctor Stauffer, the ER doctor on call. Your daughter is alive, but she's in a coma." Caroline's tense shoulders sagged in defeat and she uttered a painful moan. Dr. Stauffer placed a warm hand over her trembling fingers. "Whitney sustained some swelling to her brain, which may be the cause of the coma. We see that in cases with head trauma. She must have hit the ground rather hard, I'm afraid."

"What does that mean?" Beau leaned forward, holding his hands out helplessly toward the doctor. "Will she have . . . will she be able to . . . ?"

Dr. Stauffer gave Beau a reassuring pat on the shoulder. The anguished father sank back into his chair. "I have a few more things to tell you." The Livingstones drew in a deep breath and held it. "Whitney suffered three broken ribs, puncturing her lung. We had to put in a chest tube to re-inflate the lung. She has also sustained a broken arm. I've got an orthopedic surgeon coming in the take a look at that arm—"

"Can we see her?" Caroline asked numbly, her eyes glazed over in shock.

"Of course," Dr. Stauffer answered sympathetically. "The good news is that your daughter is both young and strong. That will make a world of difference. We are really hoping for the best." The doctor rubbed his hands together. "I hate to use this phrase as it seems like a cliché, but as in many cases, only time will tell."

The Livingstones gave an imperceptible nod.

"I'll take you to see your daughter now," the doctor added softly, steering the stunned parents to their only child's room in the intensive care unit.

James and Lucy stared after them, trying to absorb all of the medical details that they had both overheard.

"This sounds pretty bad," James said, feeling a twisting inside his stomach as he thought about Whitney's blood-encrusted hair and chilled limbs.

"She's a strong-willed young woman." Lucy sounded as though she were talking more to herself than to James. "If anyone can pull out of this, she can."

"But who . . . who could hit her like that and then just drive away?" James asked, his voice rising in anger.

Lucy stared off down the hall. "It's *got* to have something to do with Brinkley's murder. If Whitney did lie to us about not having anyone over on Labor Day, then that person must see her as a threat. Someone stole that Coumadin, James, and that someone may have tried to kill Whitney tonight. I wish she would have told me the truth." She looked at him with frightened eyes. "If the driver *was* gunning for Whitney, that was no warning tap they gave her. That car ran her down! You heard the doctor. She's in serious condition as it is—lucky to be alive." Lucy looked around wildly. "Do you think she's even safe here?"

James longed to put his arm around Lucy's shoulders, to comfort her and show her how grateful he was for her presence. As he hesitated, the sound of men's voices caused him to turn away from her. "Looks like they sent the cavalry." James jerked his head in the direction of the entrance doors.

Keith Donovan and Glenn Truett were marching double time in their direction.

"Should have known you had your nose in this mess, Lucy Hanover," Keith began, running a freckled hand through his red hair.

James didn't care for the tone with which Keith was addressing Lucy. He stepped forward an inch so that his shoulder blocked part of Lucy's body and before she could speak he said, "Actually, it's *my* mess."

Keith blinked at James in surprise. His stunned expression quickly transformed into a hostile one, however. "Oh, right. Man, for a librarian, you sure keep late hours." Behind Keith, Glenn smirked.

"Is there something *relevant* that you'd like to ask me?" James stood firm.

Keith stared hard at James, torn between continuing his bullying act and needing information quickly. Flipping a page open in a small spiral notebook, he uncapped a pen and gestured toward a group of chairs. "I'd like to hear your version of tonight's events, *Professor*."

James ignored the deputy's churlishness. He recounted the scene in which he avoided the deer and how the wink of metal from Whitney's umbrella alerted him to her presence. He gave as much detail as possible, but was unable to provide any clues regarding the actual hit and run.

"So you saw no other cars in front of you. Just the deer?" Though Keith was obviously seeking clarification, he asked his question in such an accusing tone that James felt guilt over not seeing Whitney's attacker.

"Sorry, no."

Glenn had been silent during the interview, watching James intently. Finally, he let loose a sigh and said, "Hey, man. At least you found the girl. She probably owes you her life."

"*If* she's not brain-damaged." Keith abruptly stood. "I'm gonna talk to her folks right quick. Then I'd like you to lead me back to the exact spot where you found her. Can you do that?"

James balled his fists at Keith's patronizing tone. "Of course I can. I'd do anything in my power to find out who did this." He watched the deputy swagger down the hall, his hand caressing his gun holster.

"Don't mind him," Glenn whispered to James so that Lucy couldn't hear. "He always acts like a big shot whenever there are ladies present. He thinks they're all in love with him, 'cluding Lucy."

When Keith returned, Beau Livingstone accompanied him. Beau thanked James again and promised to call with any updates on Whitney's condition.

"And don't *you* worry about anything except your daughter," Lucy said, grasping the harried father's arm. "I'm going to talk to my friend Gillian and we'll find some way to help out your family with . . ." she gestured around the room. "Just take care of yourselves."

James walked out into the parking deck, feeling like it was days, not hours, since he had pulled up in front of the emergency room doors. The rain had ceased, but the air was bitingly cold and a sharp wind wrapped around his bare neck and sent chills down his arms.

"I'll follow you!" Lucy called to James and he waved with an appreciative smile, relieved that she had decided to come along.

Driving back toward the Stony Creek Bridge, James began to feel the effects of lack of sleep. His head felt like a bowling ball and he was positive that his neck couldn't possibly support its weight for another second. Desperate to be more alert, he rolled down his window and let the crisp air slap his face into wakefulness. He longed for another hazelnut coffee to give him the strength to make it through his next face-off with Donovan.

Keith pulled in behind James and got out of his patrol car with a flashlight the size of a baseball bat.

"*Someone's* compensating," Lucy mumbled and James hid a laugh behind his hand.

"Say something, Professor?" Keith demanded forcefully.

"At least it's not raining," James replied quickly, thinking that at least "compensating" and "raining" sounded a little alike. Lucy grinned mischievously.

"Whitney was down here." James retraced his steps down toward the gulley. Keith shone the powerful beam of his flashlight around the area.

"No bike," James said to himself.

"Why should there be?" Keith looked at him carefully.

"Mrs. Livingstone said that Whitney rode to town on her bike. I told her that I hadn't seen a bike when I found her daughter."

While Keith searched the nearby underbrush, James and Lucy trudged back up the slick hill. After a few moments, Keith joined them by the side of the road.

"Those your tire tracks?" he pointed the beam of light at the erratic skid marks on the pavement.

"Yes. The deer was standing in the middle of the road about ten yards from this spot." James moved forward, pointing. "It just stood there. Never moved."

"Guess you city folk aren't used to wildlife." Keith spat his gum onto the road. "That's why it pays to drive with caution at night."

"I wasn't speeding. That deer came out of nowhere!" James retorted. His energy was falling too low to come up with a more demonstrative answer.

"Well, with your tracks crisscrossing the road from one side to the other, I doubt we'll find anyone else's tire tracks here. Got anything, Glenn?"

Glenn had been sweeping the road and both shoulders with his flashlight, methodically covering the area where Whitney had most likely been hit.

"We'll have to come back when it's light!" Glenn yelled. "I don't see anything here, Donovan."

James glanced at his watch. It was almost five in the morning. He glanced at Lucy. Her shoulders were drooping with weariness and she rubbed vigorously at her tired eyes. It was time to call it a night.

"Guess I'll head home, then," James said more to Lucy than to Keith.

Keith smirked. "I suppose *you'll* be calling in sick today, huh Lucy?"

Lucy stopped on the way to her car and pivoted to face Keith. "Damn right I am. I spent the last few hours helping folks in our community." She lowered her voice so that only James could hear the rest of her sentence. "Too bad we can't say the same thing about *you*, Keith Donovan."

TEN

POACHED EGGS

Nutrition Facts		
Serving Size 1 egg (50 g)		
Amount Per Serving		
Calories 70 Calories from Fat 45		
		% Daily Value*
Total Fat 5g		8%
Saturated Fat 1.5g		8%
Cholesterol 210 mg		70%
Sodium 150 mg		6%
Total Carbohydrate 0g		0%
Dietary Fiber 0g		0%
Sugars 0g		
Protein 6g		
Percent Daily Values are based on a 2,000 calorie diet. Your daily values may be higher or lower depending on your calorie needs.		

"WHAT HAPPENED TO MY breakfast?" Jackson Henry demanded, standing in the threshold between the hallway and James's bedroom.

James opened half an eye and read the neon digits on his clock. It was 11:00 a.m. He groaned and covered his head with his pillow. This laborious maneuver was unsuccessful in blocking out his father's complaining.

"I had to eat that God-awful cereal you bought for your big *diet*. That crap tastes like twigs and bark. Next time you're gonna sleep this late, let me know and I'll go outside and eat some pine mulch." Jackson paused, waiting for a reaction. "What are you doin' in bed anyhow? Don't tell me you got fired from the easiest job in the world? 'Cause you ain't sick. If you were, folks wouldn't be calling over here and invitin' you to breakfast. Don't they know it's almost lunchtime? Your friends on dope or somethin'?"

James pushed the pillow off of half of his face. "Who called, Pop?"

"I'm not tellin'." Jackson sounded pleased at having something to hold over his son. "I think I might have erased that message from the answering machine, too. I can't figure out all them buttons." He tapped his forehead with his finger. "Not enough college degrees, I guess."

James sat wearily up in bed. "Was it a woman named Lucy?"

Jackson pretended to think. "Nope. Why, that your girlfriend? That why you're crawlin' home at an hour when most decent folks are just wakin' up?"

James threw back the covers and slipped his feet into a pair of tattered leather slippers. He stood and pulled on an equally ratty bathrobe and shivered, feeling goose bumps erupt along his arms and legs. He would need to make sure their oil tank was full for the coming winter. The experts were calling for record-breaking amounts of snow starting later in the month. James couldn't believe it was November. He felt his new life in Quincy's Gap had actually begun years ago instead of months.

After getting dressed in his chilly room, James turned up the heater on the way downstairs and then grabbed the phone. He called the Fitzgerald brothers to explain his absence.

"Glad you're okay, Professor," Francis said, obviously relieved. "Scott and I were wondering what had happened when you weren't here this morning. I've got good news for you, though. The manager of Shenandoah Savings came over this morning with the *real* $3,000 check. We've got to figure out what to do with it!"

James perked up at the mention of the prize money. "Why don't you and Scott make a list of suggestions? You two won the money, so you should help decide where it goes. I'll be in after lunch and we'll make some decisions then."

"Right-O, Professor," Francis answered cheerily.

Next, James pressed the play button on the answering machine and was informed that he had no new messages. His father *had* deleted it on purpose. James pressed *-6-9 and recognized Gillian's voice at the other end.

"Oh, James!" she chirped. "Bennett called me first thing this morning about poor Whitney. He heard all kinds of things on his police scanner while he was reading in bed last night. Come on down to the salon. I've made you and Lucy a late breakfast. Your very *souls* must be hurt and completely drained of energy from all you went through. It's the least I can do." A cacophony of barking erupted in the background and Gillian excused herself and hurriedly rang off.

She had hung up before James could even thank her for the invitation. His stomach growled at the thought of breakfast. Looking around for his car keys, James spied a wet paintbrush sitting next to the kitchen sink. Puzzled, he picked it up and examined it. It was a small artist's brush and appeared to be of high quality. James inspected the fine, soft bristles for traces of color but there were none. He was so intent on the mysterious brush that he didn't hear his father creep up behind him. In the blink of an eye, Jackson snatched the brush from his hand, stuffed it in the front pocket of his overalls, and marched out the back door in the direction of the shed.

James followed close behind, but by the time he reached the shed door, the dead bolt was sliding into place. "We can't go on like this, Pa! You've got to rejoin society at some point!" he shouted, but the only sound he heard in return was Jackson's battery-operated television set being switched on. It was belting out the theme music to *Wheel of Fortune* as loud as its tiny speakers would allow.

———————

A buxom brunette wearing skintight pink pants and a low-cut black sweater was carrying a newly perfumed and beribboned Pomeranian out the front door of the Yuppie Puppy as James arrived.

"You're a genius, Gillian! See you next week!" the customer called over her shoulder while receiving a series of doggie licks from her grateful pet. "Yes, yes, Sophia Loren. Mommy thinks you are *so* beautiful. Who's beautiful? You are? Yes, yes! Give Mommy kisses." James could barely squeeze past the affectionate duo to enter the toasty interior of Gillian's grooming salon.

"James!" Gillian gushed, holding a hand over her heart. "I've got an herbal tea all ready for you. It's got peppermint, eucalyptus, and licorice root—just the thing to calm your nerves and exorcise all of last night's negative feelings from your consciousness."

Lucy was already perched on a purple barstool back in the Yuppie Puppy's kitchen area. While the storefront and grooming areas seemed rather clinical in their clean whites and chromes, the kitchen was an explosion of purple, yellow, and orange hues. James spied a handmade pottery platter containing an artistic display of bacon strips and what looked like poached eggs. A jar of Tabasco sauce and salt and pepper shakers sat next to the platter.

"Help yourself." Lucy smiled and beckoned at the food. "These eggs are delicious." She turned to Gillian. "I'm so sick of frying and scrambling eggs for breakfast. This is a nice treat. I thought you couldn't cook!"

"I can cook. I just got out of the habit. That's turkey bacon next to the eggs. Tastes like pig, though, so don't worry." She eyed the bacon. "Poor dear things," Gillian added mournfully while pouring tea from a porcelain kettle into a mud-colored pottery mug decorated with pink cherry blossoms. The mug's handle was so hot that James couldn't hold onto it.

"It's Japanese. They're the world's tea masters. The pottery is so thin that it retains the water's heat better." Gillian pointed at the scalding mug. "Now, Lucy, tell me more about these Pet Palaces. My next client doesn't come in 'til two. I've got to declaw a cat and I so *hate* going against nature in that way. I'd like to have something else to think about during the appointment, especially if it's a new business venture."

Lucy slid Beau's drawing across the marigold tabletop. Gillian examined it with keen interest. "This is really something!" Her eyes sparkled and she twirled a lock of hair ferociously around her finger. James thought Gillian's hair was an entirely different shade than it had been on Halloween night and that it bore an uncanny resemblance in hue to the Tabasco sauce he had just splashed on his egg. "I could put these for sale on the Internet and make a killing. Do you know how many pet owners would treat their pets to something like this?"

"Beau uses indoor-outdoor carpeting. Do you see this?" Lucy pointed to a contraption inside the house. "That's an automatic feeding and watering system. This is a place for a raised bed, fur-lined of course, and this is a toy bin that the animal can access by pressing on this lever with its paw. And look at this! There's even a place for a framed photo of the pet's family."

"So it looks like the cat houses get scratching posts on their front porches and the dog houses get chew ties on strings. I love it!" Gillian suddenly frowned. "Still, these can't be cheap to build, especially if Beau's using vinyl siding and other all-weather mate-rials. We'd have to charge a lot to have enough profit to split and cover shipping costs, marketing costs—"

"Whoa!" Lucy held out her hands. "I just thought you might like to talk things over with Beau. Maybe sell a few for him from here. They'd look great in your window." Her tone grew more som-ber. "We've got to think of some way to help that poor family out."

"We need to do more than sell a few houses for them." Gillian's expression turned rigid and determined. "They have *really* suffered. Like you told us a few days ago, Beau is already swamped with med-ical bills. Now they're going to have a lot more where those came from. But we live in Quincy's Gap, Shenandoah County, Virginia. This *whole* state is filled with good-hearted spirits. If we could bring them together somehow . . ."

"Like having a benefit or something?" James asked.

Gillian thumped him on the back. "Exactly! A Help Your Neigh-bor Day!" Her eyes shone with charitable fervor. "If we could get the local businesses to chip in some products to sell and if Dolly and Clint would cook some food, we could take in some money for the Livingstones."

"We'd need a *huge* turnout to make enough to help them with the kind of bills they're facing." Lucy looked thoughtful. "And a *lot* of help."

James piped up. "We should call Murphy Alistair. Maybe she'd like to take a break from murder headlines and use the media for good for once."

"Stellar idea, James," Lucy said. "You deal with the media and I'll help Gillian solicit the businesses. What date should we shoot for?"

"This weekend!" Gillian declared. "I know that's short notice, but if we wait any longer, people will forget. After all, one of their own has been injured and left for dead. People's hearts are overflowing with good karma right now after reading about Whitney's injuries in *The Star* and we need to take advantage of it. We can use the field right behind this strip mall. No one uses it and there's plenty of parking out front."

"I knew you'd be able to help." Lucy beamed at her carrot-topped friend. "I'll make some calls from work. I'd like to ask the Shillings if they'd let us borrow some of their ponies for rides. We need baked goods, too. I'll see if Lindy can round up some parents, and we'll get students and teachers to organize other concession stands. James, do you have time to see Murphy before you go in to work? We need her to start printing stories right away."

James glanced at his watch. He had promised the twins that he'd be in after lunch, so technically, he had a few minutes in which he could visit the officious reporter. Luckily for him, he didn't need to go far. Murphy Alistair was next door getting a manicure and practically slammed into James as she headed toward her car, flailing her hands about like a pair of startled bats.

"Professor Henry!" She gathered herself together and offered James a phony, professional smile. "I've been calling you all morning! Haven't you received my messages?"

"I've been home until now, actually. I had a rather late night."

"That's *exactly* what I'd like to speak to you about. Can I follow you back to the library?"

James thought quickly. "I've had several calls from city reporters about last night, including *The Daily Progress* from Charlottesville and Richmond's *Times-Dispatch*. I guess they see me as some kind of hero librarian," he lied, watching as Murphy's eyes grew round in alarm. "So far, I haven't talked to anyone. I'll give you the exclusive story on *one* condition."

Murphy's narrowed her eyes in suspicion. "What's that?"

"I'd like you to write two stories for tomorrow's edition." James opened the passenger door to the Bronco and gestured for the reporter to get in. "One of them is about this weekend's . . . uh . . . Neighbor Aid Festival." Murphy gave him a blank look. "Trust me, it's breaking news. I'll explain on the way." James pointed at her glistening mauve nail polish. "Watch out for your nails."

Murphy slid carefully into the car, her hands wriggling in front of her like a pair of large spiders weaving a web. She was uncharacteristically taciturn.

———

Jackson Henry threw *The Star* down on the table in disgust. "That woman spreads poison faster than a nest of water moccasins."

James looked up in surprise. He hadn't seen his father read the daily paper for months. Reaching across the table, he took the crumpled pages from Jackson and examined the latest headline. PARENTS OF HIT AND RUN LIVE IN FEAR it read.

"And what in the hell is this Neighbor Aid?" Jackson grumbled, sinking a pair of yellowed teeth into a piece of crisp raisin toast dripping with butter.

James continued scanning the front page, pleased to see that the entire bottom half of the page had been devoted to the upcoming festival. Murphy's article on the Livingstones was touching and heartfelt. The enormous photo of Whitney in pigtails standing in front of Goodbee's Drug Store with an ice cream cone in hand was perfect. Her youth, innocence, and vulnerability shone through the eyes of the sweet, knobby-kneed six-year-old, and reminded people that she was a child belonging to the community of Quincy's Gap.

"This reporter is trying to get the townsfolk together to raise money for this young woman, Whitney Livingstone." James pointed at the more recent photo of Whitney taken at her high school graduation. "She's a part-time college student and a waitress at Dolly's. She's the girl I found lying in the ditch two nights ago."

Jackson squinted at the photo. "I know her. She's from good people. Her daddy used to work for me before he started that roofin' business. Should have stayed with me, too. He could have gotten a job at . . ." Jackson couldn't speak the name of the new hardware store. "Well, he would have had insurance if he was with them when his heart gave out."

James was stunned. Not only did his father know of Beau's troubles, but he actually said something nice about the family in the same breath. "What are *you* going to do to help them out, set up a tutoring tent?" Jackson sneered, adapting his regular scowl.

So much for a change of disposition, James thought. "There's going to be a silent auction Saturday night. I'm donating all of my vintage Marvel comic books and a few signed first edition books."

"Those books worth anything?" Jackson asked.

"Folks will pay good money for these. They're horror books by really famous authors." James wondered why his father was so curious about the subject.

"Maybe you should sell them and get our roof fixed," Jackson grumbled, getting up from the table without clearing his plate. At the door leading outside, he paused and without turning said, "I'm going to leave a box in your truck for you to sell at the auction. I don't want it opened 'til you bring it out to the field on Saturday, understand?"

James stared at his father's lean back, perplexed.

"Understand?" Jackson cast a fierce stare over his bony shoulder. It was a stare that allowed for no argument.

"Yes, sir." James muttered, reduced to a seven-year-old child once again. "I understand."

———————

The Fitzgerald brothers were in a tizzy over the allotment of the float prize funds. Francis wanted to spend all the money on DVDs and audio books, Scott wanted to update the library's ancient matrix printer and buy a laser printer as well as a new copier machine. James wanted to add another computer terminal to their single computer station. In the end, they decided to purchase more audio books and some large print books for the bookmobile to take to the homebound. They also agreed to buy the laser printer and charge the patrons per printed page so that they'd make enough money to pay for ink cartridges and paper.

"If I sell the old printer on eBay, can we use the funds along with the money from our donated book sales to buy some DVDs?" Francis asked.

"Absolutely," James agreed, feeling buoyant over the changes they were making. "I was also thinking that we might start a bit of a side business to benefit this branch."

The twins gazed at him with interest.

"You're both strong in the math and sciences. I'm not so bad at English and history. What do you think about us providing some tutoring? We'll ask for donations in order to buy that new computer. We can use the meeting room for our sessions." He turned to Scott. "If we do really well, a new copier will be next."

"I'm in." Scott assented. "I'd like to add computer classes to that roster once we get another terminal. Tons of people want to learn how to use e-mail or surf the Internet, but they don't want to go to the community college to do it."

"We could also help our patrons write their resumes or fine-tune college or work applications. I'll write an ad to put in *The Star* about the tutoring." Francis jumped up. "Meeting adjourned, Professor?"

"Yes, gentlemen." James smiled. "Good work. See you tomorrow."

James was just putting on his heavy barn jacket when the phone at the circulation desk rang. He waved to Mrs. Waxman, who was just walking in to begin the evening shift, and picked up the bleating phone.

"Professor Henry?" James recognized the voice of Caroline Livingstone. "I thought you'd like to know. Whitney's awake. She'd like to see you and Miss Hanover. Can you come?"

"I'm on my way!" James answered with elation and dashed out into the cold.

———————

Lucy was already waiting outside of Whitney's room when James arrived. She held a plate of oatmeal cookies in her hands and gave him a smile.

"I only ate two spoonfuls of this cookie dough. Believe me, that's major."

"I think you're looking thinner, Lucy." James looked at her momentarily and then eyed the cookies hungrily.

"So are you, but let's not blow it by giving into sugar cravings," Lucy said, noting the direction of James's longing glance. "Anyway, I bet Whitney's parents have hardly eaten since they got here." She knocked on the wooden door.

Caroline opened it a crack, and her face clearly expressed relief at seeing James and Lucy. "Sorry," she explained, "but reporters from all over northern Virginia have been trying to get in here. Seems like Murphy Alistair made a few calls and now we're the 'big story.'"

"I think she's actually trying to help," James said in a muffled voice. Hospitals were like churches or libraries in that he felt the need to whisper within their walls.

"And I believe I know the folks behind this Neighbor Aid Festival, too." Caroline wagged a finger at them both. "There aren't enough days to thank y'all for what you've done for us. Beau raced home to finish the Pet Palace he had started before . . . Well, come in and see Whitney."

Whitney was propped up in her twin hospital bed, an IV tube coming out of her left arm and a cast on her right. Her face was swollen and bruised, but she offered a crooked grin when they entered and then quickly stopped smiling. James could only assume that the expression caused her discomfort. Lucy pulled up a chair and took Whitney's hand.

"I'll wait outside," Caroline offered, but Whitney shook her head.

"Mom," she croaked, her voice sounding scratchy and unused. "You need to hear this, too."

Warily, Caroline sat in a faded red recliner by the window. As there were no more chairs, James remained standing, feeling awkward.

"First of all, thank you." She gazed and James and attempted another smile. "I hear I owe you my life."

James reached over and patted her arm lightly, above the cast. "I'm just glad I was in the right place at the right time."

"And I owe *you* an apology," Whitney continued, turning her eyes on Lucy. "You've been so kind to me and I lied to you."

Lucy nodded silently. "I know, sweetheart. We'll make it right, okay?"

Whitney nodded weakly. "Mom, when you and Daddy went to that anniversary party, I had some friends over. Actually, they're not even friends. We just had something in common to talk about."

"Brinkley Myers?" Lucy guessed.

"Yes." Whitney released a deep sigh. "Brinkley asked me for money. He asked us all for money."

Caroline's face crumpled. "What for, darling?"

"'Cause he knew secrets about all of us, Mom. I'm going to tell you mine. It's been eatin' me up inside for months."

"Go ahead," Lucy prompted when Caroline didn't speak.

"I'm a horrible writer. When I had to write those three essays to apply to James Madison, I knew I would never get in, so I paid another girl to write them for me. Brinkley found out and threatened to call the dean of admissions and tell them." A tear trickled down her cheek. "I'm not a liar, I'm really not. If JMU ever saw my true writing, they'd know I cheated and I'd be kicked out. I've avoided that so far by not takin' any English courses." She cast James an apologetic look. "Thing is, I had no more money to give Brinkley. With JMU's tuition and helping out at home . . ."

"Honey, couldn't one of your teachers have helped you with those essays?" Caroline asked in shock.

"Yeah, sure they would have. I took the easy route out. That was before Dad's accident. I didn't see things like I do now. I was just in a rush to move on, to get out of town and become a career woman, makin' the big bucks. I'm real sorry, Mom."

"So Brinkley was blackmailing you?" Lucy clarified.

"I paid him a few hundred dollars, but he kept at me. I'd have to quit school to keep paying him and then what would be the point? I was going to call his bluff next time he bugged me about money, but then . . . he died."

Lucy asked gently. "You had nothing to do with that, right?"

Whitney's eyes grew round. "No! I really didn't, Ms. Hanover. Swear to God!"

"I believe you," Lucy assured the wounded girl. The room filled with silence.

"Do you remember what happened last night?" James finally asked, changing topics.

Whitney shook her head. "I was walking home from Dolly's. Some asshole stole my bike." She looked sheepish for having cursed. "Sorry, Mom. The rain came out of nowhere, so I walked on the road to keep my sneakers from getting soaked. Next thing I know, I'm here."

"So you never saw the car?"

"I saw headlights and I moved off to the side. I turned around, but only for a second. I feel like I saw something, something weird, but I can't remember what."

James and Lucy were silent.

"So who else was at your house the night your parents were away?" Lucy inquired in an authoritative tone. "It's time to tell me now, honey."

Whitney didn't answer.

"Amelia Flowers was there," James stated. "You might as well admit that."

"How did you know that?" Whitney was startled.

"The day Brinkley died, he was probably going to ask Amelia for money, too. What did he have on her, Whitney?"

The young woman closed her eyes. "It's not for me to spill her secrets, Professor. I'm sorry, I know I owe you more than that, but I just can't."

Even though James could see that Lucy was frustrated, he couldn't help but respect Whitney's sense of honor.

"The sheriff will be here asking you the same questions!" Lucy practically shouted. "He's not going to let you off this easily. Someone tried to kill you, Whitney! This isn't over!"

Whitney began to cry and Caroline hustled from her seat to stand protectively at her daughter's side. "That's enough for now, please. I'll try talking to her later, but right now . . . I just think she's been through enough."

Lucy bowed her head in shame. "Of course. I apologize. I just want to make sure no one else gets hurt. I'm real worried about your daughter."

Caroline nodded and then turned to enfold her daughter's head gently in her arms. She began to hum softly as she pressed a light kiss on Whitney's forehead. "Momma's here," they heard her croon as they closed the door. "No one is gonna hurt my baby ever again."

ELEVEN

CHILI CHEESE FRIES

Nutrition Facts	
Serving Size 1 package (98g)	

Amount Per Serving	
Calories 400 Calories from Fat 171	

	% Daily Value*
Total Fat 19g	29%
Saturated Fat 5g	25%
Cholesterol 10 mg	3%
Sodium 990 mg	41%
Total Carbohydrate 51g	17%
Dietary Fiber 5g	20%
Sugars 2g	
Protein 8g	
Vitamin A 8% • Vitamin C 30%	
Calcium 4% • Iron 4%	

*Percent Daily Values are based on a 2,000 calorie diet. Your daily values may be higher or lower depending on your calorie needs.

THE SPECTACLE THAT HAD become Neighbor Aid was one that James Henry would remember for the rest of his life. In just a few short days, the entire town had pitched together to set up a charity event the likes of which Quincy's Gap had never seen. The festival came to life in the unused field behind the strip mall housing the Yuppie Puppy and lasted from early in the morning until dusk.

The work began at dawn on Wednesday with a few of the farmers who drove their industrial tractors into town at 15 miles per hour in order to mow the field. Next, the county's only party rental store, Party Like It's 1999, from the nearby town of Elkton, erected their entire supply of large tents across the mowed field. Volunteers from Elkton helped the party store set up the tents and line the interiors with long tables for displaying goods as well as creating a dining area for those who wanted to sit and have a meal.

Dolly and Clint posted a sign on the diner door that they would be closed all day on Saturday and that should patrons wish to eat, they should visit the Dolly's Diner booth at Neighbor Aid. Il Pomodoro, the local Italian restaurant, did the same. These eateries were joined by the Sweet Tooth, an ice cream parlor called Cups 'n' Cones from the town of Alma, and Adam's Ribs, a barbecue joint all the way from Keezietown.

"They have the *world's* best chili cheese fries!" James heard a woman exclaim to her husband as they quickly jumped at the end of the long lunchtime line in front of the Adam's Ribs booth.

Further down the line of tents, James spied Gillian and her assistant beneath a hand-painted banner reading "On the Spot." The two women were giving baths and nail clippings to a queue of dogs. Gillian and her mall neighbor, Mary Ann Pulasky of Shear Elegance, had bought extra-long hoses and extension cords in order to provide their customers with shampoos and rinses. They were offering a "Parent and Pooch" special in which dogs and their owners could receive a simultaneous beauty treatment. Luckily for Gillian, Mary Ann, and especially the Livingstones, the weather was cooperating by providing a rare sixty-degree day replete with sunshine and cloudless November sky.

Men and women filled the fields, eating, purchasing goods donated from local businesses, or leaving bids at the silent auction tables. Children had their faces painted by a group of high school girls and someone had rented a mammoth moonwalk for the younger kids to bounce around inside. Pony rides, sponsored by Shilling's

Stables, as well as a dressage and jumping demonstration conducted by the Shilling trainers, were a big hit. James was just watching one of the stable's horse trailers back into a makeshift paddock when a woman's voice called out his name.

"Professor!" James turned to see Murphy Alistair beaming at him. "Looks like my friend from *The Washington Post* came through for us. He put a short piece on Whitney and our festival in the 'Arts & Living' section and is even sending a staff writer out to cover the event!"

James took in Murphy's triumphant expression and put a hand on her shoulder. "You did a good thing, Ms. Alistair. Look at the *positive* power media can have. I wish more reporters were like you."

Murphy's eyes shone. "I'm not all *that* bad, Professor. Not all reporters are scum any more than all librarians are prudes." She gave him a penetrating stare.

James felt his face growing warm. Was Murphy flirting with him? He took in her short, stylish, blonde-streaked brown hair and hazel eyes before the honking of a horn distracted his attention. The trailer stopped, and a woman with a puff of hair dyed a shade of platinum bordering on ghost-white and dressed in a pink skirt suit and beige leather pumps descended from the passenger seat of a white Shilling's Stables pick-up truck.

"Who is that?" James asked Murphy, who was watching the woman with intense interest. Before she could answer, a silver Porsche convertible pulled next to the trailer.

"Don't see many of those kind of cars around here," James observed.

"That must be Chase Radford, the senator's son." Murphy pointed at the tall youth as he leapt out of the car and raced around the hood to open the passenger door. "Rumor has it that he's been dating Allison Shilling. Hmm. Looks like the ladies from Shear Elegance are right for once." Murphy made a few adjustments to her digital camera as she and James watched Chase help Allison out of the car and then plant a demure kiss on her cheek. "I'd better get some shots of them." Murphy hurried away.

Without realizing it, James found himself trailing behind the energetic reporter. As he watched a trainer from Shilling's Stables unload a beautifully sleek horse from the newly arrived trailer, he spotted Lindy and a group of high school students manning a large table covered with pottery to the left of the horse paddock.

Trying to ignore the pungent combination of barbecue and horse droppings, James headed over to Lindy's booth. Lindy was busily selling her students' art. Bowls and pitchers in glossy jewel-toned glazes were flying off the table. Two high school boys were furiously unpacking vases, plates, and mugs in earth-tone glazes. At the neighboring table, two friendly female students were selling watercolor paintings, charcoal drawings, and African masks created from papier mâché.

"Hey, Lindy!" James sidled up to her table. One of the boys gazed at Lindy with interest.

"Yes, we *do* have first names, Billy. Can you wrap up this bowl for Mrs. Samson?"

"Sure, Miss Perez," the boy smirked.

"Looks like you're making a killing here." James observed.

"I've never had people throwing money at me so fast!" she exclaimed, her face flushed with exertion. "I think I could get used to it, too." She bestowed a prideful glance at the students surrounding her. "My kids have really been the heroes though. They spent so many hours making these pieces but once when they heard about Whitney, they gave them up just like that." Lucy snapped her fingers. She lowered her voice to a whisper. "We have over five hundred dollars already."

"Excuse me," a snide voice demanded attention. "My daughter and her *fiancé* would like to purchase that cobalt bowl. Do you think we could have some service?"

"Hello, Mrs. Shilling." Lindy offered the polite salutation through gritted teeth. "And hello, Allison," she said to the young woman standing behind her mother wearing a bored expression. Her tan arms were folded across her small chest and she glanced around the crowd as if searching for something or someone truly worth looking at. Finally, her icy blue eyes settled on the round face of her former art teacher.

"Hi, Miss Perez," Allison muttered.

"Congratulations on your engagement!" Lindy forced herself to sound enthusiastic. "Let's see your ring."

Allison held out her left hand limply. James couldn't help but whistle at the size of Allison's ring. He had seen smaller rocks at a limestone quarry. The diamond was so large that it appeared to be weighing down the girl's thin finger. Allison's fingernails were painted a pale pink and each nail bore a small rhinestone in the center. James wondered what kind of job a person could have and still manage to keep ten rhinestones intact on the ends of her fingernails.

"Wow! You could use that thing as a disco ball!" Lindy laughed good-naturedly. "And is this your husband-to-be?" Lindy gave the young man at Allison's elbow a sincere smile.

"Chase Radford is the son of our own *Senator* Radford," Mrs. Shilling bragged when Allison didn't respond. "He has just graduated from Georgetown University with a law degree. He plans to follow in his father's footsteps."

"Nice to meet you." Chase reached in front of his fiancée in order to shake Lindy's hand. His arm brushed Allison's and she recoiled from it in annoyance. She tugged at her mother's sleeve and said, "Let's get going, Mother." Chase seemed oblivious to his fiancée's negative body language.

Turning to her, he ran a hand through her long, wavy brown hair and gazed at her with nothing short of adoration. James and Lindy exchanged befuddled glances.

Mrs. Shilling paid for her pottery and gave her daughter a sidelong warning glare. "Come on, Chase," she said, hooking her arm in Chase's. "Let's find out how we can donate our fine mare to the silent auction. We Shillings believe very much in helping out our neighbors."

"Good luck today, ma'am." Chase gestured at the artwork as he was being led away. "You must be a mighty fine teacher to have such gifted artists in your classes. Bye now!"

"Well!" Lindy exhaled. "What is that darling boy thinking by getting himself involved with that pair of shrews?"

"They both looked like they've been raised sucking on lemons," James said, watching Allison plod sulkily along next to her mother.

"Or sour milk," Lindy sniggered. "Allison spent most of high school away at the Portsmouth School for Girls. Not to be catty, but I heard the Shilling princess left in disgrace the end of her junior year. Now she goes to Sweet Briar and is in the Equine Studies

Program. I guess Allison's on mid-term break right now." Lindy ran her hand over the surface of a pottery sap dish. "Believe it or not, she and Whitney used to be friends."

James raised his eyebrows in surprise. "I can't picture that."

Lindy shrugged. "Whitney grew up, while Allison didn't. Whitney has had to pitch in to help her parents make ends meet and Allison still just puts her hand out and then goes shopping. Must be nice."

"She certainly doesn't look happy," James said.

"No joke. I've never seen such a miserable bride-to-be. Chase is clearly nuts about her, but Allison looks like she'd rather have a cavity drilled than hang out with him." Lindy paused to hand a customer two coffee mugs to examine. "You seen any of the other Flab Fives?"

"Just Gillian. She's washing dogs like crazy. You?"

"I saw Bennett earlier," Lindy said. "He and the other county postal workers have gotten together a row of carnival games. Bennett is running the balloon toss booth where kids can pop balloons with a dart." She giggled. "He looked as white as a swan watching those darts fly all over the place. I do believe kids may scare him even more than Lucy's dogs!"

"Did I hear my name?" Lucy appeared from behind a pack of boys holding boxes of popcorn and sticks of pink and blue cotton candy. "Lindy! Your booth is wonderful! Hi, James. What are you up to?"

"I'm heading over to the silent auction tent. I've got some comic books and stuff, and my pop gave me a mystery box to donate as well."

"I'll walk you over. I've been given an unofficial job by Sheriff Huckabee to keep an 'eye on things.'" She held up a walkie-talkie. "See? I even have one of the boys' toys."

"What? No gun?" Lindy teased. "Some kid might get high off too many caramel apples and turn Bennett into a pincushion."

Lucy laughed so hard she had to put a hand on the table to steady herself. "I saw him! He is standing in a corner of his booth cowering like a little girl who's seen a *really* big spider."

"I'd better give my artists a hand," Lindy said, noting the growing line in front of the table containing the paintings and masks. "Though I don't know how I'm going to get out of here today without a funnel cake. You guys bring any duct tape? You might need to physically restrain me when I pass by that booth."

James and Lucy were in high spirits as they headed to the silent auction tent. Lucy carried one of the boxes of comic books while James struggled beneath the weight of a box of books and his father's large, rectangular box, which was firmly sealed with brown packaging tape.

The members of the Shenandoah County Historical Society had offered to run the silent auction booth, and James was amazed at the quality of goods they had managed to solicit within a few days. Jewelry, gift certificates, baskets of Virginia-made wine and gourmet foods, plane tickets, weekend getaways, antique silver and glassware, and more were tastefully arranged on maroon tablecloths. James nervously unwrapped his Marvel comics and signed horror novels, but one of the volunteers in the booth thanked him heartily for donating such valuable items.

"You've got quite a collection of items here. Very impressive," James praised the nearest volunteer and left bids for the gift certificates donated by a handyman service and a steak restaurant in Harrisonburg.

"These *are* great," the woman agreed. "But Shilling's Stables has just donated our most amazing item yet. They've given us one of their thoroughbreds! And a writer from *The Washington Post* took a picture of *me* accepting the horse! My goodness, can you believe the generosity of Mrs. Shilling?" The woman was practically shrieking with excitement.

James shook his head. "Pretty hard to believe," he said under his breath as the woman turned away. He spied Lucy on the other side of the booth, scribbling bids on several clipboards, her face alight with the enjoyment of her activity. Finally, James could turn his attention to the contents of his father's box. He tried to cut the tape using his car keys, but was unsuccessful. He was just about to ask one of the women working in the booth if she had a pair of scissors when Lucy fastened a clawlike grip on his forearm.

"There's Amelia!" she shouted. "Quick! We've got to get some information out of that girl!"

"But—" James stammered, his hand still fastened to his father's box.

"Ladies! This box is yours, too!" Lucy removed James's hand and pulled him along after her.

Lucy hustled behind Amelia's knockout figure. She was easy to spot in the crowd due to the neon-orange top she wore. James thought that most women would have looked like construction flagmen in such a shade, but Amelia seemed to wear the tight top like a runway model. In fact, she even strutted across the uneven field as if she were on a catwalk in Milan. James found himself fixating on the saucy wiggle of her curvaceous derriere.

"She's getting in line at the Adam's Ribs booth," Lucy said, finally withdrawing her hand from James's arm. She pumped her own arms in a furious, fast-paced walk and stepped into the line a few customers behind Amelia.

"Excuse me," she said sweetly to a man in a cowboy hat standing behind Amelia. "I don't want to be rude and cut in front, but do you mind if I chat with my friend here while we're all waiting?"

"Sure thing, honey," the man said, tipping his hat. Lucy smiled, momentarily beguiled. James wished he possessed the man's natural charm as well as his washboard stomach, which was clearly visible beneath the thin cotton of his white T-shirt.

"Hello, Amelia. You remember me from a few Saturdays ago?" Lucy asked.

Amelia nodded, her large, golden brown eyes flickered with fear and she took a minute step away from Lucy as if already in retreat. James examined her face for the second time. When he had seen her through the bakery window, he had formed an impression of a young woman with a plain face and a killer body, but as he looked at her more closely, he noticed that her facial features actually seemed a bit skewed. Her eyes were too far apart and her nose was narrow and too pointed. Her lips were thin and drawn and her cheeks were wide and flat.

"Don't worry," Lucy spoke up as James was giving Amelia the once-over. "We're just here for the chili cheese fries. You know Professor Henry?"

Amelia shrugged. "I've seen him at the library." She turned to James and added in a husky, flirtatious voice. "I don't go much because you don't carry enough fashion magazines. Could you order a few more, like *W* and *Glamour*?" She leaned toward him so that he had a clear view of her resplendent cleavage.

"I'll look into it," James assured her, uneasy with her abrupt change in manner when addressing him.

"I'm glad to see you out here, Amelia," Lucy intervened, a scowl on her face. She kept her tone neutral, however. "Whitney's family needs all the help they can get."

Amelia shrugged again. "I'm workin' the haunted hayride down at Miller's farm tonight. He's extended it through the weekend just for the Livingstones." She looked at the ground as the line took a step forward. "Have you seen Whitney?" she asked in a soft voice, which suddenly sounded very young.

"Yes," Lucy replied. "She's banged up, but she's going to be okay."

Amelia released a deep breath. Her tense body relaxed and a smirk came to her face. "So it wasn't that big a deal then, huh?"

James could tell that Lucy was fighting to control her temper. He could see her compact hands balling themselves up into clenched fists. "It *was* a big deal. She got run over, Amelia. She's lucky to be alive." Lucy quickly lowered her voice. "What I don't understand is why Whitney would want to protect you when you don't even give a damn that she nearly died a few nights back!"

Amelia's eyes flew open wide. "Protect me? I don't need *her* protection," she hissed.

"Let's start with the fact that you spent the night at Whitney's over Labor Day weekend. That means *you* could have stolen the drug that Brinkley was poisoned with."

The line moved forward, but Amelia stood rooted to the ground, her mouth agape as if she were sucking on an ice cream cone made of air.

"How did . . . Whitney went narc on me . . . ?" Amelia whined in disbelief.

"Someone tried to kill her, Amelia. You can hardly blame her for coming clean. So where were *you* on Halloween night?"

"I was home with my ma," Amelia snapped, regaining her confidence. "You can ask her." She looked ahead of her. Only two people stood between her and her snack. "I'm not even hungry anymore, thanks a lot!" she barked at Lucy and began to walk away.

"Whatever was on Brinkley's cell phone is still on there!" James surprised himself by calling after her.

Amelia froze as Lucy gave James a startled look. Slowly, as if she were walking through knee-deep water, Amelia headed back toward them.

"What do you mean?" she asked James, her flat face filled with a mixture of childish petulance and fear. "It was smashed."

"The memory is in a chip," James answered hurriedly, unsure of whether he even spoke the truth. "The sheriff can get it examined if someone points it out to him."

Without warning, Amelia sagged against his chest, and began to sob dramatically. "He had pictures of me! No one can ever see them!"

At that crucial moment, the threesome had reached the front of the line. Despite her confusion, Lucy ordered two plates of chili cheese fries as James led Amelia over to a row of plastic folding chairs and pulled three chairs away from the feasting customers.

"Did he ask you for money?" Lucy inquired gently.

Amelia nodded wordlessly. She pressed her face into a paper napkin and blew her nose loudly. "I had a modeling job last year, my first one. Some guy put an ad in the Charlottesville paper and

I read it while I was getting a haircut at Shear Elegance. Five hundred dollars guaranteed for swimsuit models. I knew I had to get that gig. I've wanted to be a model my whole life." Amelia picked up a cheese-laden fry and twirled it around until it resembled a limp noodle. "Everything seemed fine at first. I was there with three other girls who were chosen out of like, two hundred or something. We put on these string bikinis which were like, skin-colored and almost see-through, but not totally," she added defensively. "Things got a little weird when we had to do poses with each other. We had to act, like, well, you know . . ."

"Like you were attracted to the other girls?" Lucy guessed very quietly.

"Yeah." Amelia finally popped a fry into her mouth. "We had to sign a bunch of papers at the beginning with print so small I didn't bother to read them and we got our money right up front, in cash! That was awesome because I wanted to have a portfolio made and my mom said we couldn't afford it." She grimaced. "We can never afford *anything*. I would be lucky enough to have a drunk for a daddy. He took everything when he left, so Mom and I have had to work like dogs ever since." She glared at James and Lucy fiercely. "I hope that bastard's rotting in a gutter someplace."

"So what happened to the pictures?" Lucy prodded gently.

"They were doctored and put on this Girls Who Love Girls website. Brinkley found it, probably while he was drooling over a site just like it." She blushed and examined her plate of fries. "I never knew the pictures were for a site like that. We all look totally naked in them! My modeling career would be over for sure if a real agent ever saw those. Once you do something like that . . . And not to mention what my mom would do if she found out!"

Lucy bit into a fry, just to have something to do. "She doesn't know?" she asked, chewing.

"No way!" Amelia yelped. "Brinkley came in to ask for more money the day after Homecoming. He had the pictures on his phone—you can download all kinds of things to cell phones now—and he threatened to show them to my mom."

"That made you angry, didn't it?" James casually asked, also munching on a fry so that his question seemed less direct.

"Of course it did!" Amelia snarled. "Brinkley was a lowlife scumsucker!"

James thought she was probably accurate in her assessment. He remembered the rolled-up magazine Amelia had been holding so tightly at the crime scene. "So you hit him with a magazine," he stated, trying to remain focused on Amelia's face as the spicy chili, smooth cheese, and crisp, salty fries coated his mouth with an ambrosia-like flavor. His taste buds cried out in bliss.

Lucy paused mid-chew to stare at James. Then she turned her attention back to Amelia. "*That's* what started Brinkley's nosebleed."

Amelia began to cry again. "I didn't mean to kill him! I was just, *so mad!* I already gave him the whole five hundred dollars from that horrible job, and he still wanted more!" She gazed at Lucy and suddenly looked very much younger than her twenty years. "I don't know anything about those drugs the paper talked about, though. I swear to God I don't!"

"I believe you," Lucy said as she patted Amelia's elegant but work-worn hand. James could see tiny burns on the girl's knuckles, undoubtedly from the oven, and small nicks probably made by a serrated knife. He thought about how different Amelia's hands were from Allison's.

"Do you have to tell people about my pictures?" Amelia asked pleadingly.

"Only if it's necessary," Lucy promised. "As long as you've told me the truth about *everything* to do with Brinkley Myers, I think we can keep your secret."

"Thanks. Look, I gotta go," the young woman said hastily, glancing at her watch. "I'm one of the chain saw maniacs in the field tonight and I've got to learn the back paths and get made-up and stuff."

"Just one more question, honey, and then you can go." Lucy bit off the end of another fry. "Who else was with you guys that Labor Day weekend? Because if you didn't take the drugs and Whitney didn't, someone else did."

"Dunno," Amelia said nonchalantly, standing up. Then she straightened her shoulders and flicked a strand of long hair over her shoulder and marched away, smiling alluringly at the man with the cowboy hat before she disappeared into the milling crowd.

"Back to square one," Lucy muttered, gazing after Amelia. "Damn."

James didn't respond. His mouth was too crammed with chili cheese fries to utter a single intelligible syllable.

———————

The afternoon shadows were lengthening as James and Lucy headed off to tell the others about their conversation with Amelia. They agreed to split up, grab their friends, and meet back at the podium area for the closing of the festival at five. The mayor planned to make a speech and then send the crowd down to the Miller's Farm to contribute more funds by purchasing tickets to a spooky hayride

175

through the farmer's haunted fields. Most of the locals had already been on the ride, but Mr. Miller promised an even more fearful display created especially for the benefit.

James collected Gillian and then stopped to watch as Bennett yanked wayward darts from the surface of several wooden tables and chairs. Trying to suppress their laughter, they also saw him pull one out of the laces of his boot.

"Good thing they're steel-toed," Bennett grumbled as his friends helped him clean up his booth.

The Flab Five reunited off to the side of the platform erected for the mayor's speech. As an assistant tested the acoustics of the sound system, Lucy quickly filled the supper club members in on the information gathered from talking to Amelia.

"You're positive that this young woman is innocent of the murder?" Gillian asked, her face looking especially pale with fatigue. James noticed that her hands were wrinkled from having been submerged in soapy water all day long.

"Amelia admitted that she swung at Brinkley with her magazine, so she brought on the nosebleed, but she insists she doesn't know anything about the stolen Coumadin."

"So she claims," Bennett muttered crossly as he examined the hole in his shiny black boot.

"I can't see her planning something like that out," Lindy said. "Whitney is smart, but—and I know from having taught her—Amelia isn't the sharpest tack in the drawer. She works hard, God love her, always did as a student and now she gets up at dawn to help Megan bake. It can't be easy for a young girl."

"What's the story with her parents?" James asked Lindy.

"Megan's husband split years ago, when they lived in another town. She opened the Sweet Tooth when Amelia was a freshman in high school. I know they really struggled for a while. Even now, Megan probably can't make a go of it without her daughter's help."

"I would think that Brinkley could have made Amelia angry enough to want to take *some* kind of action." Bennett pursued his argument.

"*I'd* want a piece of him after what he's done to these innocent girls!" Gillian exclaimed. "Let's just pray he's already been reincarnated as a dung beetle."

The supper club members stared at her in bewilderment.

"Anyway," Lucy plowed on, unsure of how to respond to Gillian's bizarre comment, "We didn't find out if there was another person at this blackmail victim sleepover."

"Maybe the two girls planned the murder together." Bennett suggested wildly. "I mean, why are they so intent on covering for one another?"

"No." Lucy frowned. "We're missing something, some clue as to the identity of the killer. Whitney didn't run herself over and Amelia doesn't even own a car. If she *did* hit Whitney with Megan's delivery van, I think someone would have noticed."

"Plus, Whitney said it was a car and that it made a funny noise," James reminded his friends.

"I think we need to confront Amelia again," Lindy said firmly. "I'll get her to tell us if anyone else was being blackmailed by that little punk. It would be fun to go to the haunted hayride anyway. Maybe Principal Chavez will be there and will need my protection." She raised and lowered her eyebrows suggestively.

At that moment, the mayor stepped up to the microphone, accompanied by a fidgety Beau and Caroline Livingstone. Beau was wearing a blue suit that looked a size too large for his frame and Caroline had donned a long dress with black and white polka dots. They both looked slightly embarrassed and rather overwhelmed by the enormity of the gathered crowd.

"Welcome friends," the mayor began. "I have never been so proud to be a Virginian as I am tonight." The crowd cheered. "You folks came from all across our beautiful state to help these good people beside me. Now I know when we turn on our televisions, the news shows are filled with horrible stories about people hurting each other. Our books, magazines, newspapers, they all show how . . . how negative mankind can be. Well, I think they're showing a very small side of us. I believe that most people are good, and tonight, you all have proved me right!" Roars erupted from around the podium. The mayor held up her short arms to shush the throng. "I hold in my hand the total number of monies raised here today, so far. It's still coming in and I'm sure the fine men and women of our postal service will be delivering hundreds of letters to the Livingstones' mailbox over the next week."

The mayor turned to Beau and Caroline as she unfolded a piece of paper.

"Tonight, through the generosity of your fellow Virginians, those neighbors reaching out from the Blue Ridge Mountains to the Chesapeake Bay, those folks who saw the mistreatment done to your sweet daughter, have managed to raise over thirty-five thousand dollars!"

Caroline's hand flew over her mouth as Beau took an involuntary step backward in shock. Two reporters, Murphy Alistair and a suave-looking young man holding a mini recorder aloft, began snapping pictures.

"We owe a special debt of gratitude to Shilling's Stables for the donation of their fine thoroughbred colt. It brought the highest bid at our silent auction at ten thousand dollars! Thank you all for your heartfelt contributions." The two reporters swung their cameras in the direction of Allison Shilling and her mother, but Mrs. Shilling hid behind Allison and Chase so that the couple appeared to be the generous donors. Allison wore a pasted-on smile that never reached her eyes as Chase put a proprietary arm around his fiancée's trim waist and waved benevolently in the direction of the reporters.

The mayor then held out the microphone toward Beau, but he was too overcome to speak. Caroline, her eyes brimming with tears, profusely thanked the crowd and then sank down in a chair, still crying. The crowd whooped and hollered for another five minutes and then began to disperse.

The supper club members waited to offer their personal congratulations to Beau and Caroline. After being held in a bear hug by each of them, Lucy wriggled free and asked after Whitney's condition.

"She's finally at home," Caroline answered, relieved to be discussing a subject other than the incredible amount of money raised on their behalf. "She begged me to get her out of the hospital. Seems she doesn't like their food."

Beau chuckled. "Can't say I blame her. I think that's what *really* caused my stroke." The group laughed along with Beau.

"Anyway, it'll be quite a few weeks before she can go back to Dolly's since she's got that cast on her arm, so we told her to catch up on her schoolwork."

Beau looked suddenly thoughtful. "Though if those Pet Palaces sell as well in Harrisonburg next week as they did here, we might be able to let her go back to school full time in the near future." His eyes shone with hopefulness.

"I've got a few ideas for launching this product," Gillian gestured toward two chairs behind the podium. "Do you want to hear them?"

"Absolutely! Lead the way, ma'am."

"I'm off to the Haunted Hayride," Lindy announced. "*Someone* has got to come with me." She cast a look of appeal among her friends.

"Fine, fine. I'll go." Bennett jerked his thumb in the direction of the parking lot where a pickup truck waited to lead the out-of-towners to Miller's farm. "But don't expect me to act all scared when some teenager in bad makeup wielding a plastic axe jumps out from a row of hay."

"Maybe they'll have an eight-year-old brandishing a dart instead," Lindy teased and elbowed Bennett in the ribs.

James and Lucy watched their friends walk away. "Well, I've got to go home and cook dinner for my Pop," James explained to Caroline and Lucy.

"How is he these days?" Caroline asked. "I never see him around town."

"He doesn't come out. He's pretty much a recluse these days."

Caroline made a sad face. "Such a shame. I'd like to make some meals for the freezer for him, if that's all right. You and your friends have done so much for us and I'd like to be able to show you how grateful we are."

"Sure." James brightened at the thought of not having to cook separate meals for himself and his father for a while. Jackson never seemed to want anything James needed to eat to maintain his diet. He deliberately demanded flour pasta dishes, casseroles, potatoes, and sweets like brownies and chocolate cake, just to tempt his son into cheating, but so far, James had avoided succumbing. Suddenly remembering how he and Lucy had wolfed down the chili cheese fries, James flushed.

He was about to head toward the silent auction booth, to see whether any of the volunteers could tell him what was inside the box his father had donated, but before he could, Caroline put an arm out to restrain him.

"Oh, I almost forgot!" She said excitedly. "Whitney remembered something when she woke up this morning. Guess gettin' hit on the head made her forget some details about the accident for a few days."

"What did she remember?" Lucy asked, her blue eyes sparkling with curiosity.

"She said that she thought the driver was wearing a mask. She only remembers gettin' a quick look, like a flash, but she swears she's remembering it right."

As James turned his full attention on Caroline, his plans to visit the silent auction booth drifted away like the steam rising from a nearby booth selling roasted corn. "What kind of mask?"

Caroline's expression reflected some doubt, but she went ahead and delivered her daughter's message. "Whitney says it was a dog mask. Like, some kind of poodle."

TWELVE

BOMBAY CATFISH

Nutrition Facts	
Serving Size 1 piece (4.4 oz.)	
Amount Per Serving	
Calories 255 Calories from Fat 171	
	% Daily Value*
Total Fat 19g	29%
Saturated Fat 3g	15%
Cholesterol 58mg	19%
Sodium 896mg	37%
Total Carbohydrate 4g	1%
Dietary Fiber 1g	4%
Sugars 1g	
Protein 22g	
*Percent Daily Values are based on a 2,000 calorie diet. Your daily values may be higher or lower depending on your calorie needs.	

ON SUNDAY EVENING, LUCY was the first to arrive at the Henry residence. She knocked timidly at the front door instead of using the doorbell. When James opened it with a mighty creak, he noticed that Lucy's hands, which were holding a glass casserole dish, were shaking slightly.

"You okay?" he asked her.

She released her breath and smiled as she glanced down at her hands. "To tell you the truth, I was half expecting your daddy to come barreling out with a sawed-off shotgun, screaming at me to get off his land."

"No chance of that," James gave a forced laugh. "He's still shut up in his shed. I told him this morning that I had some friends coming over for dinner but he didn't care to comment, so who knows how he'll act when *his* dinnertime rolls around." He stepped back into the house. "Come on in."

James led his guest into the kitchen and followed Lucy's glance as she took in the sad state of the once-charming kitchen. The floral wallpaper dotted with tiny blue flowers had yellowed with age and little cracks had sprung up around the edges, especially by the stove and fridge. The beige linoleum floor was stained and peeling in the corners and though James had spent all morning cleaning, the overall impression what that of a tired and neglected room.

"You can tell men live here," Lucy said, in an effort to ease James's mind, but his eyes were hooded and unreadable as he led her to the dining room.

Unused since his mother's death, the small room was the only place where time seemed to have been kind to the old, dark pieces of wood furniture, the sage-green oriental rug, and the framed botanical prints gracing all four walls. James had dug out some green candles from the sideboard and had placed them throughout the room. The inexpensive chandelier was dimmed to a low light and a cluster of deep red chrysanthemum stalks set in a simple glass vase in the middle of the polished table created a romantic aura.

Lucy seemed to grow a trifle nervous being alone in the candlelit space with James. Her eyes kept darting to and fro as if Jackson Henry was hiding somewhere, spying on the two of them. "So . . ." she began awkwardly. "I'd better preheat the oven for the fish we're having tonight."

James grimaced involuntarily. "Ugh."

"Don't worry." Lucy punched him playfully on the arm. "It's so well-disguised with spices you'll think you're eating chicken."

Raising his hand to give her a flirtatious poke in return, James froze in mid-air as the doorbell chimed. He guiltily scurried to the door, disappointed that the others had arrived so quickly.

All three of the other supper club members waited on his front stoop, shivering in the chilly November night air.

"Finally!" Lindy exclaimed. "I get to have a look at the mysterious father of our own Professor Henry. You know, we all saw him so regularly when he had the hardware store, but I don't remember ever talking to him much."

"That's because he's never been much for talking, and don't expect him to sit down and join us for dinner, either." James draped their coats one at a time over one of the ladderback chairs in the living room. "Come on in the kitchen. Does anyone need pans or anything?"

Bennett held out a pie plate covered with aluminum foil. "I have created my own low-carb dessert and it is *good*. So good that I ate a whole one by myself last week."

"What kind of pie is it?" Gillian asked hungrily. "May the Buddha provide that it is better than those *awful* tombstones I forced y'all to eat last week."

"I'm not telling 'til it's time to serve it," Bennett said stubbornly, placing the pie in the fridge.

Gillian held up her own baking dish. "Green beans with almond slices and Parmesan cheese. I can just nuke them for a few minutes when we're ready to eat."

"I've got spinach salad with homemade bacon dressing." Lindy plunked a heavy ceramic bowl down on the dining room table. "Oh! It looks so pretty in here. James, you certainly know how to make a room warm and inviting."

"Thanks." James felt himself relaxing. If his father remained in the shed, then they might have a nice evening after all. He began taking drink orders for diet soda or water.

"When can we start having wine or something more grown up to drink?" Lucy demanded. "I'm getting sick of all this caffeine-free, diet, chemical-filled, brown, bubbly crap!"

Her friends laughed. "When you model your jeans for us, then we'll have a glass of wine to celebrate," Lindy suggested. "Deal?"

Lucy's cheeks became suddenly dappled with red, as if small raspberries had been rubbed all over them. "Deal. In fact, I think I'm not that far away from fitting in them. In two weeks we're back at my house, so I won't try them on until you're all over for dinner. Who will bring the wine in case they fit?"

James raised his hand high in the air like a kindergarten student anxious to share his show-and-tell item and then quickly dropped it, feeling stupid. "I have a great bottle of Merlot that I bought in case a celebration came up a few years ago. It's ready to drink."

"Like, a celebration with your wife?" Gillian asked, sipping a glass of water.

"Yeah. Nothing ever came up, though." James turned to Lucy, his warm brown eyes filled with generosity and a hint of sadness. "But if you get in those jeans, Lucy, that's celebration enough for me."

Lucy returned his stare, her own eyes reflecting gratitude and something stronger. James thought he saw a trace of longing there. A longing for what? To be able to lose the weight and become a deputy or, dare he believe it, a longing for him?

The others sensed something charged in the nonverbal exchange between their friends and bustled away to prepare the dinner. James began to set the table, feeling like a teenager who's been caught making out in the back seat of his parent's car. Lucy remained unfazed, checking up on her catfish and chatting away about the success of Neighbor Aid.

"All right, James!" Lucy proclaimed after they all sat down. She placed a plate of fish in front of him with a flourish. "Taste this and then dare to tell me that you don't like fish."

She served everyone else and then sat down. "Y'all, this is Bombay Catfish. It is a tad bit spicy, so get your drinks ready."

James took a hesitant bite. He loved Indian food, but felt sure the taste of fish would ruin the flavor of any of the other ingredients in the dish. He was pleasantly surprised to taste the curry, paprika, and yogurt flavors that had saturated the tender fish, but nothing disagreeable assaulted his tongue as he chewed. He still wasn't fond of the entrée's flaky texture, but he refrained from mentioning that aloud.

"Well?" Lucy looked at him with an expression of inquiry.

"It's good. Really. What's in it?" James said once his mouth was empty.

"Fat-free yogurt, curry powder, paprika, cardamom—and I had to drive twenty-five miles to find *that* one—cilantro, and salt and pepper."

"*This* is good for us?" Gillian happily stabbed at her fish with her fork.

Lucy nodded. "Yep. And easy to make. I marinated the fish in the fridge for a few hours and then cooked it for ten minutes. Nothing to it."

Everyone ate in silence for a few minutes, passing dishes back and forth and simply enjoying the food and the company.

"So what's the next step in our investigation?" Bennett asked, putting down his fork and breathing a deep sigh of contentment. As usual, he was the first person finished.

"We've got a new clue," Lucy said in a sing-song voice.

Lindy swatted at Lucy across the table with her napkin. "Don't hold out on us. Spill it!"

"Children, children," Gillian intoned as if she were saying a prayer. "Behave. Now Lucy, tell us or I'll be forced to illustrate some of my fiercer jujitsu moves on you."

James laughed. Gillian had certainly lightened up since he had first met her a few weeks ago.

"Whitney has remembered a detail about the driver who hit her. She says he or she was wearing a mask and she's pretty sure it was a poodle," Lucy explained.

"A poodle!" Lindy shrieked. "What a ridiculous mask!"

Bennett cleared his throat. "Toy poodles are ridiculous, perhaps, but did you know that the standard poodle is one of the oldest dog breeds in history? In fact, there are carvings on Roman tombs closely resembling today's poodle. A noble and loyal dog, I would say."

Lindy scowled. "I just mean it's a silly mask for a killer to wear, Mr. Representative of the Standard Poodle Association of America over there." She turned a pair of inquisitive eyes on the rest of her friends. "Does Goodbee's Drug Store sell poodle masks?"

No one knew. "Do you regularly groom anyone who owns a poodle?" James asked Gillian. "Maybe the killer chose the mask because he . . . *or she*, actually likes the breed."

Gillian frowned as she thought. "That's not an unreasonable line of thinking, actually. People do often identify with their pets on a *deep* and *spiritual* level. A bunch of my customers have both toy poodles and standard poodles. I can't bring up an image of anyone who seems particularly violent at this moment, but I'll flip through my books tomorrow and see."

Lindy wiped her mouth with her napkin and said, "I'll swing by Goodbee's after school tomorrow. Most of the masks are gone now since he put them at 75 percent off, but I'm sure he's got a record somewhere of which ones he ordered."

"How are you going to justify asking him for a list?" Lucy wondered.

Lindy waved off the question with a flick of her wrist. "I'll just say I wanted to order one to use in one of our drama productions."

Bennett chuckled. "Remind me never to play poker against you, Lindy."

"That's our only lead for now." Lucy pointed to indicate herself and James. "Did you get to talk to Amelia last night?" She directed her question to Lindy.

"Ha!" Bennett snorted. "That girl was too busy throwing her tongue down the neck of Darryl Jeffries to even bother trying to scare us!"

Lucy leaned forward on her elbows. "Brinkley's friend?"

"The same." Bennett grimaced. "Doesn't say much about Amelia's taste in men."

"Wait a minute!" Lucy startled her companions by yelling. "What if Darryl killed Brinkley in a fit of revenge? If Amelia is Darryl's girlfriend, he must have been pretty ticked about Brinkley's blackmail attempts." She twirled a lock of caramel hair around her forefinger. "James, can you fill up your truck tomorrow at the Amoco where Darryl works and try to get a read on him? I'd better not because I complained about the patch he put on my tire over the summer and his boss reamed him out about it. I don't think I'm on his list of favorite customers."

"Sure," James agreed, though he had no earthly idea how he was supposed to initiate a conversation with the young man. "Anything to keep us in the game."

Just then, the group heard the slamming of the back door. Jackson's shuffling footsteps made their way into the kitchen. No one spoke. James held his breath as his friends listened closely, their eyes round with expectation. It was as if a ravenous grizzly bear was prowling in the next room instead of an irascible old man in a pair of worn overalls and slippers.

"What in the hell?" they heard Jackson holler on the other side of the wing door leading into the kitchen. "Where's the goddamn crust on this pie?"

"Ah, who would like some coffee?" James asked, jumping out of his chair so quickly that it scraped the wooden floor. "Decaf all around?"

His friends nodded mutely as James hustled off into the kitchen. His father sat at the table, chewing on a pile of green beans and a slice of buttered bread. He was reading the paper with an air of utmost absorption and didn't give his son the slightest glance as James gathered the coffee pot and five dessert plates.

"Don't forget the Reddi-wip!" Bennett called from the dining room and James could hear the sound of his friends indulging in some low laughter at his expense. Irritated, he made one trip with the coffee and plates, and then returned for forks, the mangled pie, and a can of Reddi-wip. Jackson never moved a muscle.

"Is that a pumpkin pie?" Lindy asked. "Or should I say, *was* that a pumpkin pie?" She giggled.

"Aw, it's not that bad. The old guy just took a taste," Bennett said.

"Yeah, right from the center!" Lucy pointed out.

"So this is low carb?" Gillian asked Bennett as James served the pie.

"Sure is. Made the recipe up all by myself. Trust me, it's good stuff. 'Course, it helps to have a nice, healthy dose of Reddi-wip on top. I always put a big 'B' on all my desserts." He sprayed the can of whipped cream on his pie slice to demonstrate.

"Bennett!" Gillian exclaimed, licking her fork. "I don't know how you're still on the single's market when you can come up with something as delicious as this. I'm going to march right down to the First Baptist Church and put a notice on their bulletin board announcing that there is a single, hard-working, trivia-loving postman who enjoys experimenting with food looking for love."

"Do that and I will save everyone's junk mail for a month and deliver it to you over the next two years," Bennett quipped.

"Hey," Gillian shrugged. "If my bills can't fit in the mailbox then I won't have to pay them. Let's see the recipe for this pie, Chef Postman."

Bennett handed out copies of the recipe to his four friends.

The Flab Five's Guiltless, Crustless Pumpkin Pie
Ingredients
2 eggs slightly beaten
1 can (16 ounces) Libby's solid pack pumpkin
½ cup (or less) Splenda© or other sugar substitute made for baking
½ teaspoon salt

½ teaspoon nutmeg
1 teaspoon ground cinnamon
1 teaspoon ground ginger
¼ teaspoon ground cloves
1 teaspoon vanilla
1½ cups (12-ounce can) undiluted Carnation© evaporated milk
   (or, even better, evaporated skim milk)

Preheat oven to 425 degrees. Combine the filling ingredients in the order given. Pour into a glass pie dish. Bake 15 minutes at 425 degrees. Reduce temperature to 350 degrees. Bake an additional 40–50 minutes or until a knife inserted near the center comes out clean. Cool.

After devouring their slices of pie, the supper club members planned their next meeting at Gillian's house. When she handed out directions, James immediately recognized that the street she lived on was known for its historical homes.

"Are you in one of the houses on the National Register?" James asked.

"Not yet," Gillian said. "I'd like to be, but I need to finish some more renovations to qualify. I think the business I am starting with Beau Livingstone might just be my ticket to coming up with a little extra cash."

"That's great," Lindy enthused. "What are your plans?"

"First, we're looking to hire someone to build us a website. Beau has a bunch of photos of sample pet palaces to put on the site— stuff he built to take to the Veteran's Day parade in Harrisonburg next week. I'm then going to advertise in some of the smaller pet magazines. We can't afford to place ads in the big ones." She threw up her hands merrily. "After that, we'll just sit back and let the orders come in. I'm going to handle marketing, billing, and freight issues, and Beau is going to handle, well, the building and design side."

"You know, I think the Fitzgerald brothers could make you a website," James suggested. "They'd certainly be cheaper than hiring one of those IT guys and they'd love the experience. We're thinking about offering some computer courses at the library."

"I *will* call them. First thing tomorrow, before the library gets too busy."

James couldn't tell whether Gillian was being facetious, but decided to take her comment at face value.

"And just like that, Pet Palaces, Inc., is born!" Lucy declared and held her coffee cup aloft in a salute.

As the group of friends raised their empty cups, the back door slammed once again.

"Out to the shed he goes," James said mockingly.

"We should probably get going." Bennett glanced at James. "It's hardly fair to keep him out of his own house."

"It's by his own choice," James argued.

Lindy rose. "I'm going to try to talk to him. When was the last time someone did?" She looked at James accusingly.

Gillian answered before James could even open his mouth. "That man is grieving. He may be acting like some kind of crazed hermit, but that's just how he's coping. That might seem like an odd way of showing grief to *us*, but people all over this world have *different* ways of dealing with death. For example, in China—"

"Personally," Bennett cheerfully interrupted, "I like the way they make it into a party in New Orleans. That's what I'd want." He chuckled. "Jazz band, bright umbrellas, tons of food and booze. Yeah."

"See?" Gillian gave Bennett a smug look. "Who are we to judge?"

"Well, I'm *still* going out there." Lindy headed toward the back door.

"He probably won't unlock it for you!" James called after her. "And if he does, enter at your own risk!"

The remaining four brought their plates to the sink and began to wash up. They all waited with baited breath for Lindy to be driven from the shed, but apparently she had gained entrance and had not yet been verbally eviscerated by Jackson Henry.

"I guess I'll head for home," Gillian said as she dried off her bean dish.

"Me too." Bennett and Lucy also bid James goodbye. A few minutes later, Lindy exited the shed and pranced into the kitchen to retrieve her salad bowl.

"Well?" James was dying to know how Lindy fared with his father.

"I'm sorry, James, but I promised your daddy that our conversation would remain a secret."

"What? Why?" James spluttered in annoyance.

"I can't say anything more. That's the nature of a secret. Thanks for a great dinner. Bye!"

James watched Lindy get in her car in bewilderment.

The lights in the shed stayed on. There wasn't the slightest indication that someone had entered the lion's den and had lived to tell the tale. As James blew out the candles in the dining room, there was a light tap on the front door.

"I . . . I forgot my casserole dish," Lucy stammered, avoiding James's eyes.

"Oh. Sure. Let me get it."

When James returned with the dish, Lucy was holding a framed picture of him wearing a Batman costume.

"How old were you here?"

James looked down at the photo. "Seven or eight."

"Cute." Lucy returned the frame to the hall table and accepted her glass dish. "Thanks." She turned to go, hesitated, and then swung around to face James again. "Actually, I left it here on purpose."

James could feel his heart attempting to squeeze out of his rib cage. As if from a great distance, he saw himself reaching out to caress her thick hair, brushing it tenderly from her soft cheek. Lucy took a step toward him. He could smell her fruity perfume and the coconut scent of her shampoo. Sliding his arm behind her back, he gently brought her body close enough to his so that their lips could meet as she tilted her head upwards. He tried not to focus on how his protruding stomach rubbed up against hers or that her large breasts had closed the distance between them before any other part of her body.

Lucy tasted of coffee. James kissed her once, cautiously, and then again, with more force. Just as he was about to tell her how much he cared about her the unmistakable sounds of Jackson entering the house through the kitchen reverberated into the hall. James and Lucy jumped apart guiltily, wiping their wet lips and straightening their tousled hair.

"Good night," Lucy whispered, flashed a crooked grin, and dashed out the front door.

James stared after her, wearing a goofy smile and waving goodbye until her Jeep's taillights grew smaller and smaller, like two red stars winking through the dense row of trees, and then they disappeared.

"Christ! Are they finally gone?" Jackson demanded, sneaking up behind James.

"Yes, Pop. We won't be meeting back here until December."

Jackson closed and locked the front door. "Guess I should say a prayer for small favors," he replied with heavy sarcasm.

"So what did you talk about with Lindy?" James asked, his curiosity temporarily overcoming his desire to dwell on his romantic moment with Lucy, replaying it over and over like a movie being constantly rewound.

Jackson raised his caterpillar eyebrows and smirked. "Oh, was *that* her name?"

"Come on, Pop," James prompted gently, thinking about what Gillian had said about Jackson still working through his grief. "It's okay to talk to people again. Mom would have wanted you to."

For a second, James thought his father would erupt like a boiling teakettle, but Jackson seemed to be digesting the words his son had spoken without spitting out the first flippant reply that came into his mind.

"The best parts of me, and I know there weren't too many, died with your mother," Jackson said in a low voice and then turned away.

James held him back by placing a hand on his shoulder. "No, Pop." He reached over from behind Jackson's back and tapped in the center of his father's chest, above his heart. "The best parts of mom are living right here, in us."

Jackson pulled away, slowly, as if he were uncomfortable with being touched. Halfway up the stairs he turned and looked fully at James, as if seeing him for the first time since he had moved back home. "Well, goodnight . . . son."

THIRTEEN

BUTTERCREAM FROSTING

THE NEXT DAY, JAMES woke up with a start. He had tossed and turned the night before, wondering how to begin a casual conversation with a man he had never laid eyes on before.

The Cabin Creek Amoco station was completely out of the way for James during his short commute home, so he drove there during his lunch hour as it had only taken him five minutes to gulp down the in-

Nutrition Facts		
Serving Size 2 Tbsp (35g)		
Servings Per Container about 13		
Amount Per Serving		
Calories 140 Calories from Fat 45		
		% Daily Value*
Total Fat 5g		8%
Saturated Fat 1.5g		15%
Cholesterol 0mg		0%
Sodium 65mg		3%
Total Carbohydrate 24g		8%
Dietary Fiber 0g		0%
Sugars 21g		
Protein 0g		
*Percent Daily Values are based on a 2,000 calorie diet. Your daily values may be higher or lower depending on your calorie needs.		

side of two tacos and a beef and cheese burrito from the Quickie Mart. He threw the tortilla shells in the trash and went back inside to buy two hot dogs without buns. Draining a bottle of water, which cost $1.50 and was merely filtered tap water with a crisp, blue label,

James resigned himself to his fate. It was time to put his investigative skills to the test.

Wishing for Lucy's guidance, James pulled next to one of the pumps and began to fill up the Bronco with gas. He noticed that the gas prices were five cents lower than they were in town. No wonder the station was busy. The other three pumps were all occupied and two cars were up on lifts inside the garage bays. James filled his tank and went inside to pay. A short line of customers waited to settle up for gas and sundries, and it quickly became clear to James that the cashier was not Darryl, but a woman in her mid-fifties sucking on a lollipop while she cheerfully zipped credit cards through a machine.

James peered through the glass door connecting the Food Mart to the garage. He could see the shiny dome of a bald head sticking out from the undercarriage of a Honda Accord, but he couldn't tell who was working on the classic Camaro coming down off the lift in the far bay. James paid for his gas and then walked around the front of the garage and approached the broad back of a man wearing a denim jacket who was operating the lift.

"Excuse me," James began hesitantly.

The man turned slowly around and James knew that he had found Darryl Jeffries. Though not as captivatingly handsome as Brinkley had been, Darryl had narrow, almond-colored eyes, straight brown hair, and a childish peppering of freckles across the bridge of his nose. His upper body was wide and muscular and his hands were covered with grease and oil. Like Brinkley, he showed the beginnings of a beer belly. Darryl's cheek was filled like a squirrel's and when he turned aside to spit into a cup, James realized the twentysomething was sucking on a wad of tobacco large enough to put a professional baseball player to shame.

"Can I help you, mister?" Darryl asked, his face a mixture of impatience at being interrupted and the need to exhibit professional courtesy.

"Uh, my Bronco has this strange habit. Sometimes it keeps on running *after* I take the key out of the ignition." James answered lamely. No one in the car industry ever fully believed him when he mentioned the Bronco's odd quirk.

Darryl swung his head around to look at the cars near the gas pumps. "That yours?" He pointed at the Bronco, a spark of interest lighting in his eyes.

"Um, it's a 1985."

"Oldie but a goodie." Darryl walked over to the truck and patted the white hood as if he was greeting an old friend. "I've got a real classic at home that I'm fixin' up in my spare time. It's a '68. Even got a bikini top for her."

James had a vague mental image of a Bronco from that era. It was a true outdoorsman's truck—exposed steel frames and giant wheels crying out to be driven through the mud. He decided to act supremely impressed. "That'll be some truck when you've got it done. You can tear all over these mountains with a machine like that. What else do you need to do to it?"

Darryl chortled. "Just a little engine overhaul! Now, how long has your girl been makin' this trouble for you?"

"Ever since I bought it." The irritating habit had existed since James owned the truck. It had happened to him several times, but never in the presence of any mechanic. Even after James explained the problem to the guys at the dealership, they had examined the Bronco and then had thrown up their hands in defeat after having tried to fix it a half a dozen times. James finally gave up trying to solve the problem as the engine would eventually cut off if he jiggled the keys frantically enough.

Darryl looked thoughtful. "Might be your battery leads. Do you want me to take a look?"

"I'd sure appreciate that, if you've got the time," James answered, pretending to be extremely grateful.

"Let me pull her into the bay. Just take me a second to park that Camaro. Be right back."

James watched Darryl hustle off and tried to picture him as a killer. He seemed like a helpful and hardworking young man. True, he hadn't become a nuclear physicist after graduating from Blue Ridge High, but he was clearly a competent mechanic. Judging from the cars parked alongside the garage, Darryl seemed to have plenty of work lined up for the day and, unlike many folks, he actually appeared to enjoy his job. As James watched him park the Camaro, a convertible Beetle zipped up to the pump next to James and a leggy brunette stepped out, wearing jeans that could have been airbrushed on her gazelle-like legs and a short leather jacket that cinched tightly around her waist. She shook out her long hair and then applied some ruby-red lipstick using the car's passenger mirror.

This is my segue, James thought as Darryl walked over to the Bronco, staring openly at the comely brunette. "You get customers like that all the time?" James whispered, jerking his head toward the woman.

"Not as often as I wish!" Darryl exclaimed, eyeing the woman's legs. He got into the Bronco and drove it expertly into the bay. As he popped the hood, he cast one more glance at the brunette as she walked back to her car from the Food Mart. "Man, I love a chick in cowboy boots."

"I hope your girlfriend knows that," James joked.

"Tsss," Darryl made a sound through the mound of tobacco. "She doesn't wear boots, but she's pretty hot, too."

"Like model hot?" James prodded, feeling idiotically transparent.

"Yep," Darryl replied offhandedly, absorbed in his examination of the Bronco.

"Lucky man." James looked around the garage. Behind him was a cluttered desk bearing a half-empty liter bottle of Mountain Dew and a soiled Atlanta Braves baseball cap. Above the desk was a bulletin board covered with phone numbers, parts diagrams, and a poster of a blonde in a bikini draped over the hood of a black Ferrari.

Darryl raised his face from his inspection and laughed. "*That's not my girlfriend!*" He gestured at the poster and laughed. "She did one modeling job, but it wasn't her thing. You've probably seen her around. Her ma owns the Sweet Tooth and she works over there." Darryl sounded proud that his girlfriend held a steady job that required hard work but not a college education.

"I love that place," James said truthfully. "Sure, I think your girlfriend has helped me there before. She's great. Her name's Amelia, right?"

"That's her." Darryl climbed inside the Bronco and began tinkering within the steering column.

"I bet Amelia's had a rough time lately, huh? With that ex-football player dying in her shop. She doing okay?"

"Yeah, she's a tough nut." Darryl scowled at the steering wheel, and then turned the engine over. He removed the key and to James's astonishment, the engine kept running. Other than the frown he wore over the mechanical puzzle before him, Darryl seemed completely unfazed by much of anything, including the mention of Brinkley's death.

"You look like you might have played some ball yourself." James filled his voice with admiration.

"I was on defense. Not the same kind of glory as guys like Brinkley get." He paused. "Got," he added apologetically.

"Were you two friends?" James winced, hoping he wasn't pushing it too hard.

"We hung out now and then after we graduated, but he started acting funny a few months ago, and I started hanging out more and more with my girl. You know how it goes. Once a woman's got her hooks in you ... look out! There goes your free time." Darryl sounded delighted to be able to complain about having a relationship.

James was stumped. Not only did it appear that Darryl felt no animosity toward his one-time friend, but he gave no indication that he knew about Brinkley and his blackmail scheme.

"It must be tough to come up with the extra dough to work on your Bronco," James commiserated. "All the long hours here and then you need spending money for your girlfriend. I don't know how guys like you work so hard." James fidgeted as he prepared to lie. "The only times I saw Brinkley he was eating at the diner or lazing about the video store, checking out three or four movies. Guess he had no girlfriend to spend cash on, huh?"

Darryl shrugged. "He always claimed to have more than one. Who knows? Girls thought he was the bomb." He paused, adjusting something out of James's view behind the dashboard. "I don't know where he got his extra jack from, either. He didn't mow *that* many lawns." He grunted in exertion and then jumped out of the car and disappeared under the hood again. "I think I know what's going on here!" he announced, pulling open a drawer near the desk and fishing out a tool. James froze. His gig was up and Darryl was calling his bluff. But to James's surprise, the young man pointed excitedly to the Bronco and asked, "You leave your car outside at night?" as he slipped back inside the car.

James leaned into the driver's-side door. "Yes."

"Does it keep running like this in the summer or only in the colder months?"

James thought about the question and then exclaimed, "Only when it's cold! I never noticed that before."

"Yep, you've got a bad battery lead. It makes your battery drain in cold weather. I can fix that. I also think we should make a copy of your key. I think the original, this one that the dealer gave you, is messed up." He pointed at the ignition. "The tumblers connect to the ignition switch and I think this key pushes the tumblers on its way *out*. It's only supposed to hit them on the way in. I can file your new key down a bit and then your problem should be solved. Can you leave it here today?"

James stared at Darryl in amazement. "Man, you're a magician. I can't, because I've got to get back to work, but I can drop it off first thing in the morning and catch a ride from a friend."

"Sounds like a plan. I'll put you down for tomorrow." Darryl jotted a note in his appointment book. As he wrote, the sound of police sirens cresting the hill near the gas station broke the midday stillness.

Two brown Sheriff's Department cars pulled erratically in front of the garage and came to a grinding halt, inches behind James's truck.

"What the hell?" Darryl dropped his pencil in shock.

Sheriff Huckabee and Deputy Donovan leapt from their cars and hustled over to the young mechanic. Their faces reflected a grim determination that immediately set James on edge.

"Darryl Jeffries?" Sheriff Huckabee asked. "We've got some questions to ask you. You want to answer them here or down at the station?"

James stood frozen in shock as Donovan turned a disdainful gaze on him. "Now just what are you—?"

"What the hell is going on here?" the bald man who was working on the Honda suddenly demanded. "This boy committed a crime?"

"That's what we're tryin' to find out, Tom. We just need to ask him a few questions." Sheriff Huckabee stepped closer to Darryl.

"Well, shit! You don't need to drive in here like the place is filled with terrorists! You're scarin' all my customers. Turn off the damned sirens and sit down like civilized human beings. Does he need a lawyer?"

"No, no," Sheriff Huckabee replied in a placating tone, never taking his eyes off of Darryl. "We've got a girl missin' and we need to know if your assistant has any information for us on her whereabouts."

For the moment, the man named Tom, who James assumed was Darryl's boss, seemed satisfied with the sheriff's answer.

"What girl? What are you talking about?" Darryl asked angrily.

"Now calm down," Donovan shushed him in his patronizing tone. "You act up one mite and I *will* drag your sorry ass downtown."

James thought Donovan sounded like a complete hack, like some TV cop from a B movie reciting his lines in front of the mirror. Donovan was such an unbelievably dislikable person that James wished he could think of something to say to take him down a notch or two, but he felt it was best to remain mutely in the background.

"When was the last time you saw Amelia Flowers?" Huckabee asked.

Darryl's eyes flew open. "Saturday night. We worked Miller's Haunted Hayride. Why? What's going on? What's happening?" His voice echoed shrilly throughout the garage.

"This is the last time I'm warning you to calm down, *son*," Donovan threatened. Tapping on his gun holster, he continued. "Seems she's gone missin'. You were the last person anyone can recall seeing her with that night. You got anything you wanna tell us?"

There was a long pause. Darryl shook his head, confused and worried. "Look, we hung out for a bit after the last group went through the ride, but then we split up. She said she was catching a ride with one of her friends and that's it. I split and went home."

"What time was that?" Huckabee asked.

"Like, eleven, I guess." Darryl held out his hands helplessly. "I'm not sure exactly."

"How late do you usually stay out with Miss Flowers?" Donovan continued the grilling.

"Never past midnight. She's got to get up pretty early to go to work."

Donovan scribbled some notes in his pad. "Her mama's down at the station. She's pretty upset. There anything you'd care to say that could make that woman feel better?" Donovan barreled on without waiting for a reply. "What *exactly* were you two *doin'* after the hayrides were over?"

Darryl fidgeted with the zipper on his jacket. "We were messin' around a bit, you know. She's my girlfriend."

"No," Donovan answered meanly. "Why don't you elaborate for us?"

"Kissin' and stuff," Darryl said defensively. "We're both adults. It's no crime!"

Donovan shrugged. "Maybe things got a little rough, huh? Maybe Amelia didn't want to *mess around* anymore but *you* did. Did you get mad at her over somethin' like that, Darryl?"

Without warning, Darryl lunged at Donovan. The two men grappled with one another until Sheriff Huckabee intervened. He shoved Darryl into the back of his car and pulled Donovan aside to dress him down. James couldn't hear their conversation, but he could tell from Donovan's sagging shoulders that he was not being complimented by his superior.

"That was provoked!" Darryl's boss yelled. "I'm a witness! Where you takin' that boy?"

"Relax, Tom." Huckabee stroked his lush, walrus-like mustache. "I'm just going to bring him down to get his statement. After he signs it, we'll bring him right back." The sheriff got in his car and drove off. Tom went inside the Food Mart, cursing under his breath.

Donovan ran a hand through his hair, which was a fiery red beneath the November sunlight, and swung around. He practically spat at James, his voice a vehement hiss. "Don't you have some library cards to stamp, *Professor?*"

James waited until the second brown car had pulled out of the lot before carefully backing the Bronco out of the garage bay. He broke at least four traffic laws driving to the library, but he figured that every member of the Sheriff's Department was busy with something much more significant—the disappearance of Amelia Flowers.

"You've got mail!" James's computer announced as he raced to check his e-mail upon returning from his dramatic lunch break. Lucy had written the supper club group about the morning's events at the Sheriff's Department.

Dear F. F.s,

I feel terrible! I think that when James and I questioned Amelia, we triggered a horrible event. Megan Flowers came to the station this morning to report that her daughter never returned home from a weekend trip to a friend's lake house. When she called to speak to the friend, she was told that Amelia was never expected at their house at all!

Megan brought in a note that Amelia left under the van's windshield wiper telling her that she'd gone home with her friend Cyndi and would be heading up to Cyndi's lake house to stay over Sunday night. With the bakery being closed on Monday, Megan had no objection, even though she thought it was weird that Amelia left the note on the van instead of in the house or inside the Sweet Tooth where Megan would have found it Sunday morning. Now that Megan's had time to really examine the note, she also believes it may not even be Amelia's handwriting!

Do you all realize what this means? Brinkley's killer and the person who ran Whitney down MUST have seen Amelia talking to me and James. Now, that person has taken her, maybe even killed her, too! We have got to have an emergency meeting today to figure out what we can do. I hope you all found out what you could about that poodle mask—that's our only hope of finding out who's responsible for bringing all of this violence to Quincy's Gap.

I've got to go. Murphy Alistair is here and is demanding to know what's going on with Amelia. Apparently, they've brought in Darryl Jeffries for questioning.

James, can we come to the library after work? This is serious and it's gone way beyond me trying to play deputy. We've got to put our heads together and help this young woman.

Yours,
A Worried Lucy

James immediately wrote back to his four friends that they should come to the library as soon as they were able and that they would shut themselves in the meeting room and figure out what to do next. He then summarized his conversation with Darryl and explained that he didn't think the young man was capable of murder, but that was just a feeling. James knew that he would need to repeat the entire exchange in order to get his friends' point of view.

A few minutes before four, James told the twins to mind the fort and slipped out to the Quickie Mart to buy some kind of snack for the meeting. Truth be told, he was too restless to spend another second in the serene atmosphere of the library. He desperately needed fresh air, some loud music, and an errand to take his mind off of Amelia Flowers and her unknown fate.

As he pulled into a parking space, he noticed a beige Jeep parked a few spots over. It looked remarkably like Lucy's. Walking behind the other cars, James could see that someone was sitting in the driver's seat, but he wasn't certain if it was Lucy. All he could really see was a fuzzy pink hat with a matching scarf and a pair of shoulders covered by a black overcoat.

Slinking off to the side so that the driver wouldn't see him in the rearview mirror, James tried to get a closer look by pretending to duck down and tie his shoe. As he stood back up, slowly as if he had a hurt back, he could see through the rear window on the passenger side that it was Lucy. Even if he hadn't seen the profile of her smooth cheek, James could have identified Lucy's car by the piles of trash scattered about the back seat and floor. Just as he was about to rap on the window, James saw Lucy raise a spoon to her mouth and, having taken a large bite, sink back into her seat as if relaxing for the first time in ages.

James craned his neck forward in order to catch a glimpse of the indulgence that was giving Lucy such obvious pleasure. When her plastic spoon was licked clean, she dipped it back into a small, cylindrical container. Loading the spoon up with a creamy, vanilla-colored substance, she returned the utensil to her mouth. James backed away from the car as if he had just caught one of his former students doing lines of cocaine. Skirting around the cars between Lucy's Jeep and his Bronco, he sat back inside his truck until Lucy finally pulled away.

James hurriedly went into the Quickie Mart and chose a snack for his friends. On the way out, he walked down the last aisle containing the baking products to double-check the identity of the container he saw in Lucy's hand. It was as he feared—Lucy had been pigging out on a can of vanilla buttercream frosting.

FOURTEEN

LOW-CARB ICE CREAM

Nutrition Facts	
Serving Size 1/2 cup (70g)	

Amount Per Serving	
Calories 140 Calories from Fat 110	

	% Daily Value*
Total Fat 12g	18%
Saturated Fat 7g	35%
Cholesterol 45mg	15%
Sodium 20mg	1%
Total Carbohydrate 13g	4%
Dietary Fiber 4g	20%
Sugars 1g	
Sugar Alcohol 5g	
Protein 2g	
Vitamin A 8% • Vitamin C 0%	
Calcium 6% • Iron 0%	

*Percent Daily Values are based on a 2,000 calorie diet. Your daily values may be higher or lower depending on your calorie needs.

"I'm guilty!" Gillian wailed before the other four supper club members even had a chance to settle into the chairs in the library's only meeting room. Gillian turned to Lindy with moist eyes, and, seeing her friend's expression of befuddlement, pulled an orange candy bar wrapper from her cavernous purse and slapped it on the table.

"I have committed a food crime. I had two peanut butter cups today. I *had* to have them!" She exhaled audibly. "I called every single pet specialty shop in Virginia that might sell poodle masks. I finally got a hit from Pampered Pooches in Richmond, but they wouldn't reveal their customer list, no matter how much I begged. We're going to have to tell all we know to the sheriff if we really want to do Amelia any good. Are we at a dead end?"

"I'm a food loser, too," Bennett moaned. "Gillian called to ask me if I remembered delivering a box with a return label from Pampered Pooches. The crazy thing is, I *do* remember the label 'cause it had these little paw prints all over it. I just don't remember *where* I delivered it. Gillian and I cross-referenced her clients with my mail route and no one fits. I've been thinking about that poor girl ever since I read Lucy's e-mail on my Palm Pilot during my coffee break. Man, I drove right to the store and bought myself some donut holes." He looked down at the table. "I've still got the empty box hidden beneath my seat."

Lindy put her hands out in front of her, wrists touching as if she were preparing to be handcuffed. "You got another cheater, here. I ate the most scrumptious chocolate-caramel candy bar I've ever tasted today. Delicioso! And to add to that, I had a lollipop on the way over here." She stuck out a bright purple tongue. "Grape Tootsie Pop."

"It takes an average of 252 licks to get to the center according to a study done by Purdue University," Bennett said as he watched flashes of purple from inside Lindy's mouth as she spoke.

"Thanks, but I bite mine. No time for 252 licks." Lindy allowed her long hair to fall in front of her face and peered out through the shiny curtain. "What could we do to help Amelia at this point? We can't even control ourselves from eating junk food?"

"We *can* do something!" Lucy ran a pair of agitated hands over her hair. "First thing is to call Whitney and make that girl tell us who else was at her house with her and Amelia. She'll have to tell us once she knows Amelia's gone missing." She turned an angry gaze upon Gillian. "And we *can't* tell the sheriff now. Do you know how much trouble we'd all be in for meddling and then not sharing our information? I'd probably be fired!"

"Let's think this over calmly." James stood up and spoke with an assuring, authoritative tone. "Arguing with one another will get us, and Amelia, nowhere. It's been a hard day all around." He pointed to the grains of orange dust gathered around the beds of his fingernails. "It took three snack bags to keep me from completely freaking out. We'll all get back on track on our diet once this . . . these horrible events are over with. So we're at a dead end with the mask, for now. I'll tell you about my conversation with Darryl and then we'll make a new plan of action, okay?"

His friends nodded miserably. James returned to his seat and reviewed his meeting with Darryl from beginning to end, leaving out no detail.

"Sounds like a regular kid," Bennett observed.

"And it seems like he cares about Amelia *and* that he didn't know about the blackmail," Lindy added.

"That takes away his motive for killing Brinkley, if he really was genuine. Was he *really* sincere, James, or do you think he was working you over?" Gillian asked.

"I can't be sure as I don't know Darryl from Adam, but I think he's a decent sort," James answered. "He was both surprised and very upset when he heard about Amelia being missing. I swear he didn't have time to put on an act about that. You could have knocked him off his feet with a feather when the sheriff told him that he was the last one to be seen with Amelia."

"They've still got him at the station," Lucy sighed mournfully. "They've been questioning him for hours and his story hasn't changed at all, from the gossip I've picked up from Glenn and Luke.

You can tell Donovan *wants* it to be Darryl. After all, they dragged in Whitney first and now they've got Darryl. Sounds like, if what James says is true, they've got the wrong man *again*."

"I doubt Darryl owns a poodle mask," Gillian said flippantly and then grew anxious again. "It also means that we need to act quickly, because Amelia has been taken somewhere by the *real* killer."

"Caroline Livingstone called the sheriff this morning and told him about the mask," Lucy said tersely. "They'll be able to conduct a thorough search of Darryl's house, but you're right, Gillian, I think someone else wore that mask."

"If I could just remember *where* I brought that package, we'd have our answer." Bennett tugged roughly on his mustache. "Why is it I can recite the capital of every country in the world, but I can't recall where I delivered that box?"

Lindy grabbed Bennett's hand. "Don't be so hard on yourself. You deliver pounds of mail every day and that package went through weeks ago." She looked around at her friends. "We might not be succeeding in helping at the moment, but let's remember that there is an evil person out there doing these terrible things, not one of us. James, you saved Whitney's life already and we have a chance to save Amelia's as well. Let's not give up hope. That girl needs us to be strong and clear headed."

"You're right, Lindy. I'll start by calling Whitney." Lucy jumped up. "Can I use the phone in your office, James?"

"Of course." When Lucy left the room the others fell silent, lost in thought. "I don't suppose anyone would care for some low-carb ice cream?" James asked hesitantly. "I've got a few different flavors."

"Why not?" Gillian muttered. "My regular comfort food didn't work, so let's try something I'm *supposed* to be eating."

By the time James returned bearing Styrofoam bowls, plastic spoons, and three pints of ice cream, Lucy was off the phone.

"Too late." Her shoulders slumped. "The sheriff called her down to the station to make a statement about the mask and anything else she remembered. Beau said that Caroline was going to make sure that Whitney came clean on *everything* she knows. Beau promised that she wouldn't be mentioning telling James and I first. Thank goodness for that! I don't really want to end up flipping burgers at Hardees."

"So the sheriff will finally hear about the blackmail angle," Lindy mused, twirling her spoon around inside her cheek. "Does this mean we're out of the picture?"

Bennett said, "I can't think of anything that we can do to help."

"Me either," James admitted. He looked at Lucy. She sat, spooning ice cream absently into her mouth, her eyes staring straight ahead with an unfocused glaze. Watching her lick her spoon made him think of how she had been eating frosting in a similar manner earlier that day. Why hadn't she shared her indiscretion when everyone else had confessed about their minor falls from grace? Were there other little secrets that she was keeping to herself?

Gillian stood. "I guess there's not much else to talk about right now. Lucy, please let us know if anything new comes up on Amelia. I've got to get home and pay the painters."

"I've got a bunch of short essays on postmodernist art to correct," Lindy whined, gathering her belongings.

One by one, the supper club members slunk out of the library, solemn and dejected. James watched them go. Lucy hadn't lingered for a moment and she had barely glanced at him as she walked away alongside Bennett. James felt hurt. He knew that she felt responsible for Amelia's disappearance, but he didn't see why she had to ignore him as a response.

"I guess it's because I helped question Amelia," James mumbled to a pile of books sitting on top of the circulation desk. "Lucy blames me as well as herself."

Mrs. Waxman waved to him and headed over to the children's section where a toddler was busy pulling all of the Dr. Seuss books off the shelf with great giggles of pleasure. James turned away and began loading the reshelving cart with the strays he had collected from the reading tables.

"Excuse me?" A female voice behind his left shoulder made him turn quickly around.

It was Allison Shilling, looking as cheerless as she had at Saturday's festival. "Hello, Allison. Nice to see you again." James mustered a smile for the dispirited young woman.

Her face remained blank as she pulled out a library card from a tiny pink suede purse. "I'm supposed to pick up some books for my *mother*." She said the last word as if she were chewing on her least favorite vegetable. "She said they're on hold."

"Sure thing." James grabbed a bundle of books marked "Shilling" that were held together by a rubber band and took the card from Allison's limp hand. He noticed that she was not wearing her engagement ring. He also noticed that every book Mrs. Rachel Shilling had ordered from neighboring branches was a wedding resource book.

"*Someone* is excited about throwing you a wedding," James said, trying to lighten the mood.

"Yeah, *someone* is." Allison took the books and added a soft "thanks" before walking off.

James decided to quickly empty the book drop in front of the library before heading home. Brandishing the small key that opened the book bin, which was actually a full-sized blue mailbox painted green with the words "Books Only! No Trash or Mail" stenciled in white block letters, James opened the back of the box and paused curiously.

Allison Shilling was backing out of her parking spot and the noise coming from her car was slightly unusual. Nothing was wrong with the old Mercedes, but it was a diesel model and not many people drove diesels anymore. James was struck by a thought. What if the strange car noise Whitney heard was a diesel engine? As the car pulled out of the lot, James continued to stare after it. Allison was the same age as Whitney and Amelia. He suddenly remembered Lindy saying that Allison and Whitney were good friends during their senior year of high school.

"It was you!" James pointed an accusing finger at the receding car. "*You* were the other person at Whitney's house, I'd bet a case of cheese puffs on it."

———————

James drove straight to Lucy's home and came to such an abrupt halt on her gravel driveway that little beige pebbles flew violently in all directions onto her overgrown grass. Trotting up her walkway, his stomach bouncing with every step, James was almost at her door when Lucy's three German shepherds came racing around from the backyard, teeth bared and barking wildly as if they had just spotted their next meal.

Terrified, James jerked open the screen door and used it as a shield as he pounded desperately on the wooden front door. Lucy jerked it open and he practically fell inside, the dogs nipping at his heels. Lucy pushed their noses back outside using her foot and told them to hush up. She was holding a phone up to her ear and winced as she tried to concentrate on what the person on the other end was saying above the braying of her dogs. Finally, she managed to close the door. She motioned for James to follow her into the kitchen where they both sat down at her kitchen table, which was covered with junk mail, plastic grocery store bags, and paper napkins.

"Just sit tight," Lucy said to the caller. "I'm going to tell James what you said. Call you right back."

Grasping the phone to her chest, Lucy blurted out, "Bennett remembers where he delivered the package. He had switched routes with a friend over a month ago and that's why he couldn't think of the address. See, he doesn't usually go out there."

"You mean, to Shilling's Stables?" James asked complacently.

Lucy's mouth fell open. "How did you *know?*"

"I'm not certain or anything, but Allison came to the library this afternoon to pick up some wedding books and I heard her car as she was leaving. It's a diesel and the motor makes a unique noise. If I could replay the noise for Whitney, we could see if that's the sound she heard before she was hit."

Lucy jumped out of her seat. "If we put those two clues together, there can be no doubt that Allison's our killer!"

"But what's her motive?" James wondered.

Lucy gave him an annoyed flick of her wrist. "I'm sure Brinkley had something on Allison, too. It must be something pretty serious because not only did she murder him, but she also wants to

216

silence the other two people who know her secret. Come on!" Lucy headed toward the door. "We'd better get out there!"

"Hold on!" James grabbed her arm. "We can't just bust in the house and demand to see Amelia! We've got to have a plan!"

Lucy paused. "But we can't waste any time. James, Amelia's life is in danger!"

"So we'll call the sheriff." James sat back down and gestured to the chair opposite him. "Sit down, Lucy. Huckabee now knows about the mask, so we'll simply tell him where it was delivered. If you do that, you'll save him a lot of legwork and I'm sure he'll be grateful to you for that."

Sighing with resignation, Lucy petulantly grabbed the phone off the kitchen table and dialed her boss's direct line. "Sheriff? This is Lucy. Listen, that poodle mask Whitney saw was delivered to Shilling's Stables. My friend is a mail carrier. Um . . . I also think Allison Shilling may be responsible for Brinkley's death. Please call me back to discuss this. Thank you." Lucy left her home and cell numbers. "Voice mail. He and Keith must still be tied up with Whitney and Darryl."

"At least that keeps Whitney safe." James eyed Lucy as she began dialing again. "Now who are you calling?"

"I'm going to leave a message with the second shift assistant. She can tell Sheriff Huckabee that I left him an urgent message."

As Lucy was dictating her message to the assistant, she hurriedly finished up by saying, "I gotta go, Sheila. I've got another call coming in . . . Lindy? Hold on, hold on! I'll explain everything." Lucy summarized the information she had received from both James and Bennett. Lindy babbled about something James couldn't quite hear and then rang off.

"Now what?" he asked, feeling very much on edge.

"Lindy's got a friend who works at the Portsmouth School for Girls. She's going to call her and find out exactly why Allison was kicked out before she could graduate. That might help us figure out her motive. Obviously, if she's going to marry a senator's son, her background had better seem squeaky clean."

James frowned. "That makes sense, especially since Chase has aspirations to get involved in politics in the future. But Allison doesn't even act like she wants to marry him, so why would she commit all of these crimes to protect that relationship?"

Lucy shrugged. "She's twenty years old. Who knows what's motivating her? Maybe she's marrying him for the money. Senator Radford comes from a whole family of real estate tycoons. I don't think Allison has much interest in working, do you?"

James thought back to the sight of Allison's nails. "That certainly seems plausible. So are we waiting for Lindy to call us back?"

"You can if you want." Lucy gave him an impatient look. "But *I'm* driving out to Shilling's Stables. Lindy's calling me back on my cell phone and I've done my best to get through to the sheriff." She narrowed her blue eyes at James. "I'm not going to sit on my ass while Amelia might be in danger." And with that, she swiped her keys off the cluttered counter and headed for the door.

"I'm coming with you!" James shouted, hating how his voice betrayed a hint of desperation. Lucy's demeanor had become so downright hostile since Amelia's disappearance. As they approached Lucy's car, James spied the disheveled condition of the passenger seat. It was once again littered with papers and other trash.

"I'll drive," he offered quickly. "That way you can answer the phone."

"Fine." Lucy huffily grabbed her purse from her front seat and climbed into the Bronco.

"You don't have to get all miffed at me!" James stated as he started the engine, feeling quite miffed himself.

Lucy was silent as they backed down her driveway and headed west. "I'm sorry. I'm just going crazy, thinking that this is all my fault."

"I feel guilty, too," James admitted. "When we get there, let's just park the truck nearby and try to check out the grounds. Maybe we can find Amelia without a confrontation."

Lucy seemed unimpressed by his idea. "Maybe." The phone in her hand began to chirp. "Lindy? You found out? Tell me, quick!"

James drove through the shadowy forest leading toward the Shilling's large horse farm. It was almost six o'clock and night would fall before too long. As he listened to Lindy's incomprehensible voice through Lucy's cell phone, he felt chilled by the sight of the leafless trees, the dense, brown tufts of grass along the roadside, and the lack of other cars passing by. Drawing his coat in tighter and wishing he had zipped it before getting in the car, James coaxed the Bronco's heater to a higher setting and turned left at the next intersection, heading toward the ridge of mountains. They looked blue-black and menacing in the deepening twilight.

Finally, Lucy assured Lindy that she and James would be careful and then summarized her conversation for James's sake.

"It appears that Allison has a thing for stealing drugs," Lucy announced. "During her junior year, her roommate at the Portsmouth School was taking codeine after having knee surgery. Apparently, Allison tried a few pills and liked the affects of the painkiller. The roommate was continuously missing one jar of pills after another until she caught Allison taking them from her book bag. Allison had already been given a warning for possession of marijuana, which she claimed wasn't hers but was forced to go to counseling over, but the incident with the codeine was the last straw. She got kicked out and came back here for her senior year."

"But Allison stole Coumadin from the Livingstones' house, not codeine," James pointed out.

"It just proves that this little lady knows her drugs. She deliberately took the Coumadin with the intention of killing Brinkley." Lucy pointed toward a dirt road bearing off to the right. "Pull in here. We'll walk in through the woods and for now, we'll stick to just looking around for Amelia, but I'm not leaving here until we know what's happened to that girl."

James glanced forlornly into the thicket of barren pine trees. Their trunks seemed ragged and bristly and the forest floor was blanketed with sharp pinecones and protruding sticks. Only a small line of light remained above the horizon as James followed Lucy into the woods. He wished he shared her courage, but he was filled with fright over sneaking into the killer's territory, the daylight dying in front of him as he scrambled down the slope toward an open pasture where several horses stood like silent sentinels at the gate.

"Hurry up, James," Lucy hissed. "God, I hate horses. You never know how they're going to act."

"The horses are the least of our worries." James passed by her, leading the way to the farthest corner of the fenced field, his feet hastened by the sinking sun and the fear that grabbed a hold of his insides and wouldn't let go. "Night is falling," he said, surging forward. "And it's coming fast."

FIFTEEN

BEEF JERKY

Nutrition Facts	
Serving Size 1 oz. (28g)	
Amount Per Serving	
Calories 80 Calories from Fat 10	
	% Daily Value*
Total Fat 1g	2%
Saturated Fat 0g	0%
Cholesterol 25mg	8%
Sodium 500mg	21%
Total Carbohydrate 5g	2%
Dietary Fiber 0g	0%
Sugars 5g	
Protein 11g	
Vitamin A 0% • Vitamin C 0%	
Calcium 0% • Iron 6%	
*Percent Daily Values are based on a 2,000 calorie diet. Your daily values may be higher or lower depending on your calorie needs.	

JAMES AND LUCY TRIED to sneak through the brown-tipped field by walking carefully along the perimeter of the fence, but since neither one of them was light on their feet, they more or less plodded forward until they reached a cluster of horses. The frisky animals were waiting by the gate closest to a large stable. They tossed their heads and snapped their long tails in excitement as James and Lucy drew nearer.

"They're acting like it's dinnertime," James whispered.

Lucy eyed the restless horses nervously. "If it is, we're gonna get caught by whoever feeds them. Let's try to hide out inside that stable somewhere."

James saw no other choice. It was growing impossible to see what lay farther ahead beyond the stable. During their descent through the trees the sprawling manor house made out of stucco had been visible. James had noticed lights in the backyard, illuminating a kidney-shaped swimming pool bordering a grass tennis court. The luminosity in the yard had grown brighter with the incoming darkness, but now the only light near the fields was an inviting rectangle escaping from the back door to the stable, which stood ajar.

Keeping her back against the wall, Lucy pivoted her shoulder and took a quick look inside while James tried to get both his breathing and his heart rate under control. He noticed that Lucy's large breasts were bobbing up and down like buoys in a rough sea and he averted his eyes from her heaving chest just in time as she swung around to face him.

"I can hear someone in there," she said into his ear. "Sounds like it's a woman talking to one of the horses."

The ungainly pair trod over strewn bits of hay as they made their way toward the gentle cooing of a woman from within one of the stalls. The repetitive *whish* of what sounded like a brush running over the horse's coat and several soft whickers were the only other noises in the stable aside from the woman's voice.

James motioned for Lucy to stop as he quickly peered into the stall. Allison Shilling was busy grooming a roan-colored horse. Her back was to the door and she was humming softly to herself. Lucy moved next to James, forming a blockade of folded arms, flabby stomachs, and wide hips. At the last second, James reached out and grabbed a pitchfork hanging from a rusted hook nearby.

"Hello, Allison," Lucy said quietly.

Allison jumped in surprise, startling the horse she was brushing. Its ears twitched nervously as it pawed at the stall door in front of its feet. As Allison tried to calm the beast, the horse neighed loudly and showed the whites of its eyes as it struck out again and again with its powerful hoof against the barn door.

"What the hell do you think you're doing?" Allison yelled, grabbing the horse by its bridle and forcing its head down. "Easy, girl. Easy now," she soothed the horse while hastily stroking its glossy coat.

"I think that's a better question to put to you." Lucy took a step backward, away from the horse's dangerous hooves. "We know you were the one who stole the Coumadin out of Whitney's house the night you and Amelia stayed over."

Allison stopped her caress mid-stroke. Then, ignoring Lucy's comment, she continued brushing the mare while James watched her carefully to make sure that she wasn't about to grab a shotgun from within the pile of hay in the corner of the stall.

"The secret Brinkley knew about you must have been a pretty good one, huh?" Lucy tried again.

Allison shrugged. "Brinkley Myers was a loser. I'm not too upset that he's dead and I don't think anybody else is, either."

"Maybe not, but nearly killing your friend Whitney upset *a lot* of people," Lucy retorted sharply.

Allison put down the brush and, resting a casual arm on the horse's flank, asked, "Is that why you're here? You're *upset* about Whitney?" The girl taunted in return. Then she frowned, looking genuinely confused. "What's the big deal? She's fine now, anyway."

Lucy offered a contemptuous laugh. "Yeah, sure, until *you* can take a second shot at her. Maybe you should drive one of the stable's trucks next time you do it. She might not make it then."

Allison's lip curled and she snarled. "You're crazy. I didn't have anything to do with Whitney's accident. Why don't you go bother somebody else. There's a Golden Corral about fifteen miles from here. You and the professor could really make a dent in their All-You-Can-Eat buffet."

James watched as Lucy's fists curled into tight angry balls. "I work for the Sheriff's Department, Allison, and they're on their way here to discuss the disappearance of Amelia Flowers with you, along with a few other interesting subjects, like murder and attempted murder."

"Amelia's 'disappearance'?" Allison asked, looking less confident than she had a moment before. James was certain he saw a flicker of anxiety enter her expressionless eyes. "What do you mean?"

"Like you don't know," Lucy mocked the girl. She then turned to James. "She'd make a good actress, don't you think? Much better job for her than future senator's wife."

Allison stepped toward them, irritation reflecting in her clenched jaw. "I could give a shit about being Chase's wife. And as for Whitney and Amelia, I have no idea what you're talking about. If you work for the Sheriff's Department, then where's your uniform?" She paused, glaring at Lucy. "Where's your warrant? How about a badge?" She jerked her thumb angrily at James. "And who is this? Your K-9 unit? Get out of my way. *I've* got a life, unlike you two, apparently."

Lucy didn't budge. "Not until you admit what you did," she said evenly. James leaned conspicuously on the pitchfork.

Allison's eyes bored into Lucy's and then settled on the sharp tines of the pitchfork. She sighed in annoyance and then put her hands on her small hips. "Fine. I stole the drugs. I thought they were codeine pills, okay? I mean, I knew Whit's daddy had had some surgery so I figured he must have gotten painkillers out of the deal. I only had, like, a second to look in his medicine cabinet before Whitney called me to say that our pizza was ready. So I just grabbed the bottle." She shrugged again. "When I got home, I didn't recognize the name so I didn't take them. I'm not that stupid." She pulled a piece of straw from her hair. "I was going to check this Coumadin stuff out on the Internet but when I went to get the bottle from where I'd hidden it, the pills were gone. Oh well. I found something else to replace them soon enough."

"That's it?" Lucy asked incredulously.

"Yeah, that's it. You planning on arresting me?" she asked, still unfazed.

Lucy hesitated before saying, "But what about when you heard that Coumadin was the same drug used to kill Brinkley?"

Allison didn't speak for a moment as she processed this seemingly new information. "I didn't know that 'til now." The girl's anxiety level was clearly growing. She toyed with the horse's mane with distracted fingers. "It's not like I read the papers. Besides, so what? I'm sure lots of people around here with bad tickers use that stuff. She narrowed her eyes wickedly. "It's because most Americans are too fat."

"Stop pretending, Allison. Unfortunately for you, the bottle you stole was the only one in Quincy's Gap. That's how we know you killed Brinkley. We just followed the trail left by the pills." Lucy's tone instantly softened as she tried to work a confession out of the nervous girl. "Look, I know Brinkley did all three of you wrong, but you can fix that now, Allison. Just tell me where Amelia is and it will look really good for you later on. You've got to do something to help yourself now. You're backed into a corner."

Allison's eyes flicked back and forth between Lucy and James. Beads of sweat popped out on her forehead and she wiped them away with the back of her sleeve. "Brinkley knew about my drug problem," she finally whispered. "He threatened to tell Chase all about it, but I told him to shove his blackmailing ways up his ass and that I wouldn't pay. So, I had no reason to kill him." She kicked at a bit of straw with her riding boot. "I was actually *disappointed* when Brinkley died."

"Because you don't want to marry Chase, right?" James asked softly. "You don't even love him, do you?"

"No, I don't!" Allison's anger returned. "But he's *rich* and he's from a *powerful* family and *any girl* would consider herself *lucky* enough to have him," she said in a scathing singsong. "Isn't that right, mother?"

"That's right, Allison," said a flat, emotionless voice from behind James and Lucy.

Allison pushed past the stunned pair and moved toward her mother. Mrs. Shilling looked very different than she had a few days ago at the festival. Instead of a suit, high heels, and pearls, she wore a faded pair of jeans, a flannel shirt, and a down vest. Her white-blonde hair was tucked inside a red baseball cap and she wore black leather driving gloves on her hands.

"Welcome to our home," she said, wearing a cold smile that never reached her eyes.

"Mrs. Shilling—?" James began.

"Oh, call me Rachel. We don't need to be so formal." She uttered a strange laugh. "After all, you're guests of mine now."

"Mother? What is going on?" Allison demanded.

Rachel turned to her daughter. "*You* have caused me enough trouble for a lifetime. Go get me some duct tape from the tool shed and bring it back here."

Allison looked at her mother strangely. "But—"

"NOW!" Rachel roared, and Allison hustled off.

"It was *you*," Lucy breathed. "You found out about the blackmail and *you* killed Brinkley."

Rachel smiled crookedly. "Well done, Sherlock. Yes, I killed him. Nothing is going to stop this wedding from taking place. Not some stupid, greedy boy, not you two, and none of Allison's nitwit friends, either. My daughter is checking into a *private* rehab clinic this week and she'll get over her . . . little problem." She took a revolver from the front pocket of her vest. "Now, I'd rather not have Allison see this, as she has *no idea* of what I've sacrificed in order to ensure that she marries Chase Radford, but I *will* shoot you in front of her if you give me the slightest excuse to. Do we understand one another?"

James and Lucy nodded miserably.

Allison returned bearing a large roll of duct tape. She began disagreeing feverishly with her mother. Rachel put her hands on her hips and pointed toward the stable's back door.

"Go lock that!" she ordered, but Allison continued to argue.

"We should have told Sheriff Huckabee we were coming out here," James muttered under his breath. "I don't think our plan has gone so well."

Lucy wore an expression of dismay. "I'm sorry, James. I guess this is what happens when you're untrained in confronting suspects."

"Your heart was in the right place, Lucy," James offered kindly. "You were merely thinking of Amelia's welfare."

Allison had closed and locked the back door and was now shaking her head over her mother's next order, which James hadn't heard over his whispered exchange with Lucy.

Suddenly, Rachel grabbed her daughter by the shoulders. "I said do it! These people have done terrible things and I'm going to make sure they don't do them again!"

"What things? I don't get it!" Allison began to cry.

Her mother ran a hand over her daughter's wavy hair and gave her a quick hug. "Don't worry, honey. Mommy knows what to do about everything. Just do what I say and let me handle this."

As Allison walked toward them holding a roll of duct tape, tears glistening on both cheeks, James could foretell what was about to happen. He looked over Allison's head and tried to catch Rachel's eye.

"You don't want to do this." He forced himself to sound calm and reasonable. "You're putting your family name in even more danger. There are at least three people who know what we know. They'll call for help if we're not back by later tonight. You should let Amelia go and turn yourself in."

"I don't know what you're talking about, but you are *not* going to hurt my daughter." Rachel took a step closer to them and barked, "Put your hands behind your backs, fatsos. I heard your whole conversation with my daughter. You were fumbling in the dark when you came here. For all we know, *you're* the killers." She moved even closer to them, her blue eyes burning with a feverish intensity. "And by the time any of your so-called *friends* come looking for you, you'll be long gone." Rachel drew the heads of her two captors close together so that she could whisper in both of their ears simultaneously. "You two *and* Amelia."

Lucy jerked her head away and softly uttered, "So then she *is* still alive!"

"Hush up." Rachel walked behind them so that she could watch her daughter's handiwork with the tape. "Make it tighter, Allison. I don't want them climbing out of the trailer in the middle of Highway 33."

"What are you going to do with them?" Allison's voice rose shrilly.

"Nothing you need worry about, you hear me? Now, get yourself back in the house and tell your father that I've gone to the lake overnight. If he asks why, just tell him that I'm stressed out and needed some alone time." Rachel removed one of her gloves and examined her perfectly manicured nails. "He won't bat an eyelash at that. And if anyone else comes snooping around here, call the police. We've got nothing to hide."

"So what did you do with your poodle mask?" Lucy asked derisively while tugging at her bound hands. James also tried to free himself, but Allison had effectively rendered them useless.

Rachel took another step closer, a dangerous rage flaring in her eyes. "I'd be quiet if I were you."

"Allison! It's your mother! *She's* the killer!" Lucy quickly shouted as the girl moved toward the front door of the stable.

Allison hesitated and Rachel immediately positioned herself so that she could draw her gun and press it against Lucy's back. "One more peep out of you, and she'll see someone die right before her eyes."

"She's going to figure it out," James said to Rachel in a hushed tone.

"Maybe, maybe not, but she'll be married soon and that's all that matters. Go on, honey!" Rachel called to her daughter with false sweetness and the girl reluctantly obeyed.

"Your daughter will never forgive you," James stated plainly, and for the first time, Rachel seemed to consider the consequences of her actions. However, she seemed to shake off James's suggestion as if it were a fly buzzing around her head.

Waving the gun in front of their faces, she smiled crookedly once more. "Maybe not. But mothers know what's best and *I'm* doing what's best for my girl. Now"—she jerked the weapon toward the back door—"start walking. We're going to go on a little trip." She paused, breaking two more pieces of duct tape off of the shrunken roll. "But first, I'm going to put a stop to your endless babbling." And with a flourish, she placed a strip of tape over both of their mouths.

Opening the stable's back door, Rachel gestured at them with her gun until they had walked around to the rear of a horse trailer parked next to the stable. Rachel slid a key into the padlock, unwound a linked chain, and threw open the metal double doors.

Inside, sitting on a pile of straw, was Amelia Flowers. She shifted in alarm at the sight of Rachel Shilling and whimpered. When she spied James and Lucy, she suddenly grew silent and her head slumped to her chest. It was as if she recognized that her rescuers had arrived and that their rescue attempt had clearly failed.

———————

James was thrown roughly against a wall as the trailer made a sharp turn. Rachel had secured each of them to strong wall hooks using trailer ties as if her captives were horses. This way, they were unable to reach one another to make an attempt at untying their bonds. Lucy and Amelia had been tied to chest rails on opposite sides of the trailer and James had been fastened to the padded butt bar in the back. Though these bars were made of aluminum, they were incredibly strong and there was no hope of breaking or bending the metal.

In the darkness of the moving vehicle, James found himself mournfully staring up through the narrow windows at a distant sickle of moon. For the last half hour, he had been trying to rub the end of the duct tape covering his mouth against his shoulder in hopes of working it free. He had made some headway, but each time he regained his balance and began working on the tape, the trailer seemed to lurch in one direction, forcing him to the ground again.

Glancing once more at the moon, which seemed to be mocking him as it darted playfully in and out of string clouds, James steadied himself and pushed the tape completely off of one corner of his mouth. Within minutes, he had rubbed it off entirely.

"Lucy! Amelia!" he said loudly over the roar of the trailer moving along the highway. "Try rubbing the end of the tape that's on your mouth against your shoulder. I think you'll be able to get it off."

In the dark, James could hear his companions moving about as they worked on the tape. James investigated the floor of the trailer with his legs, but found nothing but pieces of hay scattered across the metal floor. Kicking angrily, he then explored the sidewalls, but again, came up with nothing that would help them escape.

"Got it!" Lucy exclaimed a moment later. "Boy, when I get my hands on that psychotic . . ." she began but ran out of breath.

"Are you okay?" James asked.

"Yes. I'm just mad. You?"

James swallowed. "I'm fine. I've been trying to feel out my space with my feet, but there doesn't seem to be anything I can use to cut my tape near me. Can you try searching where you're sitting?"

"Ugh!" Amelia spat. "I've been trying to get that damned tape off for like three hours. I think half of my lips are stuck to that piece!"

"Amelia! We're so glad to find you alive," Lucy said, kicking out with her legs. "How are you doing, honey?"

"I'd be better if we weren't tied up in the back of some lunatic's horse trailer!" James heard her fumbling around her space with her feet. "There's nothing here that's gonna help us. We're screwed."

James waited for Lucy to say something consoling, but she remained silent.

"Where do you think she's taking us?" Amelia asked meekly.

"I'd guess Lake Anna," James replied. "It's the most likely place for a lake house."

"That's over an hour southeast of Quincy's Gap," Lucy mumbled. "Even if any of our friends or Sheriff Huckabee realize that we went out to Shilling's Stables, they won't be able to get it out of Allison that we've all been kidnapped until it's too late."

"What does that mean?" Amelia shrieked. "What's going to happen to us?"

"Nothing," James reassured the frightened girl. "There are three of us against one. Let's focus on getting one of us untied so we have a fighting chance."

Lucy perked up. "You're right, James. Even if we can't get untied, one of us can jump on Rachel while someone else kicks the gun away." James could hear the determination in Lucy's voice. "We just have to keep our wits about us and wait for the right moment."

"We're going to get out of here, Amelia," James tried to soothe the girl across the darkened trailer. "Just hang in there. No one's giving up."

"Okay," Amelia responded bravely. "Then I won't, either."

———————

An hour and a half later, the trailer bumped to a stop and the three captives heard Rachel Shilling get out of the cab and slam the door. They heard her opening the rear door to the trailer and suddenly, the beam of a flashlight was blinding them.

Rachel climbed into the trailer and untied their ropes from the hooks on the trailer wall. Each of her prisoners had ropes tied onto their bound wrists. Rachel gathered the individual lengths of rope and tugged on the lines with one hand, leaving enough slack to allow them to walk forward even though their hands were fastened behind their backs. She held out her gun and waved it until James, Lucy, and Amelia were persuaded into moving down the trailer's ramp.

"Come on!" Rachel shouted, jerking on the rope so roughly that Amelia almost lost her footing. "I'm already tired from driving down here."

"What are you going to do with us?" Amelia wailed.

Rachel frowned in annoyance. "It was too much to hope that you'd keep that damned tape over your mouths, I suppose." She pulled them down a steep driveway that led to a narrow dock. "Still, I don't have any neighbors who make it a habit to visit their lake houses in November. And even if they did"—she gestured maniacally with the revolver—"the closest one is over a mile away, so scream if it suits you. What do I care?" Rachel paused next to a small boathouse so that she could turn on a row of lights that illuminated the boathouse and the strip of dock.

Piles of lumber, two wheelbarrows, and a large Dumpster flanked a staked construction site next to the boathouse. As they passed by the small structure, James could see that they were running out of time. With their hands bound as tightly as they were, their only chance of stopping Rachel was to ambush her while she was distracted. It was clear that they were being led straight to the lake and that Rachel did not intend to return to the trailer with any accompaniment.

Desperately, he searched for something to say that would shake the woman's frosty composure and give the three of them a chance to launch themselves upon her. "What about Allison?" he called out. "She told us she's not going to marry Chase no matter what. She's twenty years old, you know. I don't think you can force her. And then what would be the point of all of this? You'll have murdered four people for nothing. You're going to lose your daughter forever."

"Yeah, you're risking an awful lot considering that if the press gets the slightest whiff of this scandal your family name is ruined forever," Lucy chimed in, recognizing James's ploy. "Allison would be lucky to marry the garbage man."

"The press will never know. Shoot, the *police* will never know." Rachel smiled as the wooden dock drew nearer. "No one is going to find your bodies. There is no *proof.* Do you think my daughter is going to turn against me even if she's questioned? She won't say a word." She snorted. "I've *already* gotten away with it."

"Allison told me she's in love with someone else," James blurted urgently.

Rachel stopped. He had gotten her attention.

James fumbled for a name but in his increased state of anxiety, drew a complete blank.

"Yeah, Darryl Jeffries," Amelia said quickly. "He's a car mechanic."

"A mechanic?" Rachel's eyes widened in horror. "Like, at a gas station?" Her gun hand dropped down a foot as her mind tried to grapple with the idea of her daughter being involved with someone with greasy hands.

"Like, at the Amoco station outside of town," Amelia stated simply. "They've been seeing each other for months."

James was proud of the girl. She sounded very believable. Rachel's hand sank down another foot, so that the revolver was no longer pointing at any of them.

"She's planning to elope," Lucy added, her eyes never leaving the revolver. As Rachel digested the barrage of horrifying information about her daughter, James suddenly yelled "Now!" and the three bound prisoners launched themselves at their captor.

Rachel attempted to raise the gun, but James had already knocked into her with his immense stomach. He heard a satisfying skid as the weapon slid down the wooden slats of the dock. Lucy threw her weight directly into Rachel's legs, hoping to topple her, but unfortunately, so did Amelia and the two women ended up throwing each other off balance. With their hands tied, they fell backward and landed in a heap, unable to rise again with enough swiftness to catch Rachel.

Grabbing the revolver, Rachel swung it around and aimed at the center of James's chest. "Move and I shoot!" she yelled. James froze in place, exhaling deeply in defeat. "That was a nice try," she said with a hint of genuine admiration. "I do admire your spunk, but I've had enough fun for one evening." She pointed her gun at the three of them and commanded them to walk to the end of the dock, where she tied their ropes to a pylon. "I'm lucky we've started our project to expand the boathouse. It means I've got easy access to some heavy materials, if you get my drift." She laughed at herself, her voice echoing eerily across the black lake water. "I *knew* adding a guest room to the boathouse was a good idea even though my husband didn't want to spend the money on it," she prattled on to herself as she walked back up the dock and disappeared around a corner of the boathouse.

When she returned, she was driving a wheelbarrow filled with long steel bars. "My daddy was in construction, so I figured a few of these would be hanging around here. See, they go into the cement in the foundation for extra support. Tonight, however, they will be supporting you three on your descent to the bottom of the lake."

As James watched in stupefied terror, Rachel gathered several steel bars and began taping them to Lucy's body using another roll of duct tape.

"You won't get away with this!" Lucy screamed in panic.

Amelia started screaming as well. James thought surely someone must be able to hear them. He tugged at his arms again, but it was no use—he couldn't get them free. Rachel had finished with Lucy and had begun to attach the long rods to Amelia, who wriggled around as best as she could until Rachel slapped her hard on the cheek. "Stop it!" she commanded, and Amelia sagged against the poles, her face crumpling as tears dropped from her chin onto the dock.

"Almost done," Rachel said jauntily to James as she wrapped four bars around his chest. She acted as if she were casually pruning a rose bush or frosting a cake. "Just remember, you two brought this on yourselves. If you hadn't snooped around in other people's business, you'd be home having dinner by now." She shrugged. "But at least the fishes will get a real good meal out of two of you."

Howling with laughter at her own joke, Rachel grabbed onto a pylon for support. Still clinging to it, she turned to Lucy. "Any last words?" she asked, untying their ropes and raising her leg in preparation to kick Lucy forward into the water.

"Wait!" James shouted. "Push me first!"

Lucy began to sob quietly, moved by James's plea and the hopelessness of their situation.

"How sweet." Rachel turned to him. "Fine, Romeo. Here goes." She raised her leg.

James closed his eyes and prepared to hit the water, but the kick to his back never came. He opened his eyes tentatively and saw Rachel staring back up the hill toward the house. A collection of flashing blue lights and blaring sirens broke through the silent darkness.

"Shit." Rachel looked around her for an escape. She headed for the small motorboat elevated above the water beneath a tin awning and ripped the cover from it. Frantically working the controls, she began to lower the boat into the water.

Hurried footsteps thumped down the hill. "Freeze!" A man's voice ordered loudly.

Two uniformed policeman aimed their guns at Rachel as they sprinted up the dock. She ignored them and hopped in the boat, unfastening the stern line.

"Put your hands in the air! We will not ask again!"

Rachel turned the key in the ignition with one hand and pointed her gun back at James with her other hand.

"Try to stop me and I shoot him," she hissed.

The cops exchanged silent signals. Moving like lightning, the one closest to James leapt sideways and pushed him to the floor of the dock. The second cop jumped down into the boat and wrestled for Rachel's gun. A shot rang out and James heard the bullet tear a splintering hole into the side of the wooden pylon where he had just been standing.

Tossing Rachel's gun onto the dock, the officer cuffed her within seconds and shoved her face down onto the wooden surface.

"Ow!" Rachel complained and began to giggle uncontrollably. "I think I got splinter."

Two more officers helped untie James, Lucy, and Amelia. James gathered both women in his arms and they sank to their knees, weak with relief. Lucy's hands were shaking as her fingers clung to the fabric of his shirt.

A third set of footsteps came pounding up the dock. James looked up to see Lindy racing toward them, her flesh jiggling wildly as she ran. Sheriff Huckabee and Deputy Glenn Truett were following behind her at a more leisurely pace. James also caught a glimpse of Bennett and Gillian lumbering down the hill as quickly as possible.

"James! Lucy!" Lindy cried out. "Amelia!" She hugged all three of them. "Thank God you're all right!"

The little group held one another until Gillian and Bennett joined them and more embraces were exchanged.

"What are you doing here?" James finally asked, watching as Gillian wiped tears from her face.

"After Lindy and Lucy talked on the phone earlier, we figured that Lucy was going to go after Allison, so we called the sheriff, who was back from questioning Whitney." Bennett glanced over his shoulder at Huckabee, who was chatting with a member of the police force. "He already had plans to go out to Shilling's Stables. We begged him to go right away and asked to go along. Surprisingly, he listened to us. We filled him in on everything we knew in the car."

"He never responded when we were finished." Gillian looked at Lucy worriedly. "I'm not sure how he's going to react when this all settles down."

Lucy looked at Gillian and smiled. "Right now, I'm not too concerned about what those guys think."

"Come on." Lindy gestured toward the hill. "Let's get out of here."

"How did the cops end up finding out about the lake house?" James asked Bennett as they headed toward the cluster of law enforcement cars.

"Allison told them." Bennett eyed Rachel Shilling as she was shut in the rear of one of the police cars. "She didn't want to at first, but I think she figured out that her mama had a screw comin' loose tonight. Plus, Sheriff Huckabee was *very* persuasive. Never mess with a man with an impressive mustache. That's my motto." Bennett grinned and smoothed his own neat mustache. "We were only a few miles behind you guys. After all, it's mighty tough to speed in a horse trailer."

"Come on folks, we'll give y'all a lift back to Quincy's Gap," Deputy Truett offered with a friendly wave toward his brown patrol car.

"Thank you," Lucy replied. Amelia and James climbed in the back. Glenn held open the passenger door for Lucy.

"Y'all hungry?" Glenn asked. "I got some beef jerky up here. Didn't get a chance to grab any supper before we headed out to the Shillings' place," he added apologetically.

"I'll take a piece," James said. "Thanks a bunch."

Leaning back against the worn leather seats, James allowed his tense body to relax a bit as he took a bite of the jerky. He wasn't hungry, but chewing on the hickory-flavored and heavily salted meat helped his whirling mind slow down.

"James," Lucy began, turning around in the front seat and looking tenderly at him. "Thanks for what you did back there . . . trying to give me those few extra minutes." Her eyes grew moist. "I treated you terribly when what I really feel is totally the opposite."

James couldn't think of anything to say. He was too exhausted from their ordeal, so he simply smiled in return and then allowed the rhythm of the moving car to lull him back to a sense of normalcy. Sighing, James glanced out the window, searching for the moon. As if beckoned, it burst out from the thin streaks of cloud surrounded by a sprinkling of stars. The warm light fell on Amelia's sleeping face and brightened the swath of highway all the way to the mountains. It was like a welcoming path leading those who had lost their way back home.

SIXTEEN

PEPPERONI PIZZA

Nutrition Facts		
Serving Size 1 slice (117g)		
Amount Per Serving		
Calories 322 Calories from Fat 171		
		% Daily Value*
Total Fat 19g		29%
Saturated Fat 7g		35%
Cholesterol 40mg		13%
Sodium 925mg		39%
Total Carbohydrate 25g		8%
Dietary Fiber 1g		4%
Sugars 7g		
Protein 20g		
Vitamin A 7% • Vitamin C 2%		
Calcium 25% • Iron 4%		
*Percent Daily Values are based on a 2,000 calorie diet. Your daily values may be higher or lower depending on your calorie needs		

THE FLAB FIVE SPENT the remainder of the week making statements to the state police regarding their knowledge of Rachel Shilling's dealings in murder and kidnapping. Afterwards, they also had to offer and sign similar statements for the Sheriff's Department in Quincy's Gap.

"This jurisdiction stuff can get confusing," Lucy explained one morning as James and Bennett waited outside the sheriff's office for their turn to complete paperwork. "The state police handled the incident at Lake Anna, as that fell in their jurisdiction, but Brinkley's murder is still the responsibility of our department." She smiled wanly. "That is, if I can still include myself as a member of this department once Sheriff Huckabee gets done with me."

"Have you already made your statement?" Bennett asked, popping a handful of macadamia nuts into his mouth.

"I came in earlier this morning. Figured I'd get it over with," Lucy said, nonplussed.

"And how did he seem?" James wondered.

Lucy shook her head. "Dunno. Kind of, just businesslike. I think he's waiting to get all his chickens in a row before he dresses me down."

Bennett stood and began pacing the hallway. "Well, you're taking the waiting part mighty well. I feel like a criminal just being here." He checked his watch. "I don't think I've had to miss my afternoon route since I started working for the USPS."

Lucy looked at James as she answered Bennett. "I *do* feel nervous about keeping this job, but there are more important things in this life than becoming a deputy. Even if I get fired, I'll find something else to do." She stapled a stack of paperwork and laid it aside for filing. "Still, I'd miss it here. This desk is kind of the heart of this place. All of the information passes through me and I've always felt useful, even if I've never been 'one of the guys.'"

At that moment, the door to Huckabee's office opened and Lindy came bustling out. She looked especially peppy, and she embraced Bennett and James as if she hadn't seen them for weeks.

"Jesus, Lindy!" Bennett choked in the midst of her fierce embrace. "It's only been two days since you last squeezed my organs to pulp."

"I know!" Lindy cried. "But I can't stop thinking about how our little group almost shrunk in size . . . and I don't mean 'cause we're losing weight!"

She would have hugged James next, but Huckabee called him in to make his statement.

"Into the lion's den," James muttered warily, drawing his hand across his throat in a mock slicing gesture.

"Oh, he's just a big teddy bear," Lindy said cheerily. "Nothing to worry about."

Lindy was right. Huckabee was the model of courtesy and directness. He asked his questions emotionlessly and James completed his lengthy statement within thirty minutes.

"May I ask you a question, Sheriff?" James blurted out after signing several documents. Without waiting for an answer he said, "There are some loose ends about this whole thing that I can't work out, like how did Rachel Shilling find out about the blackmail and why did she try to kill Whitney? That girl was no threat to her."

Huckabee examined a paperweight in the shape of a cowboy boot on his desk and seemed to be pondering whether or not to satisfy James's curiosity. Finally, he shrugged and said, "Rachel found a note in Allison's room that was written by Brinkley. Apparently, she had been pokin' around in her daughter's drawers lookin' to see if she had any more drugs stashed around. Once she read the note, she knew that Brinkley was gonna be at the diner. Allison was supposed to give him a payment before the game that night. She never did, but Rachel went to the diner. She had no problem slippin' the drug into her own soda. She then squeezed in some lemon and switched hers with Brinkley's. She was sittin' at the next booth over and asked to borrow some napkins. Apparently, that's when she did the switch. The boys were all so busy talkin' football that they never noticed."

Deputy Truett jumped in. "As far as Whitney goes, Rachel said she didn't want a single soul knowin' about why Allison was kicked out of school. Allison told her mama that Whitney and Amelia were the only ones who knew the reason and could keep a secret. Apparently, she was lying 'cause she told Brinkley about it right after she started up at Blue Ridge High. Seems like the two of them dated for a while during their senior year. Brinkley never forgot that useful tidbit about Allison's drug problem and when he noticed her hangin' around with that senator's son, he made his move to earn some easy cash."

"And that's why Rachel needed to kidnap Amelia." James nodded his head as the pieces fell into place. "Amelia was the last person who could ruin Allison's future marriage by spilling the truth about her friend's drug problem. Thank you, gentlemen." He smiled. "I appreciate you sharing that information with me so candidly. I think not knowing the details would have kept me up at night."

"Well, we can't have that," Huckabee said flatly.

As James stood to leave, Huckabee turned to Deputy Truett and said, "Glenn, can you make a copy of that for Mr. Henry to sign? I'd like a moment alone with him."

James swallowed hard and sat back down.

"I hear you're going to be offering some computer courses at the library," Huckabee began, pouring himself a cup of coffee from a thermos. He held out the thermos to James but James politely declined. Even though his mouth was bone dry, he wanted to complete his interview with Huckabee and get back to work.

"Yes, sir." James shifted uncomfortably in his chair. "Mostly basic stuff, like word processing, using e-mail, and Internet surfing."

"I've got a couple of deputies who have never had any kind of training and they've been making a mess of our reports. You see, we've got everything online now in shared files, but these boys can't all figure out how to access these files, let alone contribute to them." He stroked his mustache thoughtfully. "One of the things I learned from this Shilling business is that our men need to be aware of *all* the important information involving our cases as it comes in. Do you think they would benefit from your course?"

James stared at Huckabee's wide face with its luxurious mustache and tried not to picture him basking on a rock while flapping a pair of wet flippers. "Absolutely. We're planning on adding a course on web page development as well. Miss Hanover expressed an interest in developing one for the department."

Huckabee smiled and resumed petting his mustache. "That would be just fine." He rose and held out a wide hand. Gripping James's hand like an iron clamp, Huckabee added, "And next time your little group gets together, I would like to suggest that you stick to safer topics like books or recipes. Understand? We actually know what we're doin' in this department, so how about leavin' the crime solvin' up to us?" Huckabee's eyes bored into James. He clearly expected no argument.

"Fair enough," James said, averting his gaze. Relieved at receiving such a mild reprimand, he reclaimed his throbbing hand and made a hasty escape.

On Sunday, it was finally Gillian's turn to host the supper club. She had written them all an e-mail earlier in the week telling them not to bring any food to her house as she was planning a little celebration in honor of the capture of Rachel Shilling and the end to Quincy's Gap's greatest mystery.

Before meeting his friends, James stopped at Dolly's Diner late Sunday afternoon to pick up a chicken pot pie for his father's dinner. The three Livingstones were sitting at the counter in the nearly empty diner, enjoying steaming cups of hot chocolate smothered by fluffy coils of whipped cream and massive slices of apple crumb pie.

"Hello, Professor!" Dolly hooted as she burst through the swinging doors leading to the kitchen. "Come in here and take a load off. You poor darlin'! We've been worried sick about you and Miss Hanover and Whitney's little friend . . ."

"Amelia," Whitney said.

"Right, Megan's gal." Dolly grabbed a mug and the coffee pot and pointed to one of the counter stools. She was almost salivating as she waited for James to give her every detail of his kidnapping ordeal. Even though James wanted to make a hasty escape, he just couldn't take his eyes off of the slices of apple crumb pie, plus he was too fond of Dolly to deny her a firsthand account of his trials. He knew she couldn't wait to tell her customers a highly embellished version over the next few days.

"You should sue Shilling's Stables!" Dolly exclaimed when James finally finished his lengthy narrative. He realized that she was directing her suggestion at the Livingstones.

"You probably *could* sue for damages, in civil court that is," James said, turning to Beau. "The criminal trial will come first I guess."

Dolly's eyes lit up. "I reckon you could get enough to pay off your medical bills *and* Whitney's schooling."

Beau shook his head. "We'd never sue those folks. That family has got enough trouble comin' its way without us addin' our two cents in."

"Yeah, poor Allison," Whitney added. "She had problems even before she found out her mother was one can short of a six-pack."

"By 'before,' you mean problems the drugs?" James asked.

"And with her mama, too," Caroline said, staring at a piece of golden brown piecrust mournfully. "Rachel was so focused on her daughter marrying into a big-shot family that she ended up causing the poor girl a whole lotta heartache instead."

Whitney sighed. "I think that's why Allison started on drugs in the first place. It seemed like everything she did was wrong in her mom's eyes. She didn't study hard enough at that fancy private school and when we were friends in high school, Allison never wanted us to hang out at her house. She said she couldn't take her mom's nagging." She put her good arm around her mother's shoulders. "I'm glad you love me for me, mom."

Caroline beamed. "Well, you make it pretty easy, sugar. Who could ask for a better child?"

James absently stirred his coffee as envy bubbled up inside his stomach. He could barely have a conversation with his father and he certainly couldn't recall the last time they had exchanged a handshake, let alone an embrace. It would be nice to have the family unity the Livingstones had for just a fraction of the time.

"Here's your pot pie." Dolly handed James a paper bag. "I threw in a fat piece of banana cake. No charge. Your Pa must be getting as skinny as you are with that diet you're on and he used to love my banana cake." Dolly patted James on the cheek as if he were a little boy. "You're a good son, Professor. You just keep working on your pa. He'll come around. He loved your mama a powerful lot, so it's gonna take him some time."

James wondered if Dolly was a mind reader as he gathered the takeout bag in his hands. "Thanks, Dolly." Her words immediately comforted him and the warmth of her smile was like a blanket placed around his cold shoulders.

As he turned to leave, the Livingstones stood and Caroline enfolded him in a hug. James accepted her embrace, awkwardly, as he balanced the bag in one hand and reached out to her with his other.

"We're mighty glad you came back to our town, Professor," Beau said. "You've done nothin' but good since you got here."

James drove home with a full heart. Jackson was locked up in the shed as usual, so James left him a note taped to the fridge about heating up the pot pie. As he gathered up his car keys once again, James spied his father's toolbox on top of the kitchen counter. As far as James was aware, Jackson hadn't touched a tool since his hardware store was sold years ago. There were no signs of a current fix-it project, but James felt hopeful simply seeing the toolbox. Opening the lid, it was clear that Jackson had meticulously cleaned off every tool within. Perhaps his father was beginning to reclaim a bit of his old life. Using his long-neglected tools would be a step in the right direction. Even if it were only a tiny step forward, James would revel in the slightest sign of improvement.

Gillian lived in a large pink Victorian house with a wraparound porch. The gingerbread trim had been painted sage green in some places and a creamy shade of beige in others. Dormant flower beds and neatly trimmed mature boxwoods surrounded the porch and two mammoth magnolia trees graced the flat rectangle of lawn. A wrought iron fence complete with a squeaky gate allowed access to a cobblestone pathway that brought visitors to a polished front door with leaded glass panes.

Inside Gillian's kitchen, which was painted a light shade of periwinkle, a cluster of pink asters arranged in a ceramic pitcher was the only item resting upon the copper-colored granite countertops. James admired the cherry cabinets and the row of violet- and green-colored candles on the fireplace mantle.

"Your house is beautiful," he said. "Everything is so colorful, but it all blends together so perfectly."

"Thanks. You know, people always expect me to be a slob." Gillian gestured around the spotless kitchen. "And I know I'm kind of flaky in some areas, but when it comes to my home and my business, I'm as compulsive and order-obsessed as an accountant during tax season."

Bennett settled himself into one of the oak chairs at the breakfast table. "So where are you hiding supper in this paradise?"

Gillian smirked. "It's a surprise. First, however, I thought we'd have a toast to celebrate the successful end of our first adventure."

"Finally!" Lucy cheered as Gillian produced a bottle of champagne from the fridge. "Some alcohol! I thought I'd have to go buy a bottle of this the other night just to celebrate the look on Donovan's face when he found out he had missed his big chance for glory by not taking down the *real* killer."

"Did he have the night off?" James asked.

"No, but he switched with Glenn so that he could bowl with the Sheriff's Department from Rockingham in some big league showdown."

"Man, he must be grumpy." Bennett laughed at the thought.

"He's been pouting all week, but every time I see him, I tell him some detail about *our* investigation." Lucy's eyes twinkled mischievously.

"So, are we celebrating our diet adventure or our sterling detecting abilities?" James quipped.

"Both," Gillian said, distributing plastic champagne flutes. "Sorry about the glasses, but I don't normally drink. *I* prefer to take myself to other planes of existence through meditation and the use of scent."

"To the Flab Five!" Lindy pronounced as the friends knocked glasses together.

"Speaking of scent"—Lindy sniffed the air—"I do declare that I can smell the tantalizing aroma of pizza somewhere around here."

As if on cue, the doorbell pealed merrily into the hallway where it bounced off the black-and-white checkered floor tiles.

"You have a fine nose, Lindy," Gillian laughed and opened the door to the town's only pizza delivery man.

"Evenin', Miss O'Malley." The boyish delivery man tipped his hat. "I thought you were mad at us or somethin'. You haven't ordered a pie in weeks!"

"I've been on a diet Danny, and it unfortunately does not include pizza. Thanks so much."

Danny looked down at his tip and smiled gratefully. "I'm glad to be comin' back, ma'am. Y'all enjoy!"

James heard his stomach gurgle with anticipation as the aroma of hot pizza wafted through the spacious kitchen.

"I've got pepperoni, vegetarian, and four cheese," Gillian announced, tossing a stack of paper plates and napkins on the table. "Dig in!"

Everyone dove for a pizza box, grabbing the warm slices as if they were the last pieces of pizza left in the known world. James bit off the end of a pepperoni slice, watching as a string of cheese at least twelve inches long stretched from his mouth back down to his grease-soaked plate.

"Oh my God," Lucy moaned. "How did we live without this for so many weeks?"

"And was it even worth it?" Lindy chimed in.

"Well," Bennett said. "Let's do a tally. Everyone write down the total amount of weight you've lost on this napkin. Don't say anything and then hand it off to the person next to you. I'll add up our total when we've all put down our numbers."

Gillian started. She wrote down a number and handed the napkin to James. He saw that she had written the number 8. He had lost nine pounds over the last five weeks, so he added his number below Lucy's and slid the napkin to Lindy. None of them stopped eating as they wrote their numbers down. Finally, Bennett jotted down his own number and then added up all five of their numbers.

"Damn, we've lost the weight of an entire six-year-old child!" He looked around at a group of blank faces. "Well, a six-year-old boy, to be specific. On average, they weigh forty-eight-and-a-half pounds."

"That's amazing!" Gillian exclaimed. "Look," she said, racing over to her pantry. She dragged two large bags of kitty litter on the floor behind her. Plopping them on the table, she shouted exuberantly, "These weigh twelve pounds each. We've lost the equivalent of four of these bags. Come over and pick one of these up and just think about that. It will make you realize the *size* of our accomplishment."

"Wow." James was impressed. He picked up both bags and tried to imagine that weight being doubled, then handed off the bags to Lucy.

"Who was the big winner with the loss of twelve pounds?" Bennett asked, examining the napkin bearing their weight loss numbers.

"Me!" Lindy exclaimed. "I've been walking to school instead of driving. Well, on days when it's not too cold. I think that's helped me lose a few extra pounds."

"You were right, then." Lucy swallowed a bite of cheese pizza. "We *do* need to start some kind of exercise."

"And a little less TV watching," Bennett grunted. "Statistically speaking, if we could replace two thirty-minute shows with some kind of activity, we'd lose more weight."

"Then that will be our *next* adventure," Gillian suggested. "Not that I'm looking forward to sweating, but it's time to kick things up a notch. After all, the Flab Five can handle any challenge!"

"I'll toast to that," James said, refilling his plastic flute with the dry champagne.

"Oh, James." Lindy suddenly wiped off her mouth and stood abruptly. "I almost forgot! Lucy told me that with all the goings on at the Neighbor Aid Festival you never had a chance to see what your daddy donated to the silent auction."

James bolted to a standing position. "Do *you* know? It would answer the question I've had for months. What does that man do all day out in our shed?"

Lindy giggled. "Not only do I know, but soon a lot of other people will, too. Wait a sec. I'll show you."

Lindy left the room and then returned again with a thin, square moving box, the kind used to pack mirrors or paintings. She slid a canvas out of the box, showing only the back to James.

"Wipe your hands off first, please," Lindy requested. "I don't want any grease on this wonderful piece of art."

"Art?" James asked, thinking back to the day he had found the paintbrush next to the kitchen sink.

"Just see for yourself." Lindy reached over him and placed the painting onto the table where the plates and glasses had been. The painting wasn't large. It was about twelve by fourteen inches in total and was unframed, but James touched the edges of the canvas with trembling hands, his mind a flurry of emotions.

Jackson had painted a pair of cardinals surrounded by dogwood blossoms. The birds and vegetation looked so lifelike that it seemed that James could have been looking out a window during the height of spring instead of at a skillful combination of paint and careful brushstrokes. He examined the ruffled feathers of the male cardinal's bright plumage, the softness of the dogwood petals, the brittle textures of the tree bark. He noticed how his father had expertly captured the glossy imperfection of the tree leaves, the way in which the sun spotted areas of foliage with a gentler light, and how minute edges of the birds' feet or curled leaves were captured with just a hint of shadow.

"He's as good as Audubon." Lindy watched James as he tried to absorb the extent of his father's gifts. "I sent a digital photo to my mother's gallery in D.C. She wants to set up an exhibit as soon as possible, if your daddy agrees. I think he could make a lot of money from these paintings, James. People were bidding over them like they were made of gold at the festival. You would have been so proud."

James could barely speak. "I had no idea. I never knew he could paint like this . . . or that he even enjoyed it." He stared at the painting again. "I'm not sure that I know him well at all," he said, his voice choked with emotion.

Lucy squeezed his arm. "I guess it's a good thing you came home, then, isn't it? Now"—she drew out a plastic bag from beneath her chair—"I *hope* you've got that wine bottle in your car, Professor Henry, 'cause I am putting on these jeans today."

"Right now?" Bennett asked in alarm.

"In the bathroom, but yeah, right now." Lucy shook out the wrinkled jeans and headed for the downstairs powder room. After a few seconds, she came back into the kitchen and asked Gillian if she could change in one of the upstairs bedrooms.

"I might need more room to get these on," Lucy said, smiling at herself.

"Of course. There are three up there. Take your pick." Gillian watched as Lucy climbed up the staircase. "I hope this works out for her," she whispered, once Lucy was out of earshot. "It seems a bit too soon for new clothes, even though we've been doing *quite* well." Gillian began biting her nails.

James heard a flapping sound coming from the back of the hall and gave Gillian a quizzical look. "What's that?"

"That's Dalai Lama, my tabby cat, coming through his cat door." Dalai trotted into the kitchen and began to meow. "He wants some pizza cheese. He's a horrible little beggar." Gillian scooped the sleek feline off the floor and covered his pink nose with kisses.

James made a ball out of some of the cheese stuck to the pizza box and tossed it on the ground. Dalai gave it a tentative lick, and then batted it with his paw until it rolled under the table where he began to chew on it in earnest. At that moment Lucy returned, her face red and slicked with sweat, as if she had just finished a marathon. She was wearing the jeans, but the seams were stretched to their limit and it appeared that at any second, the stitches would give way and Lucy's flesh would explode out of the fabric.

"You did it!" Lindy cheered a trifle doubtfully.

Lucy frowned. "I'm not sure if it counts since I can barely move in them." She tugged at the fabric bunching up between her legs.

"If you can touch your toes, then it counts," Bennett pronounced.

"I couldn't touch my toes *before* I was this fat. Who are you kidding?" Lucy scowled. "Let me tell you what it was like to even get these things on. First, I had to lie down on the bed. Then, I had to tug on one side at a time, just to get them over my humongous hips. That took me, like, five minutes. After that, I had to blow out all of the air in my lungs to get the button through the buttonhole. That was a *major* deal. Then, I had to yank on the zipper. It went up, like, two teeth at a time, so I had to take another quick breath, let out another deep one, and then pull on the zipper again. That would get it halfway up. You see where I'm going with this."

"But you got them closed," James pointed out helpfully.

Lucy lifted up her long, loose shirt. The large roll of fat that formed her lower stomach strained against the heavy material and it was clear to all of them that the zipper and button were barely holding things together. "I can't sit down, people."

Lucy dropped her shirt and sighed lugubriously as Dalai Lama approached her calves and gave them a good sniff.

"She smells your canine beasts," Bennett teased as the cat rubbed against Lucy, purring affectionately.

"What a sweet kitty!" Lucy immediately brightened at the sight of the cat. Forgetting all about the precariousness of her pants situation, Lucy bent over to pet Dalai. As her friends watched in horrified fascination, the button from Lucy's jeans popped off and flew across Gillian's kitchen floor while the zipper broke apart like a popped balloon. To make matters even more humiliating for Lucy, the seam holding together the fabric covering her generous backside gave way in a horrendous tearing of fabric. James couldn't help but notice that Lucy was wearing pink and blue striped underwear.

Lucy screamed and headed upstairs, one hand covering her stomach and the other trying to hide her exposed rear. Her four friends sat in startled silence. They were afraid to say anything, lest someone break out into laughter.

When Lucy eventually returned, she snapped the waist of her black cotton pants and, sinking into a chair, pronounced, "I am apparently not ready to end my long-term relationship with elastic."

Unable to control herself, Lindy began to smile and then her shoulders began to shake as she attempted to stifle a giggle. Clamping a hand to her mouth, she avoided Lucy's snarling eyes, but when Bennett's shoulders also began to quiver, Lucy finally gave in and began to laugh. The supper club members whooped and howled so loudly that Dalai Lama tore out of the kitchen and dove out the cat door in fear of every single one of his nine lives.

"I guess I was jumping the gun by trying to get in those jeans," Lucy said after they had all calmed down.

"Dieting *is* supposed to be a process," Gillian added, pulling at an orange curl. "Plus, now you can go shopping for new jeans *when* the time is right."

Lindy picked up a cold pizza crust. "I'm *really* glad we had tonight off. There were so many times when I wondered if it was worth it, going on this diet. I know I met all of you, but it's been really hard."

Everyone was quiet for a moment as they reflected on the ups and downs of the last few weeks.

"Look at my father's painting." James stood and walked over to where Lindy had propped Jackson's painting up on the window seat in the kitchen. The four friends gathered around the painting and glanced at James expectantly. "Your eye automatically goes to the male cardinal. His bright red feathers just call for your attention. But if you wait a bit, and you give yourself time, you really start to see the female cardinal, too. She may not be as colorful, but she is just as wonderful, maybe even more interesting due to her ability to blend in with her surroundings."

"So we're kind of like her." Bennett gestured at the group. "You don't see us at first, but when you really do, we're kind of interesting."

"And kind of beautiful." Gillian stared at the brown bird.

Lucy leaned toward the painting and pointed. "It looks like she's about to land on that branch."

James took her hand and gently lowered it away from the glossy surface. "No, Lucy," he said softly. "She's not landing." He gazed at his friends, spending a few seconds to look each one of them in the eye in order to communicate how valuable they were to him. "She's like us in another way, too. Like this amazing little bird, we are all just taking flight."

ACKNOWLEDGEMENTS

The author would like to thank the following people for lending their expertise: Anne C. Briggs, Deputy Kurt Jahnke of the Lane County Sheriff's Department, my husband Timothy Stanley and the other fine physicians of Henrico Doctor's Hospital, Barbara Hollister for her pie recipe, Judy Edwards for her equine info, Jessica Faust of Bookends, Inc., and Barbara Moore and Karl Anderson of Midnight Ink.

Read on for an excerpt from the
next Supper Club Mystery by J. B. Stanley

Fit to Die

Coming soon from Midnight Ink

ONE
ÉCLAIR

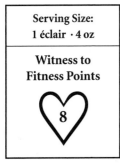

Serving Size:
1 éclair · 4 oz

**Witness to
Fitness Points**

8

"WOULD YOU CARE FOR an éclair, sir?"

James Henry stared at the attractive, chocolate-covered delight nestled in its crinkled paper cup. He knew he shouldn't even think of eating the tantalizing pastry. He was *supposed* to be on a diet. For the last six months he was *supposed* to have been on a good-carbohydrate, good-fat diet. And at first he *was* good—almost a saint—but lately, more and more, his cravings for forbidden foods had overpowered him and he had cheated. Just a little bit at first, but as the months went by, he found himself eating something deliciously fattening every day. What began with a slice of pizza once a week had morphed into a jelly donut on the way to work, a small bag of cheese puffs at lunchtime, a tub of buttered popcorn at the movies, or a candy bar during evening television. It was when he began eating the cheese puffs again that James knew his diet had officially become a failure.

All of his life, James Henry had had a love affair with cheese puffs. The crunchy, salty, cheesy ambrosia that seemed to be comprised of baked air and that addictive, electric-orange dust drove James to his knees. During the first two months of the diet, in which he was determined to lose weight alongside his new friends and supper club members, James had resolutely passed by the snack food aisle in the grocery store. If he didn't go anywhere near a bag of cheese puffs, he could resist buying them. He had been so strong and the pounds had come off. Slowly at first, just a few a week, as he had been told was healthy. In two months, he lost more than twelve of the extra fifty-plus pounds he carried on his tall frame and had felt confident and hopeful for the first time in years.

That was back in autumn, though. Then Thanksgiving had come, and Christmas. It was during the holiday season that he and the other members of the supper club, who had humorously dubbed themselves the Flab Five, could be seen sneaking little sugary treats on the sly. "What's a piece of sweet potato pie here or a little candy cane there?" they reasoned with one another. At their last supper club dinner, Gillian, the barrel-shaped pet groomer with the nest of wild orange hair and garish clothing sense, admitted that she had already gained back half of the weight she had lost over the fall. Now, in March, James Henry, head librarian of the Shenandoah County Library Branch, also ruefully confessed that he had steadily been gaining weight instead of losing it.

Shrugging his shoulders as if to brush off all thoughts of dieting, James finally accepted the éclair from the woman wearing a green apron and an artificial smile. He popped the soft pastry into his mouth and happily exhaled as warm custard oozed onto his tongue. He licked a centimeter-sized smudge of chocolate from his left knuckle and pushed his cart further up the frozen food aisle. He really had no reason to be walking down this aisle. If he admitted the truth to himself, which he wouldn't, James would have to acknowledge that the only reason he came over to this side of the store was that it took him closer to the display of jumbo-sized bags of tortilla chips, potato chips, pretzel rods, and of course, cheese puffs.

As head librarian, James made quarterly runs to the discount warehouse in Harrisonburg, Virginia. His purpose was to restock necessary office supplies such as scotch tape, staples, printer paper, ink cartridges, and the like. The small town of Quincy's Gap, where James worked, was nestled in a verdant valley beneath the Blue Ridge Mountains and didn't support a large enough population to have more than one grocery store, let alone a mammoth warehouse store. James had grown up in Quincy's Gap, so he was accustomed to driving to larger towns like Harrisonburg or Charlottesville for specialty items. And even though James worked a Monday–Friday schedule at the library, he deliberately came to the warehouse during his time off over the weekend in order to partake of the food samples.

Steering a cart the size of a compact car down the wide yet congested aisles containing refrigerated food, James paused in front of a shelf containing tubs of chocolate chip cookie dough before noticing that another green-aproned woman was serving samples of pizza bagels up ahead. James darted forward and immediately stuffed one into his mouth, ignoring the molten tomato sauce, bubbling mozzarella cheese, and the woman's sales pitch as he greedily pivoted toward the juice sampler station behind him. Tossing back the doll-sized Dixie cup filled with sugary berry juice as if he were doing a shot at a bar, James blotted his purple-stained lips with a napkin and hustled in the direction of what could only be a cart set up to offer samples of chocolate.

A clot of eager customers surrounded this particular sampling station, which was strategically located at the section of the store displaying a contradictory combination of health foods and candies. James pushed his cart into a side aisle and shoved his bulk in front of a small boy, fearing that all the free samples might be given away before he could get his share. Glancing at the stacks of cartons containing sugar-free gum, honey-roasted peanuts, and protein bars in disdain, James elbowed forward until he could see the surface of the white stand being manned by a hassled-looking elderly lady. The poor woman was cutting up squares of chocolate from a slab the size of a shoebox as fast as she could. Shoppers grabbed a square and rapidly returned to their carts, like snakes seeking some privacy in order to properly swallow their prey.

"Hey! You cut!" the boy behind James whined.

Ignoring him, James stretched a long arm between a narrow gap between the hips of two chatting women and snagged a piece of chocolate. As he attempted to retrieve both his limb and what he now saw was a caramel-filled confection, one of the women abruptly turned. Her purse, acting like a thirty-pound pendulum, smacked James roughly in the arm, which he was holding high in the air in order to avoid having his chocolate touched as he reeled it in toward his salivating mouth. He watched in horror as his caramel chocolate square flew out of his battered hand and above a tower of granola bars. Taking advantage of James's dismay, the disgruntled boy lunged forward, seized the last square on the tray and melted away into the crowd.

"Damn!" James muttered. He cast a sidelong glance at the old woman with the green apron. "Are you going to cut another piece?" he asked, hating the pathetic tone of his plea, but unable to stop himself from making it.

The woman fixed a pair of angry, blue eyes on him. "Not only am I *not* going to open a new bar," she seethed, "but I am going *right* home to read the paper."

James was confused. What did reading have to do with sampling chocolates? "The paper?"

"Yes. The classifieds! I'm going to find another job!" the woman squawked. "I've never seen such rudeness or gluttony in my whole entire life. And mine hasn't been a short one, mind you. For Pete's sake! It's just a piece of candy. I'm not handing out hundred-dollar bills here!"

James flushed, wondering why he had been fortunate enough to have been the sole recipient of this woman's tirade. Seeing the combination of an empty tray and a lack of activity on the sampler's part, most of the other shoppers had dissipated like mist.

"I'm sorry." James offered a weak apology to the woman. Then, in a final attempt to coerce her into renewing her sampling, he decided to lie. "I don't know about the rest of these people but I forgot to have breakfast today. Suddenly, that piece of chocolate looked awfully darned good to me. I guess I forgot any sense of manners in the face of hunger."

The woman eyed him as she untied her apron. "Sonny," she said, leaning toward James. "That's a bunch of horse manure and you know it. You don't look like you've *ever* missed your breakfast, or any other meal for that matter." And with that, she stomped away.

Indignantly, James reversed his cart, stormed down the main aisle, and practically skidded to a halt in front of the cheese puff display. Just as he was reaching up to pull a bag down from the shelf, he heard a familiar voice.

"James!"

As James swung around, his elbow grazed the cheese doodles display, knocking four or five bags from the shelf. They dropped into his cart with a crinkly plunk. He tried to block the cart with his body as he gave his friend Lindy a guilty smile.

"Who are *those* for?" she asked in her familiar teasing manner, her large round eyes twinkling in mischief.

"Uh . . ." James fumbled for an excuse. "Well, I *was* going to buy one bag, but those others just fell in, I swear."

"Tsk, tsk." Lindy waved a finger at him as she simultaneously tried to block his view of her cart.

Lindy was barely over five feet tall, but her round, curvaceous body was wide enough to prevent James from getting a clear look at what his fellow supper club member was trying to hide. As James noted the blush creeping into Lindy's nougat-colored cheeks, he suddenly stood on his tiptoes and spied that the high school art teacher was preparing to purchase three five-pound bags of mixed candy.

Pink roses bloomed on Lindy's full cheeks. "They're just bribes for my students." She gestured at the bags defensively, swinging a long lock of glossy, black hair over her shoulder in defiance.

James sighed as he took all the bags of cheese puffs out of his cart and replaced them on the shelf. "Well, you caught me out. Not only have I eaten every sample in this place, but I was going to gorge on cheese puffs all the way home." He looked at the snack display with longing.

"I've eaten everything in sight here, too." Lindy glumly pointed toward the checkout area. "Let's get out of this place before we get any fatter."

"Ha! We're going to lose five pounds before we ever get out of here," James said, indicating the long lines. Every shopper's cart seemed to be exploding with stacks of books, cartons holding three-dozen eggs, ten-gallon Tide bottles, steaks the size of footballs, and sixty-four rolls of toilet paper.

James and Lindy pulled into adjoining lines. The woman in front of Lindy had a similar body type to her own, being short and round with large hips and full, heavy breasts. James couldn't help but notice that the woman's cart was stuffed with cookie assortments, two cheesecakes, potato chips, ice cream bars, a giant-sized box of Frosted Flakes, rice pudding, and several varieties of candy bars. As James watched with interest, the woman opened the box of Twix bars, pulled out a single candy, and began to struggle with the foil wrapper. The gold packaging, which seemed to be illuminated with an ethereal glow beneath the fluorescent lights, was successfully preventing her from having a tasty treat while waiting in the endless line.

As James and Lindy stared, the woman tugged at the wrapper, grunting with exertion. She even put it down for a moment, then wiped her hands on her purple floral dress, and tried again. Just as her line moved forward, she was able to rip the stubborn wrapper apart, sending one of the chocolate and caramel-covered Twix bars soaring through the air and into the cart of a stick-thin brunette dressed in workout clothes standing in front of her.

Lindy's eyes grew large as she, and everyone waiting in line around the Twix Lady, ogled the brunette as she fished the candy bar out of her cart. The brunette's mouth compressed into a thin-lined smile as she turned around and looked appraisingly at the plump woman behind her.

"I'm so sorry!" Twix Lady gushed, holding out a pudgy hand in order to retrieve the offensive snack. If she was expecting to have her piece of candy returned however, she was to be disappointed.

"I'd rather stab myself in the heart than give you this"—the brunette eyed the candy as if it were a piece of dung—"disgustingly unhealthy, chemical-filled, piece of trash! Darlin'," she cooed as if talking to a baby, "you don't really want this back."

Twix Lady put her hand over her heart in shock. James and Lindy looked at one another with wide eyes. As the cashier waved James forward and he scurried around the other side of his cart so that he could unload it, he now found himself standing parallel to the brunette.

"Look at your cart, dear!" the woman continued, her voice rising in concern as she rifled through Twix Lady's cart with frantic energy. "Nothing but sugar, nasty carbohydrates, and nicely disguised lard! Honey! How can you *do* this to your body?"

Twix Lady looked around for help, but the other shoppers only stared in embarrassed fascination. It was like watching a lioness circle calmly around a wounded wildebeest.

"Don't you know that you are too beautiful to ruin yourself with food like this?" the brunette asked in a deep drawl, her hand held over her heart as if to express her earnestness. "If I were your friend, and I'm sure you have tons of friends, I wouldn't let you out this door with this cart, sugar."

"I dunno." Twix Lady looked as though she would burst into tears at any moment. She then frantically opened a new Twix bar and desperately bit off an end as if the sweetness could ward off any further attacks from the brunette. "I like this stuff. It makes me feel good."

The brunette smiled at her victim in sad disbelief. "Darlin', this doesn't *really* make you feel better. I mean, only for a few minutes. But later . . ." she let the words drift away as she took a step closer to Twix Lady. "You are killing yourself," she said so softly that James almost couldn't hear. "And it's breaking my heart." Then, smoothing back a few wisps of hair that had escaped her ponytail, the brunette perked back up and spoke in a singsong voice. "See my cart? I've got fruit, vegetables, cheese, lean meats, and sugar-free candy for when I need a little reward. My cart is why I look the way I do and your cart is why I'm real worried about your future, sweetheart. Do you live around here?"

Twix Lady blinked, overwhelmed by the brunette's concern and startled by her question.

"Um . . . not really. I live north of here."

"Anywhere near Quincy's Gap?" James and Lindy quickly exchanged wary looks.

"I live in Hamburg. It's 'bout twenty minutes drive from Quincy's Gap."

"That'll be close enough." The brunette handed Twix Lady a business card. "My name's Veronica Levitt. I'm opening a new fitness and weight loss center called Witness to Fitness in Quincy's Gap. Matter of fact, the Grand Opening is next weekend. Why don't you come by and I'll help you change what you put in your cart *and* in your mouth. I will save your life, if you give me the chance."

The brunette put a hand on Twix Lady's shoulder and squeezed it tenderly. Twix Lady began to cry, her shoulders and chest jiggling as she wept.

"You can help me?" she sobbed, a bit of chocolate drool running down her chin.

It seemed to James that Veronica hesitated for a fraction of a second before her lips curved upward into an enormous smile. "Oh, yes, my dear. Now, it's going to be tough. Real tough. But if you stick with me, you're going to be a newer, stronger, *sexier* you in just six weeks!"

"I'd like that." Twix Lady sniffed, holding the business card to her chest as if it were a treasure she might lose. "Thank you." She reached out and hugged Veronica.

"Excuse me!" Lindy called to Veronica from behind Twix Lady. "Did you say six weeks?" Lindy's tone was clearly dubious.

Veronica's bright green eyes fixed on Lindy's figure. "That's what I said. Are you interested as well, hon?"

Lindy hesitated. "I've been on a diet for over six months, actually."

Veronica began unloading her cart. "And is it working for you?" she called back, eyeing Lindy sweetly as Twix Lady turned around to get a good look at the person who might next be transformed by the magical fitness guru.

Lindy shrugged. "I've lost some weight." She pointed across the way at James. "There are five of us on the diet together. We've got a supper club going."

"Good for you!" Veronica cheered Lindy. "But now . . . is that candy a part of your supper club's menu?" she asked, using the type of chiding tone that a doting grandmother might use on a child who has eaten too many of her homemade cookies before dinner.

Lindy looked down at her cart guilty. "It's for my students! Look, I still have some curves," she added sulkily, "but we don't all have your kind of bone structure. I have always had a very full-figured build."

Veronica finished paying for her purchases. "Of course we're not all the same," she said soothingly, pushing her cart out of the way so that Twix Lady could check out. Veronica then approached Lindy as if she were a lost puppy in need of adoption, her face a perfect mixture of sympathy and friendly concern. "But you can still have the curves of Jennifer Lopez instead of the fat rolls of Jabba the Hutt. Why, with that gorgeous hair and those huge chocolate eyes, you could have men lined up for miles just to get your phone number!"

Lindy's jaw seemed to have come unhinged as her face burned red with embarrassment. Veronica seemed oblivious to the emotions she was provoking. "Here, just take my card. I'm giving discounts to all those who sign up for the six-week plan during my Grand Opening." She bent to retie the shoelace on one of her spotlessly white running shoes. "But I've got to warn you. You won't be eating any candy with me as your food advocate, so you may as well get out of this line and put it back on the shelf. That'll show you just how much you want to change your life. Go on, darlin', put it back. You don't need that candy to make you happy."

James waited for Lindy's Brazilian half to raise its hot-tempered head and verbally reduce Veronica Levitt into a smoldering pile of ash. Customarily, Lindy was an easy-going and fun-loving person, filled with a positive energy that seemed to infect all those who spent time with her, but on occasion, she could have a fit of rage not unlike to a two-year-old throwing a tantrum in the grocery store. Lindy always blamed these infrequent bouts of passionate wrath on her Brazilian mother, a former supermodel. Lindy claimed that the traits she had inherited from mother were limited to her skin tone and her ability to pitch a fit when backed into a corner. But amazingly, Lindy's temper remained completely checked. She simply nodded her head in silent agreement, scooped up the bags of candy, and left her place in line in order to return them to their proper shelf.

As a dumbfounded James began unloading his cart, Veronica appeared at his side and gave him the once over with her calculating green eyes. She placed a pair of tanned hands on her nonexistent hips and offered him a flirtatiously nudge in the side.

"So you've been on a diet for six months, too?"

James slapped a heavy carton of copier paper onto the conveyer belt. "Yes."

Veronica smiled with encouragement. "You'd do *so* well on my program. Men always do." She reached out an arm to help James empty his cart. He stared at the appendage. It looked more like a jungle vine, sinewy and leathery in texture, than a part of the human anatomy.

"You know, you've got a good frame and a *real* handsome face hidden beneath all of that cushion," Veronica said, tossing a very weighty carton filled with printer paper onto the belt as if it were a box of Kleenex. "I bet you were looker in high school and college, weren't you?"

James was amazed by her strength, considering her overall lack of body mass. He was more than a little intimidated as well. He felt more comfortable with women who had softer bodies. He liked curves and solid limbs and dimples in the cheeks. Suddenly, he had a vision of Lucy Hanover, another supper club member who worked for the Sheriff's Department. The only thing sharp about Lucy was her mind. The rest of her was all softness, like a warm and cozy chair that one longs to sink into at the end of the day. A flash of her sunlit, brown hair, eyes the shade of bachelor's buttons, and a pair of plump lips that he had dared to kiss just once a few months ago made James forget all about Veronica's presence.

Veronica was not the type of woman to be ignored, however. She shoved a business card into James's hand and then patted him on the protruding mound that formed his belly.

"Let me help you. We can change you from looking like Santa Claus to looking like one sexy . . ." she eyed his empty ring finger, "bachelor." She smiled again as James shifted uncomfortably. Veronica traced the curve of his cheek with her finger and then moved off to collect her cart. "Hope to see you next week, handsome!" she called over her shoulder as she exited the store.

James flushed as he noticed the other shoppers gawking at him. He quickly balled up Veronica's pink business card and shoved it deep into his jeans pocket just as Lindy reclaimed a place in the checkout line. James waited for her by the exit, standing close enough to the outside doors to note that the cold March rain had ceased and the formerly congealed clouds were finally showing signs of thinning.

"I thought you needed that candy for your students," James said as Lindy pulled her cart next to his.

She shrugged. "I'll have to get them something else as a reward. Truth is, I *would* have eaten half of that stash if I had it at school."

James shook his head in disbelief. "How could you listen to a sanctimonious woman like that? She's part cheerleader, part used-car salesman, part Dr. Phil."

Lindy paused in the middle of the parking lot and turned to look James in the eye. "I don't know, James. But let's face it: we haven't done so well on our own. Maybe it's time we seek professional help."

"But she's . . . she's like Richard Simmons on speed!" James spluttered in protest.

Lindy unlocked her car, a red Chevy Cavalier with a sizeable dent in the one of the rear door panels, and began loading her boxes into the trunk. "Exactly! That woman will get our energy levels up and get us to be more honest about ourselves. We haven't been accountable to one another. When was the last time we ever shared our weight loss progress?"

James fidgeted with his key chain. "At least two months," he admitted.

"That's 'cause there hasn't been any! It's time that *someone* coerced us to get back on a scale and made us exercise. If it means that Veronica's going to be the Head Diet Cheerleader, so be it. We need someone to champion us, someone who truly cares about our health and happiness. Tomorrow night, during our dinner, I'm going to suggest we all go to her Grand Opening. It's time to face the fact that we've slipped." Lindy opened her car door and squeezed inside. "The Flab Five is about to get back in the swing of things and Veronica Levitt is just the woman for the job."

James groaned. There was something about the fitness instructor that he didn't like. His instincts were warning him not to trust her, but he couldn't explain his feelings to Lindy, let alone come up with a good argument as to why they shouldn't join Veronica's program.

On the way back to Quincy's Gap, he stopped at a Food Lion and bought himself a large bag of cheese puffs.

ABOUT THE AUTHOR

J. B. Stanley has a BA in English from Franklin & Marshall College, an MA in English Literature from West Chester University, and an MLIS from North Carolina Central University. She taught sixth grade language arts in Cary, North Carolina, for the majority of her eight-year teaching career. Raised an antique-lover by her grandparents and parents, Stanley also worked part-time in an auction gallery. An eBay junkie and food-lover, Stanley now lives in Richmond, Virginia, with her husband, two young children, and three cats. Visit her website at www.jbstanley.com.